IT STARTED WITH A BOOK

CAMILLA ISLEY

Boldwood

First published in Great Britain in 2024 by Boldwood Books Ltd.

Copyright © Camilla Isley, 2024

Cover Design by Alexandra Allden

Cover Images: Shutterstock

The moral right of Camilla Isley to be identified as the author of this work has been asserted in accordance with the Copyright, Designs and Patents Act 1988.

Every effort has been made to obtain the necessary permissions with reference to copyright material, both illustrative and quoted. We apologise for any omissions in this respect and will be pleased to make the appropriate acknowledgements in any future edition.

A CIP catalogue record for this book is available from the British Library.

Paperback ISBN 978-1-83751-982-8

Large Print ISBN 978-1-83751-981-1

Hardback ISBN 978-1-83751-980-4

Ebook ISBN 978-1-83751-983-5

Kindle ISBN 978-1-83751-984-2

Audio CD ISBN 978-1-83751-975-0

MP3 CD ISBN 978-1-83751-976-7

Digital audio download ISBN 978-1-83751-978-1

Boldwood Books Ltd
23 Bowerdean Street
London SW6 3TN
www.boldwoodbooks.com

To all book lovers who have ever wished to be able to talk to a favorite character or meet them—or kiss them—in real life... this book is for us.

1

THE OUTLAW

He ghosted me. After a week with no calls, no messages, and not even a stinking like on Instagram, it's clear I've been ghosted—*again*!

No matter the staggering evidence, I still halfheartedly open the chat app to double-check if I've missed a text from Tim. I haven't had a quiet minute since this morning. This is the first chance I get to sit down and obsess over my non-existent messages.

My heart jumps in my throat at the red circle next to his name. One unread message. Hope flares in my chest as I open the chat, only for fresh humiliation to hit me because what I find on the screen is a hundred times worse than radio silence. It's one of those deleted text alerts:

FROM TIM

This message was deleted

The notification is from last night. But I must've missed the ping when it arrived because the time stamp places it at one-thirteen in the morning, when my phone is on "do not disturb." Tim must've thought I'd be good for a drunken, middle-of-the-night booty call. Then sobered up, changed his mind, and deleted all evidence of his earlier contact. Or I simply took too long to reply, and he moved on to texting some other woman he met on a dating app. Either way, Tim was never into me.

I toss the phone onto my bed, a mix of anger and dejected sadness bubbling in my chest. It isn't about Tim, per se. I'm not in love with him or anything—I wouldn't even call it a crush. He was one of the few nice-looking guys on dating apps who didn't give total creep vibes and didn't have a sweaty selfie of himself as a profile picture. Someone I felt safe to chat with and who wouldn't send unsolicited genitalia pictures. Or, at least, he *appeared* decent.

I roll over and bury my face in my pillow, letting go of a frustrated scream. I can't believe I fell for it again. That I trusted a seemingly good guy saying all the right things while meaning none of them. By the second date, they're all ready to promise me the moon. By the third date, they seem eager to introduce me to their friends and families. Then we have sex, and there are no more dates. Instead, I get a one-way ticket to ghost town.

Either I really suck in bed—I'm no sex goddess, but I'm pretty sure I don't qualify for "disaster in the sack" status—or all the guys I've dated were only after a night of fun and nothing else.

That's it. I won't have sex ever again until I'm married, or at least until I have a diamond ring on my finger. Ha ha, *as if*. I can't even get a guy to take me on a fourth date, let alone propose to me.

For a moment, I allow myself to wallow in self-pity. How could I be so naïve? So desperate for attention that I fell for the oldest trick in the book?

And now, here I am, classic me, spending another Friday night solo. No hot date, no other plans. Pathetic as I am, I'd wanted to keep my schedule clear in case Tim asked me out. I spent an entire week waiting by the phone for a call from a guy who was never going to call me.

The only consolation is that even if I *had* made other plans, I wouldn't be better off.

Most of my friends are coupled up, and the only more dreadful option than spending the night by myself, moping, would be to pass it among googly-eyed couples.

I should've gone home to see my parents. I have to go on Monday anyway for their thirtieth anniversary—talk about impossible relationship goals—because they refuse to celebrate on any day other than the actual date of the wedding. But besides holding out for Tim, I also didn't want to cancel my Monday-morning meeting with my grad advisor. Still, if I'd known this was how the weekend was going to go, I would have asked Dr. Hammond to reschedule. But now it's too late. I can't send him an email on Friday night after hours to cancel a Monday-morning meeting. It would be too short notice—unprofessional.

My last remaining single friend, Ivy, has disappeared on me as well lately. Not entirely her fault. Until the beginning of summer, we were roommates here in Evanston, a suburb thirty minutes north of Chicago, where I go to grad school. We shared this small studio apartment until June, but she moved to The Loop when she got her master's degree—she's a year older than me. Living under the same roof created a unique bond between us, one that's hard to replicate now that we're apart. She's busy with her new job. The start of the school year has been a whirl-wind for me—I'm getting my master's in computer science with a specialization in artificial intelligence. Add that the trek to down-town Chicago on the Metra takes forever and vice versa, and, understandably, we're not as inseparable as we once were.

Still, it's worth a try. I text her.

TO IVY

> Hey, girl, long time no see. I know it's last
> minute, but are you doing anything tonight?

FROM IVY

> Leigh, hi! You read my mind; I was about to
> text you.

> I have so many things to tell you. But tonight I
> can't, sorry.

> But let's meet tomorrow, six-ish? The 3 Arts
> Club?

Isn't six a little early to go clubbing? But, whatever, if Ivy wants to party early, who am I to complain? I so need a night out. I won't even whine about the commute to the Gold Coast.

I let my thumbs fly over the virtual keyboard of my phone as I reply:

TO IVY

> It's a date. See you tomorrow xxx

She texts me the location of the club, saving me from having to google it myself, and I reply with a thumbs up. In a slightly better mood, I drop on the bed and hug the phone to my chest. Saturday night is sorted. The problem remains of what to do tonight. Just the idea of opening another hook-up app—because apparently hooking up is all anyone in there is interested in—to find a last-minute date is appalling. The whole Tim debacle is still smarting too much. Never mind all the happily-ever-after stories I've heard of online flings that ended with wedding bells, I know I won't snag a long-term partner on an app.

In a burst of indignant folly—or long over-due clarity—I delete them all from my phone.

No matter that old-fashioned meet-cutes have become myths.

Folklore tales of legend. One by one, I press the little upper-corner Xs on all the colored squares that promised me love and only delivered heartbreak or, in the best cases, like Tim, searing mortification. I'm better off alone than used and scorned by the next online dirtbag.

I stare at all the new holes dotting my home screen and feel almost vindicated, free at last.

In a romance novel, this would be the moment when something exceptional happened. The heroine has just renounced dating, so of course the apartment above her would flood. The leak so severe her ceiling would collapse, and the impossibly handsome new neighbor from upstairs would literally fall in her lap.

In reality, the sky isn't about to open, and the man of my dreams is not about to drop from the heavens like a fallen angel. I throw a shady glare at my ceiling. I doubt having Mr. Calvin, my ninety-year-old neighbor from upstairs who's lived in the building since before I was born, fall in my bed would make for an epic romantic moment. At most, a hip replacement and noisy reparation works.

Since a fabled meet-cute isn't on the cards, I resign myself to a quiet night in.

I could turn the evening productive and finish a paper for my statistical language models class. But honestly, the only thing more pathetic than being alone at home on a Friday would be to be alone doing homework.

I deserve at least a dash of secondhand happiness.

I hop off the bed and go to my bookcase, searching the shelves for something to read on my never-ending TBR. On my meager grad student income, I can't afford to buy many new books, but I love to shop at thrift stores. And I have a small BookTok account where I post book reviews, so, sometimes, I receive unexpected book mail. My fingertips brush the spines on the top shelf, which is reserved for the newest arrivals. I read the titles in search of an inspiration that isn't coming. The latest YA enemies-to-lovers from my favorite author? Mmm, YA usually is low on the spice, and I'm in the mood for something steamier. A faerie romantasy? That should bring on the steam, but the world-building might take too long before it gets to the good stuff... Maybe some adult contemporary?

A thud draws my eyes to the floor, where a book has just tumbled at my feet. I pick it up and study the cover. The binding looks a little worse for wear. The author's name and the title are scratched away, unreadable. But the silhouette of a faceless cowboy is still discernible on the cover. I flip the book open, and it goes straight to Chapter One. The initial pages where the copyright and publishing info should be are missing, torn off. Even if I often shop at secondhand bookstores, I don't remember buying this book. Also, I emboss all my novels with a cute customized stamp Ivy got me last Christmas that has my BookTok handle on it. Despite the lack of front matter, if the paperback had been mine, I would've embossed page one.

Maybe the book is a leftover from when Ivy was living here—some of her socks still magically come out of the dryer in the basement sometimes. I recognize them as hers because Ivy only buys socks with ridiculous prints.

But she has excellent taste in books. So if this is one of hers, it should be good. I read the first line.

The return of Killian St. Clair, the cowboy who'd left as a scrappy eighteen-year-old and come back a ravishing billion-aire, was the talk of the town, but all Leighton could remember was the cocky teenager who'd challenged her at every turn.

Uh-huh, a cowboy romance with a hot billionaire and high school nemesis—perfect! Ravishing is exactly the kind of romance hero I need tonight. And the protagonist is called Leighton like me. If that's not a sign I should read this book, I don't know what else could be.

I consider getting my annotating kit, but nah, I just want to read and relax. If I really love the book, I can annotate it later and make a video. I've been posting on TikTok almost every day in the summer, but since school started I haven't had time to read much or review the few books I've finished.

I get ready for bed and curl under the covers, letting my mind slip into a fictional world where happy endings are always guaranteed. Soon, I get to the meet-cute scene.

> "You're trespassing," a gravelly voice informed her.
>
> Despite both of them being on horseback, Leighton still had to look up at the man towering over her from the saddle of his black stallion. Killian St. Clair was eyeing her from under his cowboy hat, gray eyes of steel almost entirely concealed in the brim's shadow.
>
> "I don't see any fences," she replied. "How can you tell this is your land?"
>
> His beautiful, cruel mouth twisted into a smug smirk. "Oh, I can tell."

I adjust under the blanket, already knowing I'm going to love this story. I'll suck up the enemies-to-lovers tension like I'm a vampire drinking straight from the vein.

Flipping through page after page, I read until my eyes are red and my lids heavy, still I push through. The tension is just too high, I want to at least get to that first kiss scene. But just as the conflict escalates and the heroine is about to confront the cocky billionaire, the pages turn blank.

I frown. Turn another page. Still blank. I quick-flip the rest of the book, but it's only blank pages—what the...? Was this a printing error? Is that why the front pages were torn? Someone got mad and ripped them off in frustration?

A giant yawn interrupts my thoughts. I'm too tired to speculate on mysterious, author-less books with three-quarters of the story missing. My lids are sliding closed. I reach out to flip off the nightlamp, welcoming the darkness. The book slides over my chest and I fall asleep with it still in my hands.

But even in my dreams, I don't let go of the story. Suddenly, I'm its protagonist. I'm the heroine entering the local bar, The Outlaw Bar & Grill, about to have a showdown with the infamous resident billionaire cowboy. It's as if my brain has decided to finish the narrative I was robbed of.

The inside of the bar is dingy and smells like cheap alcohol and bad decisions. But even in the semi-darkness, my eyes zero in on Killian St. Clair sitting at the counter, draped on a stool with an air of careless arrogance. He's the perfect romance hero in a flannel shirt with rolled-up sleeves that showcase his veiny forearms, dusty jeans that hug his toned thighs like a second skin, and cowboy boots casually hooked in the footrest. His brown, sun-kissed hair is falling over his forehead.

Killian looks exactly how I imagined him while reading the book, but now he's in high definition and there are so many new little details. The posture of his shoulders, relaxed yet unmistakably alert, as if accustomed to commanding attention without effort. There's a faint scar above his right eyebrow, a testament to a past that's both intriguing and mysterious. His jawline is sharp, covered in a day's worth of stubble, adding to his ruggedly handsome appearance.

He's nursing a glass of something amber-colored, his fingers idly turning it around on the bar top. The gesture makes me wonder how those same fingers would feel on my skin—rough and calloused from hard work, telling stories of a man not afraid of getting his hands dirty? Or would his be the smooth hands of someone who has done no real work in a long time? A man who just sits in a chair all day counting his piles of cash.

I ignore how the sight of him makes my heart race in my chest and stomp forward.

"You did it on purpose," I say.

"Hey, Luke?" the smug bastard asks the bartender without even glancing my way. "Do we have a sign out front saying annoying pixies aren't allowed inside?"

The bartender smirks behind the counter. "Not that I know of, boss."

The wretched bar owner takes a leisurely sip of his bourbon. "Then we should put one up."

Luke chuckles, and I incinerate him with a stare. At which the barman regains his composure and raises his hands. "Hey, Leigh, not my fight." He scoots sideways to go serve another patron of this dubious establishment—*sage man*, leaving me alone with his annoying boss.

Killian St. Clair finally turns toward me and drags his steely eyes over my body—from my off-the-shoulder crop top down to my cowboy boots. His gaze lingers an extra second on the hem of my shorty-shorts before he lifts his chin, locking eyes with me.

These are not clothes I'd wear in normal life, but if I'm going to live my small-town cowboy romance fantasies to the fullest, why not go all in with a little cosplay?

My nemesis raises an eyebrow at me. "Nice boots, Spoon."

Now, I'm still vaguely aware that this is a dream, and that Killian is the man I'm supposed to love to hate until we inevitably fall head over heels for each other. But I find it incredibly baffling that a fictional book boyfriend who only lives in my head still managed to pick a pet name for me that irks me to no end.

"My name is *Wither*spoon."

"Oh, really?" He takes another impossibly slow swig of bourbon. "You're so *petite* I thought I'd shorten it."

My spine stiffens, and I lift my chin. "I'm not *petite*. I buy regular-sized clothes."

"I stand corrected." One corner of his mouth curls up in a lopsided smirk that is as wicked as it is irresistible. Next, he signals for Luke to pour me a drink. "So, what are you doing here at The Outlaw? Not exactly your scene."

"One tequila soda for the lady," Luke chirrups, depositing a glass on the scarred and chipped surface of the wooden bar. Everyone knows everyone around here, down to our preferred drink choice— mine apparently being tequila sodas in this fantasy world. A drink that I've never touched in real life. I'm more of a Cosmo gal.

"No, thank you." I push the cocktail back toward Luke. "I'm not here to drink."

"What for then, Spoon? This is a bar, if you haven't noticed." Killian's grin turns feral. "Unless you're here to pick up some company for the night. In which case—"

"Finish that sentence and I'm going to have you by the balls, and not in any way you'd like."

Woah, I like fantasy me. Fierce.

Still moving deliberately slowly, Mr. Cowboy gives me another sultry once-over before nonchalantly going back to drinking his bourbon. Only this time, he takes long, drawn-out swallows that have my nerves on edge.

To avoid turning into a total cliché, I avert my gaze from his undoubtedly sexy throat and bobbing Adam's apple as he drinks.

Instead, I concentrate on the tips of his ears. By any standards, ears aren't sexy.

Killian finally drops the empty glass on the counter with a loud thud, and I judge it safe to stare at his devilishly handsome face again.

Our eyes lock, and my stomach flips. Direct eye contact with Killian St. Clair might *never* be safe.

He stands up and has to lean down considerably to whisper in my ear. "You'd be surprised by what I like, Sugar Spoon."

A shiver runs down my spine while the skin on my neck blisters in the wake of his warm breath caressing down it.

My gaze raises up to his lips which are as full as they're foul, then upward still to the leaden depth of his hard stare. Even in this crowded bar, I can pick up his scent when he stands this close. He smells like lust and ruin. Like the wilderness, like the woods and the forest and the damp, rich soil.

I behold his chiseled face, with hollowed-out cheeks and a too-straight nose. His sun-kissed brown hair, and his gray eyes brewing up a storm.

If I lifted my chin by a mere inch, I could finally kiss that sinful mouth of his. But then he straightens up, and the moment is gone.

"Goodnight, Spoon."

He makes to go away, but I stop him, grabbing him by the wrist. "Hey, I came here to talk to you."

He gently but definitively gets free of my grasp. "Pity I'm not in the mood for *talking*."

Without a second glance my way, he strolls out of the bar as if he owned it—well, he does own it, but that's irrelevant.

On impulse, I take a long drag from the tequila soda, chucking about half the glass—noting the crisp, subtly sweet agave with a hint of citrus taste that is actually pleasant, and follow him outside.

As I exit the bar, I'm disoriented for a second. I'm standing in a dirt parking lot, seemingly in the middle of nowhere. I scan the various trucks haphazardly parked across the expanse, expecting Killian to drive an old Ford Ranger or some other Nicholas Sparks-novel appropriate pickup, but the reality is much worse. Killian didn't drive here. He came on his black stallion that he's presently untying from a hitching rail. Because of course. It's a cowboy romance, after all.

I stride toward him. "Where are we?"

His gaze flickers to the piece of plywood nailed above the front door shaped in the likeness of a bandit with his face covered by a red handkerchief.

Killian throws me an alarmed glance. "The Outlaw?"

"No, what town is this?"

Now both his eyebrows rise under his tousled fringe. "Lakeville Hills?"

He gives the same fictional small-town name as the one in the book I was reading.

I chuckle. "Of course."

Killian stops adjusting the tightness of his girth and focuses all his attention on me, which is both thrilling and unnerving. "Are you alright, Spoon?"

The question unleashes a surge of fury within me I'm not entirely sure is my own—mostly that of my character, I suspect. "No, I'm not okay, you stole my shop," I accuse, mixing part of the storyline of the book I was reading with this new fictional world I've created in my head.

"Ah." Killian goes back to fixing his saddle.

"You couldn't be content with owning half the stores in this town. You had to take the one I wanted for my bakery."

FYI, I don't bake.

Killian St. Clair keeps completely still, so much so that for a moment I think he has turned to stone. When he faces me, his features are unreadable. "Tell you what, I'll rent it back to you, but only if you ask nicely."

"I don't want to rent the shop, I wanted to own it. I was just waiting for the bank to approve my loan."

Those inscrutable gray eyes are fixed on me, causing a churning low in my belly that's unsettling. "Make your business profitable for two years in a row and I'll sell the shop back to you at the same price I got it." With a preternaturally graceful move, he hoists himself up on the stallion. "But only if you say please."

I glare at him. "Is this just a game for you?"

"No games, only business, sweetheart." His voice is low and smooth as he reins in the horse. "And maybe a sprinkle of fun."

"Fun for whom?"

A smirk dances on his lips. "Let loose, Sugar Spoon, and you might enjoy the ride as well."

He winks at me before kicking his stallion into a loping canter toward the hills in the distance. I watch him disappear into the setting night and keep watching until the trail of dust he left behind has dissipated, too.

And then I wake up.

2

COUPLED HUMANS' WISDOM

Being back in the real world feels strange. I blink, still dazed by the too-realistic dream. I swear I can still feel the dust from the parking lot in the back of my throat. I pull up on my elbows, sending the book I was reading last night tumbling to the floor.

I pick it up and examine it again. The battered exterior doesn't match the modern plotline and setting.

"You're a mystery." I trace my finger over the faceless illustration of the cowboy on the fading cover.

Killian St. Clair, I'm not sure if I like you. But if you were real, I'd love to find out.

I flip the pages to check if the second half of the book is still blank, and it is. But as I return to the last chapter, it's no longer the one I left off at last night. There's a new chapter matching exactly what happened in my dream.

No, that's impossible.

Maybe last night I was so tired I was already half asleep as I read the last chapter, and then I dreamed about it too. Yes, that must be what happened. Should I re-read it just to make sure?

No. As much as I would like to stay in bed all day fantasizing about a hot cowboy who doesn't exist, real life calls. I drag myself out of bed and shuffle to the kitchen to make breakfast and prepare for a boring day ahead of catching up on homework and chores.

At least tonight I have a fun outing planned with my best friend.

I finish my paper for my statistical language models homework and then get lost for the rest of the day in the research project that's the focus of my grad studies: a natural language-processing engine driven by AI technology that can write riveting prose.

No, I'm not trying to replace human authors. I've just combined my two greatest passions in life, reading and computer science, to build a tool that will foster creativity, not kill it. Think of it as a supportive second brain or a virtual editor. At the moment, my focus is on training the engine to keep a consistent narrative voice.

I'm collaborating on the project with grad students who are getting their MA in writing. And before you ask, no, none of them are handsome hot nerds ready to sweep me off my feet. I'm working with three women, two married guys, one gay, and a dude who, as far as I know, is straight and single, but that I simply have no romantic connection with. And before you assume I'm not in a committed relationship because I'm too picky or because I don't love myself enough, please consider that it's perfectly normal for single people of the same age with interests in common and no glaring red flags simply not to fall madly in love at first sight.

Yes, I'm rambling. I admit I might be a little touchy on the subject. But try being on the receiving end of what I call "coupled humans' wisdom" for the better part of your life and you'd become oversensitive too. There's only so much well-meant advice one can take about "putting yourself out there" and "just being you" before a person starts losing her marbles at the smallest comment. I know "I'll find someone *eventually*," and that "*my time* will come," with no need to hear the cheer squad every single time we talk. And no, you cannot tell me how much you used to hate dating either, how brave I am for doing it, or how you plan to live vicariously through me.

Nope. None of that.

I put my laptop away at around four in the afternoon and take my time getting ready for my night out with Ivy. Today calls for extra pampering. My makeup gets special attention, and I tame my wild brown curls into bouncy, shiny locks. I guess I *am* a bit of a cliché. After years of hearing how I'm supposed to stumble upon my one true love when I least expect it, I like to be prepared.

I put on a purple sheath dress with a wrap skirt and high-heeled nude pumps. I finish the look with a clutch and a light jacket since the weather in Illinois has been mild this September so far.

From my apartment, I walk to the closest Metra station, take the purple line to Howard, where I switch to the red line until Clark. The entire journey takes about an hour, but tonight I'm happy to make the trip. I use the time to post a meme about never-ending TBRs on BookTok and to reply to comments on older videos. But mostly, I scroll my For-You page until I reach my stop.

Ivy texts me that she's waiting for me inside the club just as I'm getting out of the station. I hurry down Clark Street, shivering a little in the chilly wind that has picked up while I was on the train. Heavy clouds mass in the distance, potentially threatening showers for later.

I don't care, it could literally rain on my parade tonight. I'm still going to keep positive.

My optimistic attitude gets a little side-tracked when I read the full name of the bar Ivy has chosen, the 3 Arts Club *Café*. Café being the scary word here. Did I misinterpret our plans? Did she want to just meet for coffee?

I enter the old brick building, which turns out to actually be a fancy furniture store, and look around, a little disoriented.

But as I make my way into an indoor courtyard where the "club" is located, at least the place looks like a posh combination of a coffeehouse, a wine bar, and a traditional American restaurant. Under a glass-and-steel ceiling, tables are scattered amidst trickling fountains and huge vases with olive trees. Glimmering chandeliers spark extra light on the scene. The artificial illumination much needed today, seeing how the sky outside keeps getting darker and darker.

As I search the tables for my friend, I keep hoping we're here mostly for the wine bar part of the establishment.

Ivy spots me first and calls out, waving at me and beaming. A wide grin spreads on my lips in response. It's been too long since we hung out, but her moving downtown really made it harder to meet up—as per the two-hour round trip.

I cross the large indoor courtyard toward our table while Ivy stands up to hug me. My smile falters when I take in her clothes. She's wearing sophisticated matching sweatsuits in cream white while her dark-blonde hair is up in a deceitfully messy top knot. And while the outfit looks fancy enough, it sure doesn't scream girls' night out.

She gives me a gentle squeeze, and I inhale her familiar scent of jasmine and lavender.

When she pulls back, she stares down at my attire, her

eyebrows raising in her forehead. "Did you dress up like this just for coffee?"

Poof.

All the hopes and dreams I had pinned on this night evaporate. My entire body flushes with embarrassment, but I make a conscious effort not to let it show. I keep my bright smile in place, straining my lips until my cheeks hurt. "Of course not. I have a date later." The lie slips out almost too naturally for comfort.

I don't know why I lied. Ivy is the friend I used to share every humiliating first date and cringe moment with. Two months ago, I would've told her the truth. But something about her casual but expensive outfit has me on edge. She must have plans for later, but they're clearly not with me.

Ivy's eyes widen in surprise, but then she grins slyly. "Ooh, spill the tea! Who's the lucky guy?"

I feel horrible for misleading her, but I can't take the lie back now. Especially if she thought we were just meeting for coffee and she's going somewhere else later. I don't want her to feel guilty about leaving me stranded in the city.

It's my fault anyway, I should've googled the place she suggested. Then I would've known it wasn't a dancing-all-night kind of club. But a classy, designer coffee shop slash restaurant.

My bad.

"Oh, just a guy I met on Tinder," I perpetrate the lie. "First date, not much to tell yet." I cut off all lines of questioning because I'm really the worst at improvising.

Ivy sighs. "Ah, I remember those." Something in the faraway look in her eyes puts me back on high alert. "Can't say I'm going to miss dating." She confirms my ominous premonition.

Ivy has a new boyfriend, and that's why she's invited me out today to have coffee. To brag about her fantastic love story, pretend for a little longer she's not going to completely disappear into coupled life, and then move on to have dinner and mind-blowing sex with her new significant other.

She means well. They all do. Ivy doesn't want to rub her happiness in my face or anything. She's not mean. But she has that expression. That newly in love, everything is wonderful, rainbows and unicorns dreamy look we, as formerly single gals, used to gag at.

I'm not sure how the brain works, how a person, the second she gets in a relationship, forgets about what it was like to be single and on the receiving end of the dreaded "coupled humans' wisdom." I so should've gone home to Milwaukee this weekend.

At least Ivy asks about me first and has the decency to wait until after our orders have arrived before she unloads her unabashed joy on me.

She takes a sip of her latte and gets the faraway look again. *Buckle up, folks.* "You're never going to believe what happened to me..."

I brace myself for the inevitable meet-cute story, trying to guess how improbable it's going to be this time. Will it be a gym mishap where she fell off her treadmill right into his sweaty, bulging arms? Or a classic case of mistaken identity at a coffee shop where they both accidentally grabbed the same latte and their fingers brushed? Maybe the dude's name is Iverson, but he uses Ivy for short, hence the providential mix-up. No, no. I bet it'll be something even more cliché like they bumped into each other at a bookstore and reached for the same novel.

The only time I had to fight for a book in a shop was with a seventy-year-old lady who was really into her steamy romances.

Regardless, I try to smile and nod as if I am fully invested in the story.

"Two weeks ago, I was grocery shopping, minding my own business."

Ah, grocery store meet-cute, I should've guessed.

"I was a mess. Dirty hair, baggy clothes..."

Of course she was. Any respectable romance heroine has to be a hot mess for her grand meet-cute. Maybe that's where I'm going wrong. I should've come here un-showered and wearing granny underwear. Nice clothes equal no Mr. Right.

"Honestly, I had just gone out of the house to grab a carton of Ben & Jerry's because I was feeling a little lonely."

Been there, done that. Met no hot men that way.

"But then, total klutz I am, I dropped the tub."

Being clumsy also seems to be an important factor on the path to true love.

"And the tub rolled all the way down the supermarket aisle until it landed—"

"At the feet of the most gorgeous man you'd ever seen," I finish the phrase for her.

Ivy frowns as I ruin her punchline. "Have I already told you about George?"

"No." I take a sip of my coffee—decaf, to be sure I'll go to sleep early tonight and be free to live vicariously in my dreams. "I was just guessing." I try to infuse some truish enthusiasm into my words.

Thankfully, the swooning smile comes back on her face. "Anyway, I know we hated to hear this when we were single, but it's true. Love really hits you when you least expect it."

An hour and a half later, I've been treated to a few more "coupled humans' wisdom" pearls, including how I'll *surely* be next and how many fish the sea has.

When the inexplicable matchmaking instinct newly coupled people get to cure everyone near them of their singleness kicks in, I even agree to go on a double date with Ivy, her boyfriend, and his brother. Just in case my Tinder meet-up tonight turns out to be a bust. Which, seeing how the date is made up, is a given.

Ivy's enthusiasm is uncontainable. She promises George's brother will doubtlessly be perfect for me.

Ah, if I had a proverbial dollar for every time I heard that phrase. But I go along with the plan because I've learned it's just simpler. Give the newly coupled a few misfires and they'll leave you alone, *eventually*.

Once I surrender to the double date, Ivy discreetly checks her watch. "What time is your dinner?"

This probably means she has to leave soon to go have all that mind-blowing sex with her new boyfriend.

I pretend to look at the time on my phone. "Oh, I should get going if I don't want to be late. Should we ask for the check?"

Ivy believes me or pretends to believe me. We split the bill and exit the building together.

Outside, it's gotten even colder. We hug goodbye on the curb before her boyfriend pulls up in front of the café in a perfectly timed fashion. She apologizes for not introducing me right away, but she doesn't want to rush it and we have our double date to look forward to, anyway.

Yaaay.

Blind dates set up by friends and family suck even more than their well-meaning advice.

Ivy gives me a last squeeze and hops into the car, a stylish black Mercedes. I only get a peek at the handsome man at the wheel. Don't worry, I've seen plenty of pictures on her phone and can certify his "sexiest man alive" status.

A flash of gray eyes and upturned full lips pops into my head. "The *sexiest*, Sugar Spoon?"

I said alive, I chide the mental image of Killian. *Dream men don't count.*

The Mercedes merges into traffic, and the second they turn the street corner, the sky opens and a torrential downpour pummels down on me.

Again, in a romance novel, this would be my moment. The heroine has reached a new rock bottom. She's standing shivering under the pouring rain without an umbrella and dressed in fancy clothes she had no reason to wear. She's the last remaining single person in her circle of friends. A true Highlander. Surely now, something magically romantic must happen. A handsome stranger is bound to appear out of nowhere. He'd also be without an umbrella and getting soaked, but he'd still offer her his coat. They'd stare at their drenched selves and laugh, leading to a chance encounter that would change their lives forever.

But this is real life, and as I hurry down the street in the deluge, no handsome strangers are waiting for me in the rain. Just a car cutting a corner and spraying dirty street water on my bare legs and nude pumps that will almost certainly be ruined now.

3

FROM SCRATCH

At home, I take a long, soothing hot shower and eat a simple dinner of instant chicken noodle soup.

Then I'm ready for bed. Snuggled under the covers, I pick up the cowboy book from the nightstand. I open it, almost expecting a new chapter to have popped up. But of course it hasn't. I close the novel again. I could search for something else to read, but, honestly, I don't want to read somebody else's love story. Get lost into a narrative where I'm not the protagonist. I prefer to dream about my own imaginary romance.

I hug the book to my chest and close my eyes, willing the fog of sleep to take over. It takes a while. But eventually, memories and fantasies swirl together until I become lost again in a world of my own making.

This time it's daylight in Lakeville Hills and I'm standing behind the counter of a bakery, hands sunk deep into a ball of dough. I stare down at myself clad in the most ridiculous baking attire I've ever seen. Shorty-shorts again, of course, a red-and-white checkered shirt tied in a knot over my stomach that leaves my belly button exposed, and high-heeled clogs.

Who bakes in high heels?

Dreamland me, it seems.

None of my curls are falling over my eyes. I catch my reflection in the display glass to confirm that my hair is being held back by a handkerchief hair tie secured in a pretty bow just above my forehead.

I stare around at the shop, presumably the one Killian rented to me after stealing ownership of the lot.

The walls are covered in strips of brown paint and pastel pink, like the kind on the inside of chocolate boxes, while the floor is made of white tiles in a basket weave pattern with black accents. Wooden tables and chairs are arranged in a variety of shapes and sizes around an extra-long counter where two glass cases display an array of pastries, cakes, and cupcakes.

The place smells like a gingerbread house and coffee and it's adorable—but dishearteningly empty of customers.

I'm not entirely sure what to do. I pinch a small piece of the dough and taste it, confirming it's some sort of sweet preparation. Should I attempt to finish whatever this version of me was making?

I wouldn't know where to start.

Thankfully, the me in Lakeville Hills is well organized and has a handwritten recipe book open on the counter.

"Cinnamon buns—improved recipe," the annotation at the top of the page states.

So, in this world, not only do I bake in heels, but I also make up my own recipes. I quickly scan the instructions, which inform me I should knead the ball of dough for eight to ten minutes. I'm not sure how long I've been kneading it, so I decide to give it the full ten minutes. In for a penny, in for a pound of cinnamon gooeyness.

I check the time on the clock mounted on the wall opposite the counter—six-thirty.

From the way the sun is hanging low and warm in the sky outside, I'd say six-thirty in the evening.

"All right, boss." A woman comes out of the professional kitchen at my back, making me jolt. "I'm heading home. Do you want me to switch the sign on the door to closed?"

A pang of relief squeezes my chest. Maybe the shop is empty because we're near closing time.

"Yeah, please, do that. Err—" I've no idea what her name is. "Thank you."

"All right. Have a good evening, Leigh." The woman gives me a weirded-out glance but proceeds across the shop toward the exit.

"You, too. Bye." I lower my gaze to the dough to avoid making eye contact again, even more embarrassed that I don't know her name.

The bell over the door chimes.

"I'll take care of that, Suzy," a deep, masculine voice says.

My head snaps up just as the woman—Suzy—walks out of the shop, and Killian St. Clair swaggers in. He turns the sign on the windowpane from "Open" to "Closed" and locks the door behind him.

Uh-oh.

Today, he's wearing a black suit. Black shirt, black leather shoes. No tie. He looks like the dark angel of smut incarnated.

"What are you doing here? We're closed."

He smiles, wickedly. "Closed to the general public, surely not to the owner."

I narrow my eyes. "You might have stolen the property, but you don't own my business. So, again, to what do I owe the displeasure?"

"I came to collect rent."

"All right, Sheriff of Nottingham, I've deposited your tithe check this morning." My brain snaps in place providing this random bit of info. "So you can go count your doubloons or whatever it is you do when you're not busy trying to ruin my day."

Killian chuckles. "You're cute when you're annoyed."

I roll my eyes and turn my attention back to the dough, which is no longer in a nice, round ball, but it's being splattered in a death grip. "Is there something else you wanted, or are you done messing with my peace and quiet?"

He leans against the register, crossing his arms over his chest. His eyes lower to my hands. "Aren't you mishandling that poor dough?"

I drop the sticky ruin onto the counter and glare at him. "I was doing just fine before you walked into my shop."

"You mean *my* shop." He flashes me annoyingly white teeth.

I roll my eyes and grab a pinch of flour to dust my hands off. "Fine, your shop, *my* business. Now that we've established rent has been paid, is there anything else you need?"

He shakes his head. "Nope, just came to check on things. Make sure everything is running smoothly." He takes a seat on one of the stools that line the other side of the counter. "What are you making?"

"Testing a new recipe for cinnamon buns."

"Oh, my favorite."

I flash him a viciously sweet smile. "Pity you won't taste any."

He smirks. "Of course I will. You need an expert's opinion if you're trying a new recipe."

I sigh. "Whatever I say, you're not going to go away, are you?"

"Nope." He opens one of my display cases and pops a mini donut into his mouth.

"That's two dollars fifty."

Killian shrugs. "Add it to my tab."

"You don't have a tab here."

"I do now."

Aaargh. This man is so insufferable, so frustrating. On impulse, I grab another pinch of flour and throw it at him.

The shocked expression on his face and consequent sneeze are priceless.

While he's busy cleaning himself with a paper napkin, I transfer the reformed dough ball into a well-oiled bowl, as per the recipe instructions, and cover it with plastic wrap and a kitchen towel.

When I turn around to place the bowl into a turned-off oven in the kitchen, I find Killian standing behind me.

He drops his hands on the counter, one on either side of me, effectively caging me in. The only thing providing a sliver of space between us is the bowl in my arms.

"W-what are y-you doing?"

He flashes me a grin—the evil kind. "You ruined my suit."

"I'm sure you can afford more designer suits."

"With all my ill-gotten doubloons?" He leans in ever so slightly, but in our current state, even half an inch makes all the difference. The heat between us is palpable. So much so I'm worried the dough in my hands won't simply double in size, it will grow to fill the whole shop. "I'm more of an eye-for-an-eye kind of guy."

While I was distracted by his proximity, he must've reached behind me and coated his right hand in flour because now he smears it over my face. His fingers spread the powdery substance over my cheek and then down my nose to my mouth. His thumb lingers on my lower lip especially long, doing a thorough job of spreading the white powder.

Revenge accomplished, Killian drops his hand back on the counter. A self-satisfied smirk curling his devious mouth.

My heart is pounding at a million beats per minute, but I'm not about to let him see that. Since I'm still holding the bowl, and have no other means to clean myself, I lean forward and wipe my face as best as I can on his black shirt—mouth and all.

I meant the move to be retaliation, but the sensation of his hard chest under my cheek... I don't hate it.

When I meet his gaze again, he's looking at me with a mixture of surprise and amusement and some other emotion under the surface that I'm not touching.

"Are you asking for more, Sugar Spoon?"

"I'm not going to food fight with you." I wish the warning had come out steady and collected, but there's only so much a woman can take, and my words resembled more of a squeak.

Killian is so little intimidated that he drops his mouth to within a breath of my ear. "What else are you *not* going to do with me?"

Finally, I regain some grit and shove him away. "Talk to you. This conversation is over."

I cross into the kitchen, slamming the metal door in his face. I lock it, and, through the small glass windowpane, I point at the red "staff only" sign on the other side.

The door is pretty thick and almost soundproof. But I can still see Killian as he brings his hands to his chest, pouts, and mouths, "You wound me."

I wave at him through the glass and disappear into a corner of the kitchen where he can't track me.

I push the dough into a random empty oven and slam the door shut. The cinnamon buns experiment will have to wait. The real me can't bake on a good day, let alone after that kind of incendiary interaction.

I stare around the kitchen and hope that Suzy took care of whatever safety measures one needs in place in a bakery before going home. That's when I spot a handbag in a corner, I pick it up and explore the contents: a wallet with only some cash inside, tissues, a small notebook with a worn leather cover, a pen, and a bunch of keys, including those of a car. No phone.

Excitement pulses through me. Do I own a car in this world?

The logo on the key is Chevrolet. I exit the shop from the back, search for the right key to lock up, and find it on the third try. Then I peek out from the side alley to check if the coast is clear of devastatingly handsome billionaire cowboys.

It is.

The street is empty except for an old light-blue Chevy K20 pickup parked near the front of the shop that would *totally* be appropriate for a Nicholas Sparks movie.

I sneak out of the alley and lock the main door of the store as well. Then I turn to my car. I have a car! In twenty-four years of life, I've never owned a car. My parents couldn't afford to buy me one when I was sixteen. For undergrad, I went to Notre Dame in Indiana, where everything of interest was within walking distance from campus or reachable with public transportation. Same in Evanston. The Metra might take forever, but it gets me everywhere. Still also can't afford a car, especially not now that Ivy has moved out.

But I can't deny that the idea of owning a car has always been appealing to me. And this Chevy is a beauty. It's not perfect, there are a few scratches and dings, but it's got character. And it's mine! I unlock the door and climb inside, inhaling the scent of old leather and motor oil.

The pickup only has a front bench seat, which makes me love it even more. Bursting with anticipation, I turn the key in the ignition. But when I go to put the car into D for drive, there is no

D. Also there's an extra pedal at the bottom that my foot slips on. The pickup rattles forward and then dies.

It's a stick shift.

Deflated, I drop my forehead on the wheel. Not that I had anywhere important to be. But why does my first car have to be one I can't drive?

Wait. Maybe my brain in this dream world will have muscle memory and I can actually drive a stick. I turn the pickup back on and fiddle with the clutch and gear stick. But after several tries, I only manage to lurch forward to the sound of screeching tires and almost run into a nearby streetlight. Panicking, I hit the brakes, and the pickup comes to a halt only a few inches away from a fender bender.

I turn the engine back off and decide that maybe it's best if I leave the driving for another day. Just like the cinnamon buns.

I'm about to exit the pickup when a knock on my window makes me jolt. My heart trips in my chest as I turn to find Killian leaning over, one arm braced on the roof, with a mischievous expression on his beautiful face.

"Need a hand?" he asks, just a second before my alarm goes off in the real world.

4

ENDS THAT DON'T MEET

Why? Who sets their alarm on a Sunday morning? I swear I didn't.

I roll on the bed and register that it's not an alarm that woke me, but my phone ringing, an unknown number on the screen.

"Hello?"

"Leigh, hi," a woman's voice says on the other side. "Did I wake you?" She sounds unimpressed, as if—I check the time—nine-thirty on a Sunday morning was a totally inappropriate hour to still be sleeping.

"No, I'm awake. Who is this?"

"Oh, it's Maggie?"

"Maggie?" I lower the phone to stare again at the unknown number. "Did you change your number?"

"Yeah, a month ago. I was doing a purge of the unwanted people in my life and kept only the contacts of the people I cared about. I gave the others a clean break. Haven't I texted you the change?"

"No."

"Really? Then it's clearly been too long since we hung out."

Maggie was my dorm roommate at Notre Dame. Now, she's a realtor who still lives in South Bend and a "coupled wise human." Since I moved to Illinois, we've kept in touch, done the occasional girl trip when she was still single, but we don't have the talk-every-day kind of relationship we used to. It's morphed into more of a text-every-other-month deal.

"You're right, life's gotten hectic," I say, noting how I wasn't on top of her list of people to notify about the new phone number.

"You should come up one weekend, for old times' sake. Hang out with the gang. Watch a football game."

"I'd love to." I fidget with a loose thread on the comforter. "But you know finding a place for a game weekend is impossible."

"Nonsense, you can always stay with us. We have a spare bedroom."

Hearing people my age casually toss into a conversation that they have spare bedrooms when I can barely afford to rent a tiny studio apartment makes me feel like I've failed at adulting. If I had to witness first-hand the put-together life Maggie leads, I'd probably lose faith that going to grad school was a sound career choice. Plus, playing third wheel for an entire weekend is my idea of a nightmare. "Oh, wow, thanks. I'll think about it. See how crazy my schedule gets and if I can get away for a weekend."

"And if you have a boyfriend, you can bring him, too."

Real subtle, Maggie.

"No, still single," I trill.

"How hasn't anyone grabbed you up yet?" She regales me with a classic coupled human nugget. "We need to find you a partner! Corey has a lot of single friends who would just be perfect for you."

And there goes another evergreen. Everybody always knows

the perfect friend, relative, or friend of a friend who'd be right for me. Except, they never are.

"Actually, I already have a date this week," I reassure her. The notion that "I'm putting myself out there" always seems to comfort "coupled wise humans." And it's not even a lie this time. I have the double date from hell planned with Ivy, her boyfriend, and his brother. Or I will have soon once I tell Ivy my non-existent date of last night didn't deliver The One. "So, what's up with you?"

A long, anticipatory sigh.

Please don't say you're getting married. Please don't say you're getting married.

"I'm engaged," Maggie chirps. "Corey proposed last night."

"That's amazing." I force the happiness into my voice.

I'm not a horrible person, and while I think that, yeah, misery loves company, I don't actually wish any of my friends to be miserable.

But weddings? Those are hard.

I drag a hand over my face. Next, she's going to ask me to be a bridesmaid. For which I will have to spend money I don't have on a pricey bridesmaid dress I won't choose and that I will only be able to wear once. Then there'll be the wedding gift. Bridal shower gift. And bachelorette party getaway. I can't afford any of these things. As a TA, I have a salary, but with rent—Evanston, regardless of being a suburb, is crazy expensive—food, and other necessities, I'm barely scraping by.

A wedding could mean financial ruin for me or a forced diet of instant ramen and white rice. Maybe I should accept I must go back to having a roommate. With Ivy gone, I switched our twin beds for a queen one. I thought I could afford to stay here alone. But my financial plans didn't include random celebrations of love.

Maggie is still being quiet on the line. I probably haven't supplied the necessary level of ecstasy in my felicitations. She must expect more from me, I oblige. "Oh, wow! Congrats! I'm so happy for you." I force a smile, then realize she can't see me and go back to pouting.

"Thanks! I can't wait to start planning. You'll be a bridesmaid, of course? I already have a Pinterest board full of wedding ideas."

I'm screwed.

"Of course, I'd be honored."

The squeal of joy on the other side almost perforates my eardrum. "Amazing. I'm going to add you to the bridesmaids' chat group. Right away."

Would I be considered evil if I muted the group?

"Can't wait."

"Listen, I gotta go now. So many other phone calls to make. But I'll be in touch soon with all the deets."

"Yay." I don't think she picks up on my being ironic.

"Talk later, bye."

I toss the phone on the bed, bring a pillow over my face, and scream.

Besides being a hurdle financially, weddings are also emotionally draining. I will have to sit—no, not even that, I'll be standing right next to the altar the entire time—watching two people promise eternal love to each other while I can't even get a guy to commit to a fourth date. I'll dream, I'll hope, I'll cry. My feet will hurt.

Hope is the worst. Whenever I attend a wedding, I always tell myself I'll finally turn into a bridesmaid-and-best-man trope. But the best men are never handsome strangers, and even when they are, they're already taken.

If I'm lucky, someone else in the wedding party will be single and not completely obnoxious. So that I won't be the seventh or ninth wheel at the table. But with my unfortunate track record, Maggie won't even have a wedding party table, and I'll end up at the singles one, sitting with guests all under the age of fourteen.

I hate my life.

My phone pings from its position at the foot of the bed where I tossed it.

I almost dread looking at who it is.

I roll the pillow over my face underneath me and reach for the phone. It's Ivy.

> FROM IVY
>
> Hey, hon, how was your date last night?

Made up.

> TO IVY
>
> Nothing special

> FROM IVY
>
> So, no second dates in sight?

Am I being paranoid, or does she sound almost optimistic?

> TO IVY
>
> No, no second dates

> FROM IVY
>
> Don't hate me if I say I'm happy because you have to meet George's brother. He will be truly perfect for you. Can I set us up for a double date on Friday night? Dinner?

Ah, the dreaded double date. Right. I'm already at rock bottom, so it's not like I have any further to fall. I might at least get a free dinner out of it.

TO IVY

Sure. Let me know the time and place

FROM IVY

Fantastic, you're going to love Oliver

I'm 99 per cent sure that I won't, but I send her a thumbs-up emoji all the same.

After a quick breakfast, I take out my laptop and make an estimate of how much Maggie's wedding is going to set me back. I open a file on what the last wedding I went to cost me and use the old data to jot estimations for the dress, gifts, accommodation, and travel expenses—assuming the wedding will be in South Bend and not somewhere extravagant.

The grand total is over a thousand dollars. And if I have to adjust for inflation, it's twelve hundred bucks I don't have.

I scan the list of items again and remove a hundred bucks of bridesmaid dress accessories. I'll wear old shoes and refuse to add any sparkle. But even like this, I'm going to have to pinch every penny from now on. Maybe I'll keep the heating off all winter. It's not like it gets that cold around here in December, right? Lake Michigan doesn't completely freeze over. There's always a blotch of unfrozen water in the middle somewhere. And no heating is better than taking on another student loan.

I should've gone to grad school in Texas, where it's always warm.

With a small crack in my heart, I cancel my Netflix subscription. With an even bigger fracture, I also cancel my e-book subscription. From now on, I'll borrow e-books from the library only. That should save me about twenty bucks a month, which means that in a year, I'll be able to afford the trip and overnight stay in South Bend, and a smaller bridal shower gift. To pay for the rest of the wedding expenses, I'll have to get creative.

Re-sell some old clothes online? Or maybe take a bunch of stuff to the consignment store down the block? Online, I might have more reach, but shipping costs are going to cut heavily into any profit I can scrape by, so maybe the consignment store is better.

That's how I spend the rest of my Sunday, leafing through my possessions to decide what has re-selling potential. By mid-afternoon, I drag two sacks of clothes to the secondhand store alongside a small cabinet I no longer use. It takes me three trips to bring all the stuff over, and by the time I've priced everything together with the cashier, I'm beat.

Back at my apartment, I pack a small overnight bag for my short trip home tomorrow and cook some white rice—I can't go cheaper than that. After dinner, I enjoy a few hours of streaming TV before my subscription expires before tucking in for the night.

I curl under the covers in fetal position, hugging my mysterious book to my chest, and close my eyes.

When I open them again, I'm back in Lakeville Hills right where I left off last time. With Killian St. Clair knocking on my pickup window, gray eyes twinkling with mischief.

5

CLOGS AND CLUTCHES

"Need a hand?" Killian makes a roll-down-your-window gesture.

I shake my head from the safety of behind the glass.

"Come on." He knocks on the pickup window. "What's the matter?"

"No matter at all," I shout to be heard through the glass barrier.

Killian tries the handle next, but thank goodness, I'm locked in.

Still, I think it wiser to just roll down my window and shoo him away. I actually have to manually roll the glass down as per the lack of modern electronics in my Chevy pickup.

"Leave my truck alone," I threaten.

Unperturbed by my menacing tone, Killian drops his elbows on the sill. "Have you forgotten how to drive a stick?"

More I never learned how.

"Of course not."

"Then why was your car jerking about worse than a rodeo bull?"

"My foot slipped over the clutch, that's all," I reply, feeling a little defensive. "Clogs are not the best driving shoes."

Killian's eyes trail down my mostly naked legs to my feet, shrouded in darkness under the dashboard. His gaze on me feels physical, scorching a path down my legs.

I clutch the wheel harder, suppressing a shiver.

He laughs, and my annoyance grows. "Sure thing, princess. Need me to give you some lessons?"

"I don't need any lessons from you," I snap back.

He stands back up, crossing his arms over his ruined shirt, still matted with white flour, and takes a step back. "Then, please, drive. I'm not standing in your way."

Right now, I really wish I could drive a stick. That I could simply tell him, "Watch your feet," and speed off.

But I can't, so I debate my other options. There's no way I can move this car forward without him knowing I don't have the faintest idea what I'm doing.

"No, I think I'll just take a break."

"In your car?" His frown is almost victorious. "In front of the shop?"

"Yes, it's not illegal."

His eyes narrow and he braces his arm on the roof of the car, leaning in again. "What's going on with you lately?"

"What do you mean?"

"You forget things. Half the time, you look like you've suddenly woken up out of place. And now you've forgotten how to drive a stick shift when I've seen you do it a million times before."

Ha. Sorry if I have a few gaps in the narrative.

"I'm fine, I promise. It's only the stress of starting a new business and having to deal with an awful landlord."

"Oh, come on, would an awful landlord offer to drive you home?"

Before I can react, he's pulled up the lock from the inside and is opening the car door.

"Scooch," he orders.

When I don't move, he forces his way into the truck, pushing me sideways with his butt.

"What are you doing?" I protest.

"I'm taking you home." Killian grins at me as he pulls the door closed after himself. And it's an actual grin this time. No smirk. This genuine smile illuminates his face, softening the usual intensity in his gaze and lending him a boyish charm that enhances his rugged features. The corners of his eyes crinkle in a way that makes it hard to breathe.

I scowl and pout, crossing my arms over my chest. "You're not driving me home."

Killian shrugs. "Fine with me."

He puts the car into gear and seamlessly pulls onto the street because, of course, he can drive a stick like a NASCAR racer.

We speed past what I suppose is the small downtown of Lakeville Hills. Soon, shops give way to houses and then endless pastures.

"Where are you taking me?"

He flashes me that heart-stopping grin again. "*Not* home."

"You know, some may consider this kidnapping."

"You need to loosen up, Sugar Spoon. A little adventure won't kill you."

No, but falling for him might. Especially because, in the back of my head, I still know that he's not real.

We drive through the countryside, the sun a red ball of fire directly in front of us. Warm yellow light filters through the pickup windows as we merge onto a dusty track. As we go deeper into the forest, the sun's rays are cut off by the taller, older pines.

Killian has kept his window down, and a warm breeze brings in the smell of rich earth and wildflowers. It mixes with Killian's unique masculine scent of sandalwood and impossible dreams.

And I know romance heroines are supposed to smell like honeysuckle and peaches, but I might be developing an unpleasant body odor instead. The worn leather of the pickup bench has gone sticky under my bare thighs. I hope my armpits won't be next. Why is nervous sweating a thing for me even in fictional worlds?

I look over at my supposed enemy, who's driving me away into the sunset.

I take in his strong profile and firm jaw. The perfect line of his mouth, and the way his sun-kissed hair falls in gentle waves over his forehead. He's dangerously, infuriatingly handsome.

Imaginary love interest, I repeat to myself. *Wiser not to fall for him for real.*

But right now, with the breeze tousling his hair, he seems so real, so alive. Killian is driving with his arm casually draped out the open window. On any other man, I'd find the position tacky. But *he* couldn't look more at ease in his dirty designer suit driving a ratty old pickup.

As I keep ogling him, Killian's gaze flickers to me.

"Don't stare at me like that, Sugar Spoon."

"Like what?"

Eyes on the road, he brushes a knuckle on the outside of my knee. "Like you're regretting not finishing those cinnamon buns and taking a bite out of a warm one."

Eeeeeeeeee.

Stars are shooting straight up my leg from where he's

touching me, and he's right. I wouldn't mind biting that sensual, pouty lower lip of his.

"Would you be the cinnamon bun in this scenario? 'Cause you're the furthest thing from a cinnamon roll hero, I promise."

Side glare. "What's a cinnamon roll hero?"

"A golden retriever kind of sweet guy in a romance novel. Ideally, he'd be a veterinarian, a middle-grade teacher, or a single dad. The cinnamon roll is goofily hot, possibly even a hot nerd. He has some heartbreak in his past but has never stopped being open to love. And he's spectacular in bed, of course."

Raised brow. "And what's my archetype?"

"Oh, you're definitely a beautiful bastard."

A quick glance at me, and the corners of his mouth curl up. "Beautiful, uh?"

"Of course you'd concentrate on that part of the sentence."

"If you want me to concentrate on something else, I could ask you how the beautiful bastards do in bed?"

They're wicked, toe-curlingly devastating, and ruthlessly addictive.

"I'd rather not discuss that part."

"Fine by me." He oh-so-casually brushes that wretched knuckle on the outside of my knee again, making starlight explode in my belly once more. "I've always been more of a show-don't-tell kind of guy, anyway."

And he's started to make literary puns. My clothes might spontaneously rip off at this point.

Thankfully, we soon arrive at our secret destination, and the parking maneuvering requires Killian to keep his hands to himself.

We're standing at the edge of a small lake with a rickety pier that looks like it hasn't been used in forever.

Killian kills the engine and hops out of the car.

"Come on, or you're going to miss it."

Begrudgingly, I exit the car. "Miss what?"

He looks back at me over his shoulder with a face that's pure damnation. "The best sunset in the world."

I follow him to the pier, my steps tentative at first, wanting to make sure the boards won't give under my weight. Not that I really need to, if they can withstand all six-foot-four of muscled cowboy billionaire they sure can support me.

We sit side by side at the edge of the pier, our feet dangling over the water but not touching it.

The view is truly spectacular. Hues of red, pink, and orange paint the sky and bleed into each other, casting a golden light over the lake. The surface is still as glass, with only a gentle ripple breaking the reflection.

It's breathtaking.

"Is this where you bring all your women to seduce them?"

Killian tilts his head toward me, mischief dancing in his eyes. "So I'm trying to seduce you now?"

I shrug in an I've-no-idea way. Is he?

Killian glances away, gazing at the horizon, his expression unreadable. "I haven't come here since my wife died."

My heart stops, breaks, and falls apart. The reaction feels too real for a dream. I shouldn't be so upset about the death of an unseen character. But... he had a wife? She died? I'm simultaneously jealous and sad. "You had a wife?"

His mouth twists. Oh my gosh, is he going to cry?

But when he presses his lips harder together as if he were trying to suppress a smile, I shove his shoulder. "You jerk. You've never been married. You're just messing with me."

Killian lets go of the laugh he'd been holding, throwing his head back. The sound of him laughing is like a ray of sunshine that cuts through the clouds on a rainy day to make a rainbow.

And it's a punch to the solar plexus.

"Sorry." He shakes his head. "You always fall for my tricks. I couldn't resist."

How long exactly have we known each other? In the book I was reading, since high school. But I'm not her, and this feels like a completely different story. Because a story is all that we are, right? All of this is just a fantasy.

"Don't look so upset, it was only a joke," Killian says, misinterpreting my downcast expression.

"You make terrible jokes. Dead spouses shouldn't be part of your repertoire."

"Noted." He turns serious again and looks back at the water. "But to answer your question, you're the first woman I've brought here. I used to come as a boy with my dog, Crumbles. We'd swim out to the center of the lake and then race to the shore." I try to imagine Killian as a boy. I bet he was just as much of a daredevil. "We came almost every afternoon, but I haven't been back in a long time."

"Why?"

"One day, Crumbles didn't come back with me."

Did he lose his puppy? "What do you mean?"

"A whirlpool got him, or so I think." He throws a pebble in the water. "Guess I'll never know." Deep sigh.

I narrow my eyes at him. "What breed was Crumbles?"

With a straight face, he looks me right in the eyes. "A Labradoodle."

We burst out laughing together this time, then he says, "The Labradoodle was taking it too far, wasn't it?"

Still chuckling, I nod. "Yep. And dead dog jokes are just as bad as dead spouses," I say, standing up.

Killian jumps up next to me. "Don't go. I promise it was the last one."

We stare at each other for a long beat. Slowly, the smile dies on my face. The mood shifts and the air in my lungs thins. All I can hear is the steady thump of my heart. The way Killian is looking at me sends alarmed tingles shooting down my spine. I take a small step back, but collide with a thick pier piling—and just as well, or I might've splashed right into the water.

"What do I have to do to make you stay?" Killian asks.

"Tell me something real," I whisper, bracing my arms backward onto the piling for support.

Killian reaches out and unties the bow of the hair tie on top of my head. My curls tumble loose.

"Right at this moment, you're the most beautiful woman I've ever seen."

He takes my neck, cupping my nape with his warm palm.

"Killian—" I gasp as he steps closer. "What are you doing?"

His other hand slides into my hair, tousling my curls. Then he pulls on a lock at the front, straightening it only to let it bounce back.

"I'm pulling your hair. Don't girls love it when boys pull their hair?"

"I'm not a girl, so I wouldn't know."

"Oh, I think you know." He pins me down with a wicked smirk. "Do you want me to kiss you, Sugar Spoon?"

His eyes search mine for a sign of resistance, but all he's going to find is a desire to surrender completely to him.

I can't think straight. My heart is pounding, my skin tingling with anticipation and a strange sense of longing.

Then his gaze lowers to my mouth and *beep, beep, beep...*

6

EARLY BIRDS DON'T GET KISSES

"Noooooo," I howl in my bed, kicking the covers away in protest.

I rage against my pillows next, punch them and throw them across the room. I've never hated a Monday morning more.

Killian was about to kiss me. It was going to be the kind of worth-dying-for, all-consuming, earth-shattering kiss that only happens in romance novels. I was about to experience that—*almost*. Dreams count, too.

But no. My stupid alarm had to go off at that precise moment. I'm half tempted to ignore my responsibilities and go back to sleep, but I can't.

I have the meeting at nine with my advisor, and one class to teach at ten. Then I need to hurry to the station to catch the train to Milwaukee.

Real life sucks.

My loathing of reality worsens when, at nine fifteen, I'm still standing outside my advisor's office door, and he's nowhere in sight.

I'm seething. Fifteen extra minutes is all I would've needed to be kissed senseless by Killian. I could've pushed the alarm back and gotten my grand romantic moment.

And I know that I'm being ridiculous. That I'm digging myself deeper and deeper into an impossible situation where I'm falling for a man who doesn't exist, losing myself into a fantasy where I wear crop tops, bake, and drive pickups.

But if all the real world has to offer me are the Tims of Tinder, can anyone really blame me?

Killian aside, my advisor being late is extra annoying today. If I'd known he was going to blow me off, I could've gone home for the weekend on Friday. Spent more time with my parents instead of rushing there today to come straight back tomorrow. And I also would've been spared the rainy debacle of Saturday night. Yeah, I have a class to teach later, but I could've asked one of the other TAs to substitute for me. We do each other favors all the time.

And Dr. Hammond being late is just plain disrespectful in itself. Either he thinks his time is more valuable than mine or he assumes I don't have better things to do than sit and wait for him. He might be an accomplished scientist, having published plenty of papers on artificial intelligence, but he's officially the most inconsiderate human being on the planet.

Maybe he forgot about our meeting entirely, because it's just gone nine thirty, and still no sign of him.

I finally spot him ambling down the corridor at nine thirty-seven—not even hurrying—absorbed in conversation with another student, Trevor Calkin.

Oh, so Dr. Hammond probably decided my time was less valuable than their male bonding. I swear sometimes he still appears surprised there are women in his classes.

And before you ask why I didn't pick someone less of a jerk as an advisor, Dr. Hammond is *the* authority on AI-driven model languages. He was the best academic choice. Also he didn't come with a misogynistic warning sticker—I had to find out the hard way.

"Ah, Leighton," he says when he spots me. "Sorry to have kept you waiting. Trevor and I got caught up discussing deep neural networks. You don't mind, do you?"

Microaggression number one, implying I should be okay with wasting almost an hour of my time. Why? Because I have a uterus?

"Actually, I have a class to teach at ten." I pointedly stare at my watch. "I can only give you a quick update, as I prefer not to be late for my appointments."

Dr. Hammond and Trevor exchange a look, probably communicating some telepathic anti-female sentiment like "The witch must be on her period."

I do my best to stay chill and not react. There'd be no point. If I called them out, they'd just deny it and probably call me emotional to my face.

When Dr. Hammond finally gets to the door, I squash down my irritation as I follow him into his office and sit across from him at his desk.

I skip the part where I update him on my progress and goals for the year and go straight to asking him if he had any luck having a paper I wrote on evaluating the efficacy of generative language models in natural language processing published.

Dr. Hammond takes his time turning on his computer. I'm not sure if he didn't hear me say I have to leave in ten minutes or if he's simply ignoring the fact.

"That, yes," he says eventually, still half-distractedly looking at his screen. "I've submitted it to a few scientific magazines. We'll just have to wait and see."

Okay, I'm fed up with being ignored and I really have to go, anyway. "Well, thank you, professor." I don't think he'll pick up on the irony in my voice. "But I have to leave now."

"Before you go." He finally looks at me. "I have a group of potential students coming in at eleven thirty. Would you mind giving them a tour of the lab?"

Microaggression number two, always asking one of the two female students in his class to give tours.

"Sorry, but I can't." Technically, I could squeeze in the tour before heading to the train station. But I don't want to. And even if I didn't have a trip planned, my time would be better spent working on my projects rather than chaperoning incomings.

He frowns at me as if my refusal came as a total shocker. "Can you ask Shayla, then?"

Ah, of course.

Since I didn't intend to palm off the tour on her, I deflect. "Maybe I'll ask Trevor."

"Trevor?" Now the shock on Dr. Hammond's face is true and complete.

I flash him my sweetest smile. "Yeah, why not?"

And since he can't very well tell me to my face, because he's a man, I get away with it.

I leave his office feeling victorious, at least until I remember that lab tours come with refreshments and I could've gotten a free lunch out of it.

* * *

A few hours later, I hustle through the train station, the heels of my ankle boots clicking on the pavement with each step. The early afternoon sunlight reflects off the waiting train's windows as I make my way to the platform. Just in time, I board the express to Milwaukee and settle into a window seat. I drop my handbag, with the cowboy book tucked safely inside, on the aisle seat while I shove my overnight bag in the overhead compartment. I'm not really reading the book anymore—as per its lack of pages—but it feels like my only connection to Killian, so I brought it along.

"Mind if I sit here, dear?" a sweet old lady asks, gesturing to the seat next to me.

"Of course not," I reply with a smile, sitting down and moving my handbag onto my lap.

As the train chugs along, we engage in light conversation. I tell her I'm headed home to Milwaukee for my parents' anniversary, and she tells me she's en route to Minneapolis to visit a friend.

Eventually, the gentle rocking of the carriage lulls me into a drowsy state. With one last glance at my handbag, I let my eyes close and drift off to sleep.

"Past your bedtime, Sugar?" a deep voice rumbles, waking me up with a start mere seconds later.

Blinking away my confusion, I realize I'm no longer on the train, but in a different vehicle. My pickup truck. I'm in the passenger seat, and Killian is once again behind the wheel, smirking at me with twinkly eyes and tousled hair.

7

TWILIGHT TWISTS AND TURNS

"Wha—how did I—" I stammer, trying to make sense of this sudden change. It takes me a minute to readjust. Usually, when I go to bed, I'm looking forward to what my dreams will bring, but I wasn't expecting to fall asleep on the train and wake up in my fantasy world with Killian driving me around.

Did we kiss? Are we just coming back from the lake? We must be, at least judging from the fact that I'm still wearing my shorty-shorts and Killian his dirty black suit. Only the sky has gone completely dark now. Why didn't I go back to the moment when we were about to kiss? Is this a closed-door romance? Because in that case, I want out.

Well, not really. Even without the smut, *not* being kissed by Killian is still ten times hotter than anything that has happened to me in real life lately, including sex with Tim.

"Relax, darlin'," he chuckles, his gray eyes sparkling with amusement. "You were out cold. Must've been one hell of a day."

"Just a regular day," I retort, trying to regain my composure. "I'm a baker. I have to get up at dawn. Tuck in early."

Killian inclines his head slightly as if conceding to my point.

"A baker, uh?" he says, his gaze returning to the road that stretches out before us, illuminated by the truck's headlights cutting through the darkness like twin lances. "That your archetype?"

"No." I pout, crossing my arms over my chest. "I'm clearly a boss girl."

Killian throws his head back and laughs. "Is that right?" he says, the laughter still clear in his voice. "Well, boss girl, where to now? Are you finally ready to admit you need me to drive you home because you've forgotten how to drive a stick for some mysterious reason?"

Before I can come up with a proper rebuke, a plume of smoke billows out from under the hood of my pickup.

"Uh, Sugar," Killian says, concern lacing his voice, "is your ride just a little temperamental like its owner or do we have a problem?"

The pickup responds with angry gurgling sounds.

"Great," I mutter under my breath as he guides the sputtering truck to the side of the road.

We both get out to go check the damage. The heat radiating off the engine is palpable as Killian pops the hood and grimaces.

"Looks like you've got yourself a busted radiator," he declares, wiping his hands on his jeans. He reaches for his phone but frowns when he realizes there's no service. "We're in a dead zone, too. Do you have your phone?"

"No." There wasn't one in the handbag at the shop.

"We can walk down the road, see if there's better reception ahead." He lifts his phone and angles it in different directions. "But, no, my battery just died."

"Are you kidding me?" I exclaim, frustration building. "This is all your fault. I just wanted to be left alone in my parked car in front of my shop."

"Whoa, hold up, Sugar," Killian interrupts, raising his hands defensively. "Last time I checked, it was your truck, not mine. Maybe if you'd taken better care of it, we wouldn't be in this mess."

"Excuse me?" I snap back, indignation flaring. "I'll have you know I am very diligent about maintaining my truck!"

"Really?" Killian smirks, arching an eyebrow. "When was the last time you checked your coolant levels?"

"Um—" I falter, trying to recall if I ever even popped the hood.

Then I remember I don't really own a car, and this engine malfunction is clearly a fictional setup to keep the main couple in a forced proximity scenario.

"Thought so." He chuckles, clearly enjoying himself.

"Enough with the bickering," I huff, crossing my arms. "We need to find a solution."

"Alright, alright," Killian concedes, scanning the area. "There's a motel a few miles down the road. We can walk there."

"Walk? In these shoes?" I protest, glancing down at my fashionable but completely impractical clogs.

"Got any better ideas, Sugar?"

I stomp my foot down. "We're not walking to a random motel."

"Why not?"

"Because I know exactly how this is going to end."

Killian crosses his arms over his chest. "Enlighten me. I'm curious."

"We'll get there, and whoever is manning the place will tell you that the tow company won't be available until tomorrow—because small town and all..." I kick a pebble off the road. "Then our only choice will be to spend the night at the motel, and guess what?"

He raises his eyebrows. "Please continue, the suspense is killing me."

"They will only have one room available. And the room will only have one bed. So, thanks, but no, thanks. I'm not sharing a bed with you."

Killian shrugs. "Fine, if you prefer to sleep in your car. I'm going to the motel."

He walks off.

I trudge after him. "Are you serious right now? You'd just leave me alone in the middle of a dark road?"

He doesn't even turn as he replies, "No, Sugar, I've invited you to come along. You're leaving yourself alone on a dark road, *boss girl.*"

"Fine," I grumble, begrudgingly following him, knowing I have little choice.

When I catch up to him, the satisfied smirk he gives me is exasperating. "FYI, we're not sleeping in a motel."

He's deluded. I want to see him fight against the romance gods. "Wanna bet?"

"What do I get if I win?" Killian asks, his stride confident and steady as we walk down the dimly lit road, his silhouette outlined by the occasional streetlight.

"What do you want?" I counter, trying to match his pace despite my impractical shoes.

"You'll owe me a boon." He glances at me, the moonlight casting shadows across his face, giving him an ethereal look.

"A boon?" I chuckle. "No way."

"Why not?"

"You're not a faerie prince, in case you haven't noticed. And even if you were, I'd say no."

"You haven't heard what I'm offering in return?"

"What?"

"I'll sell you the shop if you win, at cost." His tone is solemn now, and he stops walking for a moment, turning to face me fully. The earnestness in his eyes is unmistakable.

"Are you being serious?"

"Yes."

"You bet all your properties away?" I cross my arms, unable to hide the skepticism in my voice.

"It's not a bet if you know you're going to win." His smile is confident, almost cocky, as he resumes walking.

I don't really care about owning a fantasy bakery, but I care about winning. "Okay, I accept."

We continue in silence after that. As we make our way down the road, the discomfort in my feet quickly turns to pain. The leather straps bite into my flesh, blisters forming with each agonizing step.

"How bad are those clogs treating you?"

"It's okay," I blurt, wincing as I take another tender step.

"You're the worst liar, Spoon." He sighs, almost resigned as he stops again, bending down slightly. "Here, hop on. I'll give you a piggyback ride."

"Absolutely not!" I exclaim, pride overcoming my misery. "I can walk on my own, thank you very much."

"Suit yourself." Killian shrugs, continuing to stride effortlessly down the road.

But as the pain becomes nearly unbearable, I finally relent, swallowing my pride. "Alright, fine," I admit, defeated. "I could use some help."

"Thought you'd come around." Killian smirks, helping me onto his back.

As we continue toward the motel, my pain eases, and I can concentrate more on the warmth of his muscular arms wrapped under my naked thighs. Or the fact that my boobs are squashed against his back. Or how solid his shoulders feel under my arms.

"Having a good time back there?" Killian asks as if he could read my mind.

"Yeah, you make for a great pack mule, St. Clair."

"A mule?" he huffs, his voice carrying a hint of teasing as he adjusts his stride, making sure I'm secure on his back. "I thought I'd be at least a stallion."

I rest my chin on his shoulder. "Do you want to be demoted to a donkey?"

He chuckles, a low rumble that I can feel against my chest. "I suppose a mule will do," he concedes with mock solemnity.

We fall into a comfortable rhythm, the only sounds around us the gravel crunching beneath Killian's feet and the occasional call of night birds. I relax against him as an unexpected sense of safety and contentment engulfs me.

"Is that the motel up ahead?" I ask as a neon sign flickers into view.

"Yep," Killian replies curtly, his voice strained from carrying me for the past twenty minutes.

We make our way across the parking lot, Killian nearly stumbling twice over the cracks in the concrete.

"Here we are," he announces as we reach the motel reception. The dingy lobby awaits us behind a dirty glass door, its faded wallpaper peeling at the edges. "Ready to get down?"

I'm not entirely sure. But before I can reply, Killian gently lowers me to the ground. I wobble a bit before finding my footing. After being carried for the last mile, my legs feel like jelly.

"Steady?" he asks.

"Yep, sorry. My legs fell asleep back there. Thanks for the ride." I force a laugh to cover my fluttering nerves and push open the door to the lobby.

"Anytime," Killian says with a mock bow, and I can't help but smile as we step inside together, ready to face whatever this motel has in store for us.

"This place looks like it hasn't been updated since the fifties," I whisper as we walk into the dimly lit reception. The smell of stale air mixed with cheap air freshener assaults my senses.

I suppose it could be worse. At least it's not some creepy Bates Motel. Still, as a faded "Vacancy" sign blinks in my face, my stomach knots at the thought of spending the night here with Killian. Just the two of us. Alone. In one bed. Because that's how it's going to go. I'm in a romance novel, after all, I'm sure.

"Hopefully, they have a phone that still works." Killian smirks and approaches the reception desk where an older woman sits, flipping through a gossip magazine.

"Excuse me, ma'am." I speak before he can, taking control of the situation. "My pickup broke about a mile or two down the road. Any chance we could use your phone to call a tow truck?"

She looks up from her magazine, sizing us up before answering. "Sorry, darling, but the towing company doesn't work this late. However, I do have one room left if y'all need it."

Aha!

I tap my foot on the floor, suppressing a grin. "Well, would you listen to that?" I say, trying not to sound too smug. The bet is as good as won.

But Killian leans on the counter, slipping the receptionist a fifty. "Mind if I try the phone anyway, sweetheart? I'd be much obliged." He gives her a wink.

The woman hesitates for a split second before accepting the money and sliding an old dial phone across the counter. Killian composes a number, speaking in hushed tones when the line connects, while I wait, impatiently tapping my foot faster. After a brief conversation, he hangs up, thanks the receptionist, and motions for me to follow him outside.

"Where are we going now?" I ask, my curiosity getting the better of me.

"Patience, Spoon. You'll see soon enough." He grins, leading me to the parking lot.

We wait in the crisp night air. I'm beginning to shiver when headlights cut through the darkness. Two luxury SUVs roll up and stop in front of us.

A muscular guy hops out of the first truck and hands the keys to Killian. "She's all gassed up for you, boss."

"Thanks," Killian replies, tossing the driver the keys to my pickup. "We left an old Chevy pickup just down the road. Can you tow it to the repair shop?"

"Sure thing, boss." Short of giving Killian a military salute, the man turns around and leaves. He climbs into the other SUV and they drive off.

Twirling the new set of keys over a finger, Killian faces me with a grin. "Need a ride home?"

He moves to the SUV and holds the passenger door open for me.

I huff, arms crossed, and curse that lopsided smile. I've lost this round, but the game is far from over.

I slide into the passenger seat, secretly wondering if I'm more relieved or disappointed that the one-bed scenario isn't happening.

While I brood, Killian smoothly takes the driver's seat and starts the engine.

We cruise along the quiet streets back to my place. Even if we're supposedly driving to my house, I've no idea where we're going, so I'm unprepared when the car stops. Even more so when, before I can take in the unfamiliar trees and houses on my block, Killian is suddenly at my door, opening it for me like a true gentleman.

"Thanks for the ride," I say, dismounting, surprised by his chivalry.

"Of course," he replies casually, shutting the door behind me. "So, is this goodnight?"

"Yep." I nod. "Goodnight, Killian."

He smirks, raising an eyebrow. "You're not going to invite me in for coffee?" His suggestive tone implies he's after more than caffeine.

"Is that code for something?" I ask coyly, fully aware of the innuendo. "Because I will definitely not be inviting you in for '*coffee.*'"

"Are you sure?" he presses, leaning in ever so slightly. The mischievous glint in his eyes is tempting.

Just as I open my mouth to retort, viselike hands grab my arms from behind and yank me backward. My heart leaps into my throat as I'm ripped away from the safety of Killian and my doorway into nothingness.

8

HOME SWEET UNKNOWN

My eyelids flutter open to the pressing tug on my arm. "Miss, miss, this is your station. You're going to miss your stop," the older woman next to me urges.

My foggy mind snaps alert, and I scramble to my feet. The train is already slowing as we pull into the station.

"Thanks so much," I tell the woman, my voice croaky with the remnants of sleep as I fumble for my overnight bag squished into the overhead compartment. It comes down with a thud. I clutch my handbag close, checking nothing spilled out—especially Killian's book—and nod to the kind stranger. "Really, thank you."

"Of course, dear." She smiles, revealing a treasure trove of laugh lines around her eyes.

"Have a nice trip." I wave goodbye and hurriedly step off the train onto the crowded platform.

As I walk along the track, the skin of my heels feels chafed against the soft leather of my boots in the same places where the blisters were in my dream.

That's impossible. I'm being ridiculous. Still, I can't shake off the sensation. I have to check. I stop and balance on one foot as I remove one boot. Squatting in a four pose, I drop my ankle on my bent knee and lower the sock to check my heel. There are no blisters.

Of course there are no blisters. Still, the skin feels a little tender. I shake my head and put my boot back on. Those too-realistic dreams are really scrambling with my head.

When I make it to the station's main entrance, Mom and Dad stand waiting, big smiles on their faces as they spot me. Warmth spreads through me, seeing them both here to welcome me home.

"Leighton!" Mom exclaims, her arms outstretched as if she could gather all my worries and tuck them away in her embrace.

I rush to them, and we hug tight.

"Hey, kiddo," Dad chimes in, his arms enveloping me with a warmth that seeps into my bones.

"Guys, I can't believe you're both here." My voice wavers, a cocktail of gratitude and guilt. They must be swamped with the party preparations.

"Wouldn't miss picking up our girl," Dad says, pride glowing in his eyes.

"We're so proud of you, honey," Mom adds, and it's as if she's stapling gold stars on my forehead, except I don't feel like I've earned them.

"Thanks." I force a smile, touched yet feeling like a fraud. If they knew how broke and directionless I've been lately, would they still beam with pride?

"How's grad school coming along?" Dad asks.

"Oh, you know, lots of research and writing," I say, not wanting to get into how my advisor doesn't respect me.

"Got anything new published?"

"Nope."

"Ah, never mind. Let's get you home and you can tell us more about your research," Dad says, ushering us toward the car parked just outside the station.

I slide into the backseat. The Honda smells just like I remember—Dad's minty gum, Mom's lavender perfume. It's a scent that reminds me of being young and carefree—safe. If only I could stay here in this backseat forever.

But all too soon, we're pulling up to my parents' house, a cozy one-story with wood siding, its yellow paint cheerful even in the fading light. This isn't the house where I grew up. The moment I tossed my graduation cap, Mom and Dad downsized to this lovable one-bedroom nest out of the expensive school district where we used to live, which they couldn't really afford. I'll be forever grateful for all the sacrifices they made to send me to a good high school.

"Home sweet home," Dad announces cheerily.

I grab my bags from the seat and follow them inside, resigning myself to the couch-sleeping fate that awaits me post-party. Since I've no bedroom, I'll have to wait for everyone to be gone before I can conk in. But it's fine; Midwestern parties end early.

The smell of cheese curds is the first thing that hits me as I enter the house.

"I made all your favorites," Mom says, dropping her jacket and heading straight for the kitchen. I follow.

The counters are covered with trays of appetizers—bacon-wrapped dates, mini butter burgers, cheese and crackers... My mouth waters.

"Anything I can do to help?" I ask.

"Oh no, dear. You just relax. Tell me all about school," Mom says.

I launch into a highly edited version, focusing on classes and campus life. No need to worry her with my advisor issues or money woes.

"And are you seeing anyone special?" she asks hopefully.

I blush, thoughts going to Killian. Do dream men count? I'm afraid not. "Not at the moment."

Her face falls.

"But I have a date this Friday," I comfort her, picking up a mini quiche.

"Oh." She brightens immediately, her hands busy arranging the cheese and crackers into a more appealing display. "Someone from school?"

"No, he's the brother of Ivy's new boyfriend." I take a small bite. "She swears we'll be perfect for each other."

"Ivy is such a nice young lady." Mom nods approvingly as she slides a tray of canapés into the oven, her movements fluid and practiced. "How are things going at her new job?"

Before I can answer, the doorbell rings. Mom straightens her apron and pats down her dress. "Here we go!"

Guests stream in—my parents' friends, colleagues, our old neighbors. I paste on a smile, bracing myself for a long night of small talk with wise coupled humans.

* * *

I'm wandering around the party, wine glass in hand, trying not to visibly cringe as yet another of my parents' friends asks if I have a boyfriend. "Not at the moment," I reply with a tight smile, taking a generous sip of cabernet.

"Such a shame," another chimes in, shaking her head. "A pretty girl like you should have someone special."

"Actually, I'm focusing on my studies right now," I counter, moving to a different area of the living room even if, with the house so small, there's nowhere to escape. If I had had a bedroom, I'd be holed up in there.

"Leighton, dear!" Mom's friend, Mrs. Thompson, calls me over. She's showing a baby picture to my mother.

"Oh my gosh, did Kelly have a baby?" I ask excitedly.

Kelly's mom gives me a puzzled look. "A baby? This is her third!"

My eyes widen in surprise. Kelly's only a couple of years older than me. How does she already have *three* kids? I force a smile. "Wow, congrats to her! They grow up so fast, don't they?" I gulp down the rest of my wine, suddenly feeling out of place in my own skin, like I've missed a crucial memo on how to live life properly.

"Thank you, dear." Mrs. Thompson beams.

I hide out in the kitchen for the second half of the night, loading the dishwasher multiple times so Mom and Dad won't have to deal with the dishes later. Finally, it's time for the presents. I made my parents a video montage of their relationship, knowing they'd appreciate something heartfelt more than an expensive gift—also I couldn't afford anything of value. As the photo reel of their years together plays, everyone coos at the memories flashing by, and some even wipe away tears.

The video is the night's grand finale, and afterward, the guests start to disperse, offering warm wishes for my parents' anniversary as they go. I feel a little unsteady on my feet. Maybe I shouldn't have had that last glass of wine.

With my mom's help, I make up the sofa bed.

"Goodnight, honey." She kisses my forehead before leaving me alone in the dimly lit room that's spinning a little.

I collapse into bed, slightly dizzy. Just as I'm about to pass out, I remember my cowboy book in my bag. I grab it and curl up contentedly. Within moments, I'm drifting off, my head still spinning as I wake up mid-pirouette on a crowded barn bar dance floor where *I'm line dancing*?

Oh, gosh!

9

DANCE THE LINE

I bump into the person on my left, then the one on my right stomps on my toes as I move in the wrong direction. Panic flutters in my chest as I fumble with the steps, desperately trying to find an escape. But I'm blocked by a wall of people on all sides.

I've never line danced before in my life. I don't know the steps. My best option to get a hang of the choreography is to copy the people in front of me and try to keep up as best as I can. Step to the right, step behind, step to the side. Knee up. Left, left, left. Knee up. A step forward, knee up. Again. Three steps back, knee up. Move the hips. Turn to a new wall.

I do better on the second wall, and by the third, I'm able to enjoy the dance. And even add a flare of removing my cowboy hat as I touch step forward, touch step backward. Yee-haw!

The wooden floorboards thrum under my feet. The air is thick and warm, mingling scents of sawdust and the sweet tang of spilled beer. Laughter and whoops fill the space, echoing off the high rafters as the barn bar pulsates with energy, every corner alive with the rhythm of loud, upbeat country music.

With every knee jerk and hip sway, the heat from the

surrounding bodies, once overwhelming, fuels my stamina. My feet move fluidly now, in sync with the crowd. Boots scoot in perfect unison, and I sing along with the chorus of a song I didn't even know I knew.

I spin, my cowboy hat held high, as a fresh wave of laughter bubbles up from my chest. I clap and stomp along until the song ends, and a new one begins. There's a brief pause in the room where we all catch our breath, sharing smiles and nods with strangers. Then, as the first chords of the next slower ballad ring out, the ranks break and people pair up instead.

Fun as this has been, I take the new song as my cue to edge off the dance floor.

Exhausted, I scan the dingy bar for a clue who I might be here with when my gaze inadvertently locks onto Killian's. He's perched on a high stool, elbows nonchalantly resting on the table behind him, beer bottle in hand. His lopsided smirk pulls me in like a magnet as he carelessly drops his beer on the table and slides off the stool. Never breaking eye contact, he stalks toward me, weaving effortlessly through the crowd. I dry my palms on my jeans as he approaches, not sure if I should keep completely still or try to make a run for it.

My heart races as I stand there, waiting for him to close the gap between us with each purposeful stride. He stops only when our toes nearly touch. He's so close I smell his woodsy cologne.

"Sugar." He nods.

"Evil landlord." I nod back. "Isn't there anyone else you'd rather pester?"

"Not when you're the only one wearing my hat. May I have it back?" he drawls in that honeyed voice, plucking the cowboy hat from my head.

So I was wearing *his* hat? Which I stole to go line dancing—

fantasy me is a riot. I bite my lip to hide a smile as he puts the hat back on.

"Of course." I feign confidence despite my pounding heart. "But I must say, it looked better on me." As I drink him in, I try to recall how or why on earth I thought it was a good idea to steal his hat. I hate missing bits and pieces of this fantasy life. Hate. It. So. Much.

"Sure thing. But I still prefer to have the hat back." His eyes sparkle with amusement. "I suppose I'll forgive the theft if you save me a dance."

He's funny. "You're funny." I edge to the side, reading my escape. "Not happening."

Killian blocks my path with his body. "You don't have a choice, Spoon."

I blink up at him. "Meaning?"

"You owe me."

"Seriously? You'd use your boon just for a dance with me?"

"I can't think of anything better."

For a moment, I consider protesting, but there's something about the way he's looking at me that makes it hard to refuse. I give him a small nod and offer my hand.

Killian goes for my waist instead, pulling our bodies flush on the dance floor. His other hand intertwines with mine, holding it gently yet securely. As we begin to move to the music, the hand on my waist slides to the small of my back, guiding our movements. We sway together, our steps matching the rhythm of the slow song playing in the background.

Heat radiates off him, and every brush of his body against mine sends waves of electricity through me. Okay, now that he puts it like this, a dance seems very... mmm... *worthy.*

Killian's eyes are locked on mine, and the rest of the world fades in the distance, leaving just the two of us gliding across the floor.

His thumb strokes a knot on my spine, and I involuntarily shiver under his touch. His smile is barely there, just the hint of something more playing at the corners of his lips.

"Why do you look at me like that?" I ask on a breath.

"Because I can," he whispers back, his voice low and husky. "Because you want me to." He leans closer now, his lips grazing the shell of my ear. "Because you look at me the same."

There's an unspoken promise hanging in the air between us, a challenge I'm not sure I'm ready to confront.

But there's also an undeniable truth in his words, a recognition that sends a jolt of anticipation through me. I'm aware of the pressure of his fingers on my back, the scent of him that wraps around me like a cloak. My pulse quickens, and I realize that this isn't just a dance anymore. Or even a fantasy.

Because the way I feel about him right now is anything but fictional.

I let go of his hand and push back, shaking my head. "I can't do this."

In a panic, I rush off the dance floor and across the barn, scanning the walls until I find an exit.

The cool night air greets me like a slap as I burst through the doors, a stark contrast to the warmth left behind by Killian's touch. I turn the corner and lean against the barn's rough exterior, my breaths coming in short bursts as I try to calm the storm within me.

The music fades into a muffled throb behind me. Above, the stars twinkle like a multitude of watchful eyes, none offering any guidance or solace.

I hear the barn door open and then bang shut, but I don't need to turn to know that he's standing behind me.

"Running away?"

Killian's voice isn't loud, but it cuts through the quiet of the night with the precision of a knife. I don't answer, but my silence speaks volumes.

He doesn't come any closer. Instead, his footsteps crunch softly on the gravel as he moves to stand opposite me. One shoulder leaning against the wall, arms crossed over his chest, expression pissed off, ready to blow a fuse.

"Can we just not?" I scoff.

"Why?"

"Because none of this matters, it's all just a dream. You're just a dream…"

He reaches out and pinches my arm.

"Ouch." I jolt back. "What did you do that for?"

"Last I checked, dream men can't pinch arms."

Arms, maybe not. Hearts? I'm pretty sure they can.

I cast a wary glance at him, rubbing the spot where his fingers have dug in.

Killian pushes himself off the barn and takes a step closer. I plaster my back against the side of the building, trying to find support or to feel less exposed, I don't know. But it's not a brilliant move because next thing, Killian is caging me in, his palms flat on the wall on either side of my face.

"Tell me I'm the only one in this, that you want nothing to do with me, and I'll leave you alone."

I swallow. I know kissing him would be a mistake, that I'll regret it later when no real man will compare to a perfectly constructed fantasy hero. But gosh, for once in my life, I want to let go, to get lost in this dream. Just for a minute. An hour. Just until morning.

He's so close now I can count the individual dark lashes around his eyes, take in every detail of his beautiful face. I'm dying to trace my finger over that faint scar above his right eyebrow. To ask him how he got it, to learn everything about him there is to learn.

I try not to let my gaze drop to his lips, but it's darn near impossible. He notices, and that sinful mouth of his quirks up at one corner.

It's the last straw. I want this. I want *him*.

And so I give myself permission. I surrender to the now, to the dream of being wrapped in the arms of my personal book boyfriend, a living, breathing embodiment of every fictional romance hero I've ever swooned over.

I close my eyes, and welcome the warmth radiating from his body. I tilt my head up slightly. A silent invitation. His breath hitches, a sound barely audible yet monumental in the stillness between us before he closes the remaining distance. His lips are soft against mine, but commanding in their movements, a gentle pressure that feels like the sealing of a promise I'm not sure I should be making.

I tangle my hands in his hair, sending his hat flying to the ground, but neither of us bothers to even look at it.

Time slows to a crawl, every sensation magnified. The soft texture of his hair between my fingers; the faint scent of hay and horse that clings to him; the pressure of his lips on mine. Killian's hands slide from the wall to wrap around my waist, pulling me closer until there's no space left between us.

I lose myself in the kiss, in the feeling of being held so close, in the way his body molds to mine. He deepens the kiss, and a thrill courses through me, igniting every nerve ending. Our breaths mingle. His heartbeat echoes against my chest, a steady drumming that matches the pounding of my heart.

I pull back slightly, gasping for air, my forehead resting against his. Killian's eyes are dark with desire, a mirror of my own emotions. But there's a vulnerability in his gaze that makes my heart clench.

"Why can't you be real?" I whisper, the words escaping me before I can think better of them.

Killian's thumb strokes my cheek softly. "Does it matter?" His voice is low, filled with a raw honesty that strips away any pretense.

I shake my head slowly, knowing it shouldn't matter, but also knowing it does. Because this moment, this connection, feels more profound than any fleeting fantasy.

"I don't know what this is," I admit, my voice trembling. "But I don't want it to end."

His lips curve into a tender smile. "Then let's not end it."

And with that, he pulls me back into his arms, his kiss a reassurance that, for now, we're both here in this moment together. The world outside this embrace fades away, leaving only the two of us, caught in a timeless space where nothing else exists but the warmth of his lips and the beat of our hearts. We kiss until we're out of breath. Until our lips are too tender and swollen. Until it's time to wake up.

10

MORNING GLOW AND NIGHT SHADOWS

I wake to the smell of sizzling bacon and the clanking of pans. Blinking, I stare up at the familiar ceiling of my parents' living room. Even if I should be disappointed at being back in the real world, I can't stop a smile from spreading across my face as memories of last night replay in my head. Killian's mouth on mine, his fingers tangled in my hair... I touch two fingers to my lips; they almost feel swollen as if I really spent the entire night making out with a hot cowboy...

I let out a contented sigh.

"Is that you, honey?" Mom calls from the kitchen. "Breakfast is almost ready. Hope you're hungry."

My cheeks flush as I sit up on the lumpy couch. I finger-comb my tangled hair. "Starving," I call back, my voice still raspy with sleep.

Mom appears in the doorway, spatula in hand. She eyes my messy bedhead and grinning face. "Morning, darling." And she's gone again.

I push myself up from the couch and make my way to the kitchen. Mom's humming to herself as she flips pancakes on the griddle. Dad sits at the table, sipping his coffee and reading the morning paper.

"Good morning, sunshine," he says, looking up from his paper and smiling at me.

"Morning," I reply, pouring myself a cup of coffee and taking a seat next to him.

Mom sets a plate of pancakes and bacon in front of me, and I just can't stop smiling.

"So, what's got you in such a good mood this morning?" Mom asks, sitting across from me.

Since I can't tell them I'm fantasizing about a kiss that didn't happen with a man who doesn't exist, I deflect. "Oh, nothing, an email from school with potentially good news. But it's too early to say."

Dad raises an eyebrow but doesn't press me for details. Instead, he changes the subject to something more mundane, discussing the headlines from the paper, the weather forecast promising sunshine and clear skies, and the neighbor's cat who seems to have taken a liking to our garden. Their voices become a comfortable background hum as my mind drifts back to Killian. I can still feel the ghost of his touch on my skin, sending shivers down my spine despite the warm kitchen.

I take a bite of pancake, the sweetness of syrup mingling with the savory bacon. I chew slowly, savoring the flavors as memories of last night continue to fill my mind.

"Honey? Did you hear your dad ask you about helping us with the garden later?" Mom's voice pulls me back to the present, her eyes filled with a mix of curiosity and amusement.

"Oh, um, yeah. Sure, I can help out," I manage to say, as my cheeks warm.

My parents have taken half a day off to be with me, gardening is just an excuse to do something together. That's how we spend the morning, and I make a conscious effort to actually pay attention to them and not get lost in my dream world again. Then, after a quick lunch of leftovers from the party, they have to drive me back to the station.

Dad parks the car, and we share one last hug before I board the train.

Since no one is sitting next to me, I set an alarm for my expected arrival time and try to nap. But sleep evades me for the entire journey.

The rhythmic clacking of the train's wheels on the tracks keeps time with my racing thoughts. Outside the window, landscapes blur into an indistinct tapestry of greens and browns, punctuated by infrequent splashes of color from passing towns. But all I can think about is going back to Lakeville Hills, back to *him*.

I finally make it home mid-afternoon. I unpack and do a load of laundry in the basement while I check my emails—mostly bizarre excuses from students on why they're late with their assignments, which I don't reply to.

With all the research hours I've missed by going home, I should be working late tonight. Instead, I find myself pondering what time would be considered too early to go to bed? Is 6 p.m. acceptable? That I'm contemplating hitting the sack before the sun has even fully set is a blaring red flag.

Besides research, I've still got a ton of papers to read and homework to grade.

I really shouldn't brush all that off to escape to dreamland. But... Killian kissed me... and I can make up for the lost work over the weekend. It's not like I have a social life that will get in the way.

It's decided. I'm tucking in early.

I slip into my coziest pajamas and slide under the covers. At once, my mind snags back to Killian, to the kiss that's so vivid in my memory it seems too real to have just been a fantasy.

I pick up the mystery book without opening it, hug it to my chest, and close my eyes. But sleep keeps eluding me for the longest time. Partly because it's way too early to be napping—my sleep hormones haven't caught up to my new irresponsible life-style. And partly because the excitement mixed with anxiety at the prospect of kissing Killian again isn't exactly conducive to sleep.

It takes a while, but finally, my lids become heavy, my head lolls on the pillow, and then I'm dreaming...

11

HIGH HEELS AND HOSTAGES

I expect to wake up still in Killian's arms outside the barn or perhaps somewhere cozier where it's just the two of us. But instead of the warm festive bar I left behind, I come to in a ghostly open space where I'm tied to a chair and gagged with duct tape.

Whaaaaat?

In the semi-darkness, I strain my eyes to better assess my surroundings. The building I'm imprisoned in has a tall ceiling and walls made of dilapidated wooden planks. If I had to guess, I'd say I'm being held in a run-down barn. Half abandoned, judging from the way the structure is coated in years of dust and dirt and the cobwebs that spread over the beams. The air is thick with the stench of manure and rotting hay.

A pitchfork and other rusted farming tools rest against a stall alongside hooks and iron hoops. At least there are no chains nailed to the wall, making me hope I haven't suddenly traveled to a horror novel.

Still, as I look down at myself, my ankles are each tied to one of the chair's legs with a coarse rope, and my hands painfully stretched behind my back and bound as well.

Not exactly your typical rom-com setting. The clothes are the same, though. I'm dressed in my country uniform of a knotted checkered shirt and jeans—longer than shorty-shorts this time. The hem reaches to about mid-calf, but it still isn't long enough to spare the skin of my ankles from being brutally bitten in by the rope. And I'm still wearing those ridiculously high-heeled clogs I had at the bakery.

Blisters or not, fantasy me doesn't give up on her fashion. But problematic footwear is the least of my concerns now. What the heck am I doing here? I keep looking at my surroundings for any clues.

The barn is almost completely dark. The only light filters in through the cracked sidings at the front of the room, where a massive door rests crooked on its hinges. From the cold glow, I can tell the light is artificial, which makes me assume it must be night in Lakeville Hills.

I eye the door again. It seems to be the only way out of the barn, except for a too-high window, and so my only viable escape route.

What am I supposed to do here? Engineer an escape? MacGyver some explosive out of cow poo and twine and blast my way out? Or patiently wait to be rescued by my dashing hero?

I find myself hoping this isn't too much of a feminist book. I'll happily play the damsel in distress and let myself be rescued, thank you very much. Half the time, I think I'm just making up stories in my head while I dream, but then something like this happens—something I'd never dream up for myself—and I almost feel like I've literally splashed through the blank pages of Killian's book. It's almost as if we're completing the unfinished story together.

The sound of a padlock being jostled brings my focus back to the door. Next, I hear a metallic snap and a dull thud.

Adrenaline floods my system when the door opens a crack and then shuts again just as quickly.

My eyes take a second to readjust to the near-total obscurity after the blinding flash of light. But even in the semi-darkness, I can distinguish the livid face of the man advancing on me. Killian looks like he's struggling to keep himself from exploding.

He's utterly terrifying in his fury, but I'm not scared, not of him.

I'm pretty sure he isn't the one who tied me to this chair, but he definitely isn't happy with me, or how I've ended up here supposedly.

He's almost on me now, gray eyes glittering in the dark like those of a cat, which turns me into the mouse in this scenario. Memories from the last time we were alone assail me. His lips on mine, my hands in his hair, our chests pressing together. What happened since then? Are we an item now? Are we dating?

"Explain to me how you got yourself captured by the worst criminal gang in the state," he barks, interrupting my speculations.

Contrary to me, Killian isn't in an amorous mood. Which immediately sets me in a temper of my own. I don't know what it is about this man, but he sure can push all my buttons.

With the duct tape gagging me, I can't talk, but I can glare.

Killian stalks toward me, closing the last of the distance, and with a precise jerk of his hand, he removes three-quarters of the tape, freeing my mouth. It stings like a bitch, but the adrenaline helps to manage the pain.

"They were torturing a poor calf, they would've killed him for fun," I sputter. It appears that my dream brain, while not remembering how to drive a stick, how to line dance, or what my relationship status with Killian is, keeps up to speed with whatever else is going on in this fictional world.

"A calf?" Killian taps his foot. "You're here because you were trying to save *cattle*?"

"I wasn't going to let a baby animal be tortured and killed for sport."

"Yeah?" he snaps, face truly lethal now. "And what do you think those gentlemen are planning to do to you, *for sport*?"

"I didn't think," I say. "I just acted, and I'd do it again a million times, even knowing I'd end up here."

"Well-the-heck-aware," Killian hisses.

And I get the distinct impression that he'd be shouting at me if not for the "gentlemen" outside he just mentioned.

The outburst shocks me a little. Every other time I've seen him, he's always appeared so cold, so in control. But there's a dark fury blazing in his eyes now.

Killian sucks in a breath as if he's just as startled by his reaction. Then, shaking his head, he kneels between my thighs. My first instinct is to close my legs or open them wider—I'm not even sure which at this point. But of course, I can't do either. So I keep perfectly still as a blade flashes in his hands, and he gets to work on cutting the rope on my right ankle. "You were reckless."

"I don't care." I lift my chin. "They were playing matadors with a baby cow. I wasn't just going to turn my head and—"

In a swift move, the duct tape is back on my mouth.

"I prefer you gagged," Killian says, the harshness in his voice a contrast to the gentle way his fingers are soothing the sensitive skin of my ankle where the rope chafed me.

The distracting touch prevents me from hauling a stream of profanities at him, even from under the gag. A tingle shoots up my leg, landing straight between my thighs.

Killian flashes me a mocking stare, as if he knows exactly

what kind of power a simple graze of his fingers holds, and gets to work on freeing the other leg.

Then he's at my back, bent at a weird angle so that his hands are on mine and his lips brush my left ear.

"In another scenario," he whispers down my neck, "I wouldn't mind having you all trussed up for me, Sugar Spoon."

The moment my wrists are free, I kick the chair backward and stand up, removing the tape from my mouth once again.

Killian dodges the chair projectile and stalks toward me. "Be quiet, will you?"

I shove him. "You gagged me."

"And you got yourself almost killed, if not worse. I'd say we're even."

I massage my wrists where the ropes were just an instant ago, the motion not nearly as pleasant as when Killian was performing it on my ankles. "What's the plan now?" I ask begrudgingly.

"We get out of here, *quietly*." The strain he puts on the word quietly is insufferable. "The sheriff is on his way, but we can't be too careful."

"If the cops are coming, why didn't you just wait for *them* to rescue me?"

The glare he throws me in response is full of frustration and some other powerful emotion I can't place. But it's fierce enough to stun me into silence.

Did something else happen after we kissed yesterday? Was it yesterday for him, too, or before? What else has transpired between us in the meantime? Like always, I've missed entire chapters and I loathe it.

"Keep close behind me," Killian orders as he strides toward the only exit.

I follow him, heart beating in my chest as he opens the door a crack, overlooking a peeling farmhouse and cornfields.

Killian slips through the opening with unnatural grace for a man so tall. I trail after him, moving a lot less gracefully on my high heels. We cross the illuminated dirt patch in front of the barn, aiming for the safety of the shadows at the edge of the fields.

We've almost made it when the door to the farmhouse bangs open and someone noisily spits to the ground. Before I even have time to realize what's happening, Killian has grabbed me and pulled me behind a tree. My back flush to his front, while one of his large hands covers my mouth to stifle my surprised cry.

I have to say, I prefer this modality of gagging to duct tape tenfold. Still, because I'm an asshole, I gently nibble on one of his fingers.

Initially, he goes rigid against me. But as we listen to the man on the porch undo his fly and relieve himself on the ground, Killian shifts his stance ever so slightly. The fingers of his left hand dig into my hip and then move up to flatten on my stomach, his knuckles grazing the underside of my breast as he moves.

And then his thumb starts to draw slow, lazy circles on my belly.

Every hair on my body stands to alert. Normally, I'd whimper and struggle to wiggle free, unable to bear the tension. But the me of this world is bold and fierce, and she certainly isn't one to de-escalate situations. So I close my teeth on the flesh of his finger and suck.

Killian buries his face in my curls, clearly struggling to suppress a groan. I rejoice knowing that I'm the one responsible for making him this worked up. To have him spin out of control.

"You'd better stop this little game of yours, Sugar Spoon." The words are so soft-spoken even I strain to hear them. "Or I might decide to come out and play for real."

In response, I give him another nibble.

This time, he spins me around and cages me against the tree, taking my breath away—and not because of the impact of my back with the trunk.

He has my wrists imprisoned above my head, eyes ablaze even against the dark night.

At this moment, I don't care if we're trying to escape a den of infamous criminals. All I care about is that if he doesn't kiss me right now, I might burst up in flames.

A strong gush of wind picks up, cooling my heated skin. I revel in the sensation, at least until I hear the barn door bang in its frame behind us. Killian tenses against me. His head snaps to the side, probably to check if the man outside has heard it, too. Our only hope is that he is too drunk to notice. But luck is not on our side.

"Hey, Dirk," the man calls out in a drawl. "Did you leave the barn door unlocked?"

I don't hear the full response, but the words *bitch* and *inside* clearly carry over the wind.

"Well, I'm afraid the bitch has escaped then."

A heartbeat of silence and then we hear the cocking of a shotgun. Seconds later, chips of wood explode a mere few inches above our heads.

Killian grabs my hand and pulls me into the cornfield, uttering a single word, "Run."

12

DOUBLE DATES AND DREAM STATES

My eyes fly open, my heart still pumping from the adrenaline of the dream. And never have I ever been more disappointed to be safe in bed instead of running across cornfields being shot at by criminals.

I sag against the pillow and cover my face with the blankets, aware I'm developing an unhealthy habit of preferring my life when I'm not living it. Unconsciousness has become my happy place.

Going to bed and escaping to Lakeville Hills is the highlight of my day, every day.

I'm also worried I might be falling head over heels in love with a fictional man who doesn't exist. But, gosh, if the dreams don't seem real. If I close my eyes, I can still sense the press of his hard body against mine. The flat of his hand on my stomach. His thumb torturing me in slow motion. And that brush of knuckles underneath my breast.

My skin breaks into goosebumps, and I'm tempted to simply ignore real life and go back to sleep. But then the alarm snoozes and I groan, forcing myself to sit up. I run a hand through my messy curls and rub the drowsiness from my eyes before getting out of bed.

I might want to ignore real life, but reality has a way of catching up. Throughout the day, I struggle. Taking a short time off has been enough for tasks to pile up.

I haven't finished grading homework assignments; I still have those million unanswered emails in my inbox. I need to come up with a lesson plan for tomorrow's lecture. And I have homework for my graduate courses to finish, too.

This means that if I'm lucky and no one shows up for office hours, I could catch up with all that and maybe carve out an hour for my research—not nearly enough to make any significant progress.

I hate how I've let things slide.

Keeping my head in the game is crucial. I can't control my love life or lack thereof outside my dreams. But I'm in charge of how well I do in my academic career, and what results my research will produce.

That's why, despite every fiber of my body protesting against it, on Wednesday night, I don't take my book with me when I go to sleep at midnight—a respectable hour for an overworked grad student. In fact, I hide the paperback under the bed—out of sight, out of mind. I struggle to fall asleep, but when I do, it's to complete darkness.

No dreams. No Killian.

I do the same the following night. I'm wretchedly efficient and utterly unhappy. But my academic future is secured.

In a blink, it's Friday night and time for my double date with Ivy, her boyfriend, George, and his brother, Oliver.

I'd like to say that I have no expectations for the evening, that I'm aware the only worse thing than a blind date is a blind *double* date where I can't bail halfway through dinner with an excuse in case it sucks.

But Ivy has sent me a picture of Oliver, and he's, well, gorgeous. Dark hair, bright green eyes, and a smile that could light up a room.

A mild Google stalking has brought up no red flags, and even his Insta is cool—artsy but not pretentious, with a dash of humor thrown in.

And so my old enemy has reared its head: hope. Hope that this time will be different. Hope that for once, there might be a spark, some chemistry. Hope that maybe, just maybe, Oliver could be the one. A real man I can have a proper relationship with.

After all my past disappointments, I should know better. But no, I'm still as naïve as a googly-eyed five-year-old watching Cinderella go to the ball and marry her Prince Charming.

I try to shake off my expectations as I get dressed for the evening. Ivy and I agreed on casual outfits. I settle for a cute floral sweater, jeans, and ankle boots. I don't spend too much time on my makeup. Still, I domesticate my curls into shiny ringlets, which I hope will resist the humidity and train ride downtown.

The restaurant Ivy chose is cozy and warm. When I see her waving from a corner table with a big grin on her face, I relax a little. George and Oliver are already there, each nursing a beer.

Ivy introduces us and we awkwardly shake hands across the table. Oliver's hand feels warm and strong in mine—dry, no sweaty palms for him. In person, he's tall and fit. Broad shoulders, firm handshake but not bone-crushing, smile as bright as in his pictures.

And is that a flutter in my belly? I can't help but beam back at Oliver as he brings my chair backward, politely waiting for me to sit. Handsome and a gentleman.

I catch Ivy's eye across the table, and she winks at me from behind her water glass, hardly suppressing a smug smirk.

Okay, I have to hand it to her. He's easy on the eyes, well-mannered, and confident. No BO that I can detect except maybe something fresh with a hint of spice, pleasing to the senses. Oliver seems like a catch.

Gray eyes flash in my mind. *A better catch than me, Sugar Spoon?*

I mentally swat Killian away. I'm in a recovery program to forget all about him. And Oliver might just be the perfect distraction I need to move on.

Our eyes meet and I quickly divert my gaze to the menu, feeling a bit flustered.

We settle into conversation over drinks and appetizers. Oliver tells me the basics about himself—studies, job, hobbies—and asks the same of me, actually listening when I reply. I'm impressed.

Talking to him is easy, it comes naturally.

As the night progresses, I laugh at his jokes and share more intimate details about myself than I intended. But he doesn't seem to mind. In fact, he seems genuinely interested.

A server brings our main course and the conversation turns to our favorite books. I'm pleasantly surprised when Oliver reveals that he's an avid reader.

When I go to take a sip of wine, my cheeks hurt slightly and I realize it's because I haven't stopped smiling for a second since I sat down.

The night is going overwhelmingly well. Still, I can't shake the pang of wrongness lodged in my heart.

Those gray eyes invade my mind again. *Bet you can't.*

Am I seriously so wrung up in my fantasies that I feel like I'm cheating on an imaginary man?

Yep!

I need a minute so I excuse myself to the bathroom.

In the restrooms, I beeline for the sink and let a jet of cool water flow over my wrists, also dabbing the fresh liquid over my neck. Looking in the mirror, I give myself a pep talk, reinforcing the concept that I must live in the real world and forget all about non-existent billionaire cowboys.

Right.

I exit the restroom, having decided to give Oliver my undivided attention for the rest of the evening.

When I come back to the table, the desserts have already arrived. We've taken the chef selection, so there's a handful of bite-sized cakes to try.

I pop a mini slice of carrot pie into my mouth and savor its sweetness on my tongue. Oliver smiles at me from across the table, his charm radiating through those gorgeous eyes, and suddenly all my doubts vanish.

I should give this a real chance.

We get lost in conversation again—and not just on a superficial level, but with genuine curiosity from both sides.

Dinner ends with the two of us laughing at some silly joke he made. I can tell he's had a great time too by the twinkle in his eye when he looks at me.

Outside the restaurant, Oliver offers to drive me home, even though it's half an hour out of his way. I don't protest too hard as I'm not too keen on taking public transportation this late at night.

Ivy winks at me, and her departing salvo is, "Don't do anything I wouldn't do!"

She kisses me goodnight and then she and George are gone, leaving me alone with Oliver.

"I'm this way." He gestures to the parking lot down the road.

Once we get to his car, he opens the door for me and offers

me his hand to help me get inside, making me feel like a fairy tale princess being escorted into a carriage by a prince.

The ride north is quieter than dinner. I notice Oliver keeps shooting me sideways glances. Is he as nervous as I am? Is it because he plans to kiss me goodnight?

We soon arrive at my neighborhood in the suburbs. Oliver pulls up in front of my building, killing the engine and turning to me with a new intensity in his green eyes. His hand softly captures mine from its perch resting on the armrest, and he brushes a thumb over my knuckles. His gaze drops to where our hands are connected for what feels like an eternity before meeting mine again when he finally asks, "Is it okay if I kiss you goodnight?"

I nod.

His grip on my hand changes, our fingers interlacing. And while the touch isn't unpleasant, there's no lick of flames. No tingles shooting up my arms. Barely a flutter in my belly as Oliver leans in and presses his lips on mine.

I don't hate the kiss, but there are no fireworks.

Oliver pulls back after a short while, avoiding my eye and keeping his gaze on his lap. "I'm sorry," he whispers.

"Sorry? What for?" .

He looks up at me, dismayed.

I smile at him because, for some inexplicable reason, I feel comfortable around this man I've just met. I'm not afraid to be vulnerable, and I can be honest. "Was the kiss so bad?"

"No!" His eyes widen. "I just didn't..."

"Feel the spark?" I finish for him.

A gentle shake of his head. "I'm sorry for trying."

"Why? How were we going to find out if we never kissed?"

Oliver shifts in his seat. "If I tell you something, can you promise not to tell Ivy or my brother?"

His expression is grave, so I match his seriousness when I say, "Of course."

"I shouldn't have kissed you because I was 99 per cent sure it would not work."

"Why?"

"I'm not sure I'm into women."

My first reaction is surprise, immediately followed by immense empathy.

I reach across the seat and hug him. Oliver keeps stiff at first, then his arms wrap around my torso and he squeezes. I let him decide when to break the hug, and when he does, Oliver is smiling. "That's not the reaction I was expecting. Why the hug?"

I beam back. "I was imagining how I'd cope if my friends and family kept setting me up with women instead of men. Why haven't you told them you're gay?"

"That's the thing. I'm not even sure I'm gay. Maybe I'm just asexual. I never seem to get a spark with anyone."

"You've kissed men, too?"

"Yeah, and still nothing."

"Then you're fine." I swat him playfully. "According to 'coupled humans' wisdom,' you're either too picky or trying too hard." I grab my chin, pretending to think. "Or you have to work on yourself because the fact that you're still single is a clear sign you have issues."

I keep a straight face for about a second and then we both burst out laughing.

"Imagine having a dollar for every time someone told us that," he says, between chuckles.

"I would at least still be able to afford my Netflix subscription."

He raises a brow at me. "Grad school that bad?"

I beam. "No, but other people's nuptials are turning me destitute."

We laugh again.

When the chortles die down, I turn serious again. "Do you have to have this conversation at the end of every date your family sends you on?"

"No." Oliver grins widely at me. "Usually the dates are so tragic I don't even need to bother."

I beat a fist on my chest. "I feel you, man. Tonight, I was actually surprised you didn't have any weird BO, or that you hadn't casually forgotten your wallet. Thank you again for paying for dinner, by the way, you really didn't need to."

"But I wanted to. You're a wonderful person, Leigh, and I felt this immediate connection to you."

"Yeah, same here, even without a romantic spark."

"The lack of a spark is clearly your fault for not loving yourself enough."

I throw my head back and laugh. "Oliver, can we become best friends, please? I haven't had this much fun in forever."

"I'd love nothing more."

We exchange phone numbers and when I make to exit the car, Oliver precedes me and circles around to get my door.

"Thank you." I curtsey to him. "It's a shame that spark didn't hit us because you'd be a perfect Prince Charming."

"And you an amazing Cinderella."

"Jokes aside, I don't know why you haven't told your family how you really feel—"

"Because I'm not sure," he interrupts me. "I don't want to tell them I'm gay when I'm not positive that's the case. I still find women attractive. And imagine if I told them I'm just confused, or that I'm bi, and they started setting me up on dates with *both*

men and women. There's only so much blind dating I can take."
His eyes spark. "Present people excluded, of course."

"Of course." I hug him again. "But if you need to talk to
someone or just vent, I'm here. Anytime."

He squeezes me one last time. "Thank you." And we say
goodnight.

As I get back inside of my apartment and shuffle out of my
clothes, I'm not sure how I feel. Even without a spark, it was a
good night. I had fun, I met an incredible person and felt a little
less alone.

But the hole in my chest where the spark should be is gaping.

I see those teasing gray eyes again. *I give plenty sparkles, Sugar
Spoon.*

And tonight, I don't have the strength to resist the pull.
Maybe my fairy tale isn't *Cinderella*. I'm not destined to find a
Prince Charming that will save me from all the ugliness of the
world. I'm Sleeping Beauty. Some wicked fairy will eventually
curse me, and I'll get to sleep a hundred years and spend them
blissfully in my dreams with Killian.

Bullets be damned, I want to go back to my love story. And
seeing how I sometimes chapter-hop in that world, I'll probably
end up in a completely different scene from the kidnapping,
anyway.

In my bedroom, I reach under the bed, dust off the poor
paperback I left rotting on the floor for days. I trace the faceless
cowboy on the cover.

"Why can't you be real?"

I open the book and my eyes bulge when I find more written
pages than last time. Now there's a chapter on the bakery, one at
the lake, the motel, the line dancing, the barn rescue... all my
dreams have magically appeared in black ink over white paper.

I frown. Did I miss all these chapters that first night? Am I just re-dreaming stuff I read while half asleep? But I clearly remember checking the book that first morning, and only the chapter about my showdown with Killian at The Outlaw was there.

Where did all the extra text come from? Did I develop some sort of somnambulism where I get out of bed and type my dreams out? But how would I even print them inside the book?

I grab my phone and search for how to print inside a book. The only viable option would be to create a stencil mockup of the page and then transfer it to the white paper. But I wouldn't even have the supplies to do so in the house.

My next Google search is even more outlandish: a book that writes itself. The only search results are on writing advice for authors. Of course, because books don't write themselves. Except this one.

I go to the end of the text and shoot a picture to check back tomorrow. Just to make sure I'm not going insane and hallucinating new chapters. The last word on the page is Killian telling me to run.

13

ABLAZE

My heel sinks into the mud as corn leaves mercilessly whip my face and arms.

Of course, if I'm being shot at, I'm going to land straight back into *this* scene. I don't even remember falling asleep in the real world. I was still studying the book, but I must've conked out at some point.

I don't have time to reflect on it now as I take another step forward and stumble, my useless heels sinking in a patch of softer terrain. I almost face plant to the ground, but Killian is holding my hand so I manage to keep upright.

"You're too slow," he complains.

"I'd like to see you trying to run in heels through a field."

"Then wear more sensible shoes."

"A, I didn't know I was going to be kidnapped. And B, I'm not in charge of fashion choices here."

Killian frowns. "What does that even mean?"

I'm about to reply when a stalk not three feet away from me is decapitated by a flying bullet.

Killian's expression changes from irritated to scared then back to irked.

"Never mind. We don't have time for this."

He half squats down and unceremoniously tosses me over his shoulder.

"Hey," I try to protest as he starts running again. "Put me down."

"Sorry, Sugar Spoon, no can do." Now that he has my extra weight to carry, the words come out labored. "Not unless you want a new lead decoration for this pretty behind." Despite sprinting down the field at breakneck speed, he still manages to slap said behind for emphasis.

I'm indignant and miserably uncomfortable. In this position, the lashes from the corn leaves are even worse, and I'm bobbing up and down so much, I might throw up.

To steady myself, I grab onto the only available thing, namely Killian's butt.

"Seriously, Sugar? Feeling me up?"

Before I can reply, we swerve right, now cutting through the field perpendicularly to the rows of corn. The amount of vegetation coming at my face is so dire that I think it best to keep my mouth shut and bury my face in Killian's back for protection.

I'm not sure how long we run. I only know that when he finally stops, everything aches. We're out of the cornfield, hiding in a patch of tall grass.

Killian gently lowers me to the grass, laying me on the ground like a princess on a bed of flowers. I make to sit up, but he pushes me back down, getting half on top of me to keep me in place.

My eyes widen, and before I can protest, he presses a finger to my lips, lowering his mouth to my ear. "Shhh, we have to keep quiet and stay hidden until the sheriff arrives."

Suddenly, I become very conscious of the muscular thigh he has lodged between my legs.

The moon is almost full tonight. So that even with no artificial illumination, I can distinguish every plane and angle of Killian's face.

The intensity in his eyes draws me in, making it difficult to focus on anything else. He's so close that our breaths mingle, his hot exhales tickling my neck.

As my heart beats wildly in my chest, the warmth radiating from his body seeps into me. The heat between us smolders and smolders until I catch fire. Plenty of sparkles, indeed.

The electricity coursing through my veins isn't a mere lick of flames, it's a full-on conflagration. My entire body is ablaze, burning from my toes to the tips of my hair.

I can't breathe. My lungs are no longer filled with air but smoke, dark and churning.

I reach up and sink my fingers into Killian's silky hair, almost daring him to stop me. I play with the soft curls at his nape, watching as the intensity in his eyes escalates.

A wicked smile dances on his lips and his hand moves. Up my side, to my cheek, then into my hair, fanning them out.

I watch his beautiful face, mesmerized as he reverses the path, tracing a finger over my collarbone, then down over my sternum, missing all the important places where I want to feel his hands, and finally to the sliver of uncovered skin over my belly.

More, I need more. I squirm in the grass, but I can't move, trapped as I am under his weight. So I retaliate by sneaking my hand under his flannel shirt and dragging my nails down his back.

Dangerous doesn't begin to cover what I see in his gray eyes in response. But then the gray flashes with blue and red. Police cars have arrived on the dirt road above us. We're saved. Or maybe I'm forever doomed because next thing, Killian's lips descend on mine.

14

COFFEE BREAK

Our kiss is frenzied, all-consuming, and overwhelming. The taste of him—hot and spicy—fills my senses. He entwines his fingers with mine and pins my hands above my head. In the dirt. I don't care.

I can savor the danger on his lips. I'm consumed by him. My body arches against his, craving more of him.

Killian groans as he deepens the kiss, his mouth battling with mine for dominance. I moan, feeling his weight press down harder, but not even close to quenching the fire in my core.

The sound of footsteps interrupts our kiss.

We've barely pulled apart when someone drawls, "Well, it looks like you folks are doing just fine." The sheriff scowls at us from under his cowboy hat. "But you'd better move this some-where else before I arrest you both for public indecency."

Killian springs up and helps me off the ground, and I avoid meeting his gaze as I dust myself off.

"I'm going to need statements from both of you at the station," the sheriff continues. "But it can wait until tomorrow."

He gives us another dubious once-over. "Are either of you in need of medical attention?"

Only if extreme embarrassment can be considered a health concern. I just shake my head no.

"Then move it along." The unimpressed officer makes a circular gesture with his arm.

Killian wraps me in a side hug as we make our way back to his truck, the heat from his body warming me on the chilly night. We keep quiet as we climb in, both of us lost in our own thoughts.

"Should I drive you home?" Killian asks once we merge on a larger road.

"Yes, please," I reply, even if I've no idea where "home" is. I barely saw the place before I was yanked back to reality last time.

Fifteen minutes later, Killian pulls up in front of a little cozy blue farmhouse and kills the engine.

I unbuckle my seatbelt, feeling a strange mix of relief and disappointment. I don't want the night to end, but I'm not sure I'm brave enough to voice that thought out loud.

"Thanks for the ride," I blurt, and, at his weirded-out expression, I quickly add, "And for saving my life, I guess."

"Anytime, Sugar."

"So this is goodnight, then?"

That wicked grin again. "No goodnight kiss?"

I watch as Killian's eyes drop from my face to my lips. The tension builds between us, electric and undeniable. He leans forward and captures my mouth in a searing kiss, his hand tangling in my hair.

When he releases me, and patiently waits for me to exit the truck, I don't move. I want more of these kisses. And not just kisses if I'm being completely honest.

"Are you thirsty?" I blurt the first thing that pops into my head, remembering his innuendo of the other night. "I mean, do you want to come in for a cup of coffee or something?"

His smile turns feral. "*Coffee*, yeah, sure."

And I hope that by "coffee" he really means wild living-room-floor sex because we're both too horny to reach the bedroom.

But Killian follows me meekly inside the house, keeping a respectful distance. The front door is unlocked. Bands of criminals or not, this is still that kind of small town where no one ever locks their doors.

As I push the door open, I take in the narrow hall that ends in a flight of stairs and the two arched passages on each side, trying to orient myself.

The interior of the house is pretty in a country chic way with distressed wood finishes and vintage touches. In any other circumstance, I'd be thrilled to discover this is my home, but my mind is too consumed with thoughts of Killian to appreciate any of it.

Where's the kitchen? So that I can get that coffee started. Because, apparently, a late nightcap is why we're here. I walk under the arch on the right and enter the living room. I immediately backtrack, smashing into a rock-hard chest and almost falling on my butt.

Killian steadies me with two solid hands on my shoulders.

"Sorry," I say. "Kitchen's that way."

Killian arches a brow at me.

I shrug free and finally make it to the stove.

I open only two wrong cabinets before I find the coffee tin. The coffee maker looks suspiciously ancient, but maybe it'll add flavor to the blend?

"How do you take your coffee?" I call to Killian.

The air behind me shifts as he cages me in between the kitchen counter and his hard chest.

Cold fingers wrap gently around my throat from behind. Killian applies gentle pressure to tilt my head upward and backward. "I like my coffee long and dark." He drops a closed-mouth kiss on the side of my neck. "With just a splash of sugar."

Are we still talking drink preferences or have we moved on to sexual kinks?

"Th-that sounds i-interesting..." I trail off as the coffee tin explodes in my hands. Maybe I was squeezing too hard. The counter is a mess, dark-brown powder everywhere.

Killian removes the tin from my still-shaking hands and drops it next to the sink with a loud thud. "I'm not really here for coffee, Spoon."

Praise be!

While he's still caging me in from behind, his deft fingers find the collar of my shirt and rip it away from my throat. Buttons pop and fabric tears. A shiver of fear and excitement courses through my body, and when he pulls me tighter into him, other impulses battle within me—a primal and thrilling need to both stay and flee.

His fingers dig into my hip, and all preservation instincts fly out the window.

I drop my head back on his shoulder to give him better access to kiss me... and I suddenly blink awake.

15

RINGING REGRETS

My phone's ringing. I swear I'm going to destroy that wretched thing. Crush it under a hammer. Pancake it under a bulldozer.

I snatch the phone from the nightstand ready to throw it down the fire escape but answer by accident instead.

"Leigh? Hello? Are you there?" Ivy's voice drifts up from the speakers.

"Ivy, hi." I do my best to keep the extreme annoyance out of my tone. "What can I do for you?"

"Are you okay? Am I interrupting something?" She screeches enthusiastically. "Were you having morning sex with Oliver?"

More I was about to have fantasy sex with Killian.

"Of course not."

"Oh. But the date last night went great." She sounds downcast now. "Didn't it?"

"Yeah," I say sincerely. Oliver might not be my one true love, but I'm happy to have a new friend. "Oliver is wonderful."

"Are you going on a second date?"

"I need coffee before we have this conversation," I stall.

I lower the phone from my ear and shoot a quick text to Oliver:

> TO OLIVER
>
> SOS. Ivy is asking if we're going on a second date. What should I tell her?

As I wait for him to reply, I shuffle the five steps from my bed to the kitchen, actually making coffee while Ivy drawls on and on about what a great guy he is.

Oliver's reply arrives shortly after.

> FROM OLIVER
>
> Please say we're going on a second date. At least my family will back off me for a short while

I hardly suppress a smile.

> TO OLIVER
>
> Fake dating, uh? Why, Oliver, we might still fall madly in love after all

> FROM OLIVER
>
> If only we could

I know exactly what he means. It seems unjust that we like each other so much and still have no spark.

I give Ivy the happy, fake news and after a million other questions—the only one I can answer truthfully is if Oliver and I kissed last night—she lets me go.

I sit on one of the two stools at the impish kitchen bar—which doubles as the only table in the house—and stare at the mug of coffee in my hands.

Long.

Dark.

With just a splash of sugar.

I can almost feel Killian's fingers at my throat.

Real life sucks.

I want to go back to sleep.

Then I probably shouldn't drink coffee. I empty the mug in the sink and hop back into bed. But before I try to sleep again, I check the book. And sure enough there's a new chapter. Cornfield escape, hot kisses, shirt ripping and all. The last passage before the blank pages ends on a sexy cliffhanger.

I grab my phone and check my picture of last night. These words definitely weren't there yesterday. What is going on?

Sleep now is the furthest thing from my mind. I go down a rabbit hole of researching legends and folklore about magical books that write themselves. But all I come up with is either more non-fiction books on writing advice or straight-out fantasy novels.

Next, I google: signs of a nervous breakdown, hallucinations, hyper-real dream states, schizophrenia, water pollutants causing hallucinations, possible causes for distorted reality.

Unless the local water supply has been contaminated by heavy metals there is no plausible explanation for what's happening.

I take a picture of the book and send it to Ivy.

TO IVY

Is this yours?

My phone pings two minutes later with a negative response.

I keep staring at the book. "How did you get here? Are you magical?"

The book, of course, doesn't reply.

I give up trying to find a logical explanation a couple of hours later. I should probably book a psych evaluation. But I'm afraid that if I tell a doctor what I'm seeing, they'd just lock me up in a mental institution. And, frankly, I don't have the time for a sojourn in an asylum.

So, I do what I do best and bury all my worries in my work.

I soldier through the day in a zombie haze; I stay up until late. At this point, I'm equally eager to go back to Lakeville Hills and scared of what will happen if I do.

I'm half-convinced I'm losing my mind. Should I throw the book away, never to open it again? Make it someone else's problem? Destroy it?

But the thought of never seeing Killian again is impossible to bear. So is the idea of never again being able to escape to an adventurous dream world where I'm happy. Where I can have third-date, guilt-free sex. No chance of Killian losing my number because I never gave it to him. This is *my* fantasy, so he's stuck with me.

I sigh and pick up the book, decided to give in to my madness. As I lie down to sleep, I keep my fingers crossed that I'll land right back in my kitchen with a ripped shirt missing a few buttons and about to have the night of my life.

16

YOU'RE NOT REAL

Obviously, I don't land in my kitchen with a ripped shirt. Instead, I wake up stark naked over a plaid quilt and under a blanket of sunshine. At once, I feel like I've landed on the wrong side of this fantasy.

I push myself up on an elbow and find Killian next to me, eyes closed, chin tilted up toward the sun, chest moving up and down in a regular rhythm. He's sleeping. And he's buck naked, too.

BAWHAM.

That definitely is not the kind of male body I'm used to seeing in real life. He's a statue. All smooth skin and defined muscles, with just a dusting of light hair on his chest, arms, and legs.

The sculptor must've spent a particular amount of time on his stomach. His abs are taut, rippled, and as mouthwatering as the V of muscles leading down to—

No, I can't look.

I whip my eyes away from his hipbones and study his face instead.

The artist must've spent even more time sculpting his mouth. Those full lips are carved straight out of a dream.

I remember how it felt to have that mouth on mine and flush from head to toe. I search the blanket to find something to cover myself with. We're lying on the pier near the little lake where Killian showed me the most romantic sunset of my life.

I find a yellow slip dress and, still sitting, I pull it over my head. I can't locate any underwear. But I recover a flannel shirt and toss it over his midriff.

Eyes still closed, that perfect mouth curls at the corners.

"Getting shy now, Sugar Spoon?"

I've no idea what just happened between us, but if the lack of clothes is any indication, we may or may not have done the most intimate thing two people can do. How do I react? Was it even the first time? Or did we do it the other night at my house, too?

At my silence, he rolls toward me—eyes focused, the smirk gone. "What's going on?"

"Why did you steal the bakery from me?" I blurt out. I don't know why, but that seems like an important point to clear up.

He sighs. "If you're still upset about that, I can sell it back to you?"

"Why now? Because I've put out?"

"What? No!" Real shock flashes in his eyes, but there's a brief, almost imperceptible pause before he speaks, as if he's carefully choosing his words. "I've wanted to give it to you since that first night at The Outlaw." A fleeting look of something akin to guilt crosses his face before he can hide it.

"Why do *you* have to give it to me?" I narrow my eyes. Does he think from the high tower of his billions that I'm unable to run a business without his help? "Why couldn't I get it on my own?"

"If we really have to do this now." He sits up, the flannel shirt mercifully staying in place. "If I hadn't bought the bakery, another investor would've gotten it, and they wouldn't have rented it to you. They wanted to open a chain coffeeshop."

"What? That's not possible. I had a deal with the realtor. He was going to hold it for me until I got my bank loan approved."

Killian arches a brow. "Same way they held it when I put in my offer?" There's a challenge in his tone, but also something else—resignation, perhaps?

My mouth dangles open. "I thought you'd turned the screws on the real-estate agency. No one can say no to Killian St. Clair in this town."

"And that's why they took my offer over that of the other investor." His gaze is scarily intense. "But it would've never been yours." The finality in his voice is unsettling, and for a moment, I catch a glimpse of something like regret shadowing his features.

Of course he had some noble reason to be a jackass.

I try to process all this new information. He's telling the truth, I'm sure. I only have one last question: "Why?"

His eyes show a flicker of hurt, and his entire demeanor turns almost shy. Killian takes hold of my hand, brushing his thumb over my knuckles. "Do you really still have to ask why?"

I nod.

"Because I love you." He cups my cheek. "I've been falling for you since the first day I found you trespassing over my land atop your mare. I love you."

My heart swells and cracks. It detonates, leaving back only devastation. It's a cruel joke. I finally hear those three little words, and they're not really for me. I've never been atop a horse in my life, but I remember reading that scene in the book Killian is part of… It was his meet-cute with my namesake. He doesn't love me. He's in love with some fictional woman mashup that doesn't exist. And all this—the lake, the pier, the man before me—they're all just echoes of a fantasy I clung to, a dream I painted with desperate, vivid strokes. A dream that I ache to be real so bad it hurts. It's a longing so deep it carves hollows in my chest.

And the worst part? Killian might not be real, but how I feel about him is.

I should've thrown away the book when I had the chance. Now it's already too late.

I swore I'd never fall for an imaginary book boyfriend, yet here I am, heart pounding against the stark reality that he's nothing but smoke. My emotions rage, tangible and fierce, but he's a mirage.

And I'm not the heroine of his story. The version of me he claims to love doesn't exist. I'm not a horse-riding, pastry-baking, country belle. I'm a slightly cynical, jaded computer science grad student who can't afford to go to a friend's wedding, let alone start a business.

The pressure of his thumb on the back of my hand increases. "Sugar, what's wrong?" His concern feels like another layer of this illusion.

I look into his soulful gray eyes and don't know what to say. A sob bubbles up, ripping its way out of my chest. It's a raw sound of breaking, of letting go.

"Why are you crying?" Killian asks, his voice soft, patient. "Is me telling you I love you so bad?"

"Yes, it is," I bawl.

"Why?"

"Because you're not real!" I push away from him and stand up, the truth a blade slicing through the fantasy. "None of this is real. This lake, the sun, this pier. It's all fake."

"I'm real."

"No, you're not." Desperation sharpens my voice.

Killian pushes off the floor and stalks toward me with determination etched in his features. He grabs my hand and brings it to his chest, where he flattens it over his heart. "This is real. My heart beating for you."

"No, it's not." I try to get my hand back, but he's not budging.

So I shove him away with all the strength I have. Killian loses his footing but doesn't let go of me.

In slow motion, I watch as he windmills his free arm, trying to keep his balance while still stumbling backward. In a last-ditch effort to keep upright, he grabs for me. Only his hand grasps my thin slip dress and rips it all the way through while still pulling me along with him.

We careen toward the edge of the pier, and then we're falling overboard.

The impact of the cool water on my sun-heated skin is shocking. The world turns muted as my head sinks below the surface. I open my eyes, but the water is too dark to see past a few inches. The lake shouldn't be this dark. Suddenly, I feel compressed by the rushing absence of sound. Deaf and blind, instinct takes over. I kick my feet toward the surface.

When I clear the first intake of breath, I'm no longer swimming in a lake, but at home lying in my bed.

My first reaction is relief, but then a cool shiver runs down my spine as I realize I'm soaking wet under the covers and naked as if I'd actually just come out of the water.

"What the—?"

I turn to my right and find Killian lying under the covers next to me, wet hair plastered to his forehead, gray eyes on me.

And then I start screaming.

17

OPEN THE KIMONO

"Will you calm down?" Killian tries to reach out and touch my shoulder, but I flinch away from him.

I barrel-roll to the other side of the bed, wanting to get out, but my feet get caught in the sheets and I stumble to the floor. I crab-walk away from him and grab an oversized T-shirt to cover myself. Thankfully the bedsheets have dried most of my skin, so the top doesn't get wet.

"Are you alright?" Killian asks. "Did you hurt yourself?"

"Oh my gosh, I'm having a psychotic breakdown," I say to myself. "I've spent too much time fantasizing about a different life, and now I've completely lost touch with reality. Imagining books writing themselves wasn't enough. Oh, nooo..." I grab a pair of panties from the chest of drawers and pull them on in a quick snag. "Nope. Now I also have to bring fictional men to life."

Killian jerks the covers away from himself and gets out of bed. "What the hell are you talking about?"

For a moment, I'm distracted by the six-foot-four of naked man standing in my bedroom. Ripped abs are still there, enticing

V of muscle as well, only this time there's no flannel shirt to cover his—I press the heels of my palms over my eyes.

"Deep breaths, Leigh, you're just having a little hallucination is all. Nothing too bad."

I silently count to ten, willing Killian to disappear from my bedroom. But when I lower my hands away from my face, he's still there, still looking pissed, still very much *exposed*.

"You're still here."

His stare is mutinous. "And where should I have gone?"

"Away."

"Why?"

"Because you're not real."

"Again with this." He crosses the room and plants my hand over his heart just like he did at the lake. "Does this not feel real to you?"

There's warm, wet skin under my palm and a heartbeat. Oh gosh, I'm hallucinating at a level where not only my sight is compromised, but my other senses, too.

"Spoon?"

I shriek away and put a chair between us as a sort of barrier.

"Go away."

"I'm not going anywhere."

From the chair, I grab my satin kimono and throw it at him. "At least cover yourself up."

He snatches the kimono out of the air and regards it with disgust. "I'm not wearing this."

"Well, I don't have any clothes in my house that would fit you, so."

"Where are we, anyway?"

"Dress first, I can't talk to you if you're..." I wave toward his nether regions.

With angry jerks, he shoves his arms into the kimono sleeves and ties the belt over his stomach. "Happy now?"

"Far from it." I glare.

"So where are we?"

"Evanston."

"Where's that?"

"Illinois."

"How did we travel all the way here from Kansas?"

I never even wondered what state Lakeville Hills was in, but Kansas seems hilariously fitting. A hysterical laugh bubbles out of me.

Killian scowls. "What's so funny?"

Still chuckling, I chortle out, "I was just checking if I had my red slippers on. Do you think Toto is going to join us soon?"

"You're not making any sense."

I grip the backrest of the chair. "On that we can agree. Single-hood finally bested me. I'm about to earn my crazy-cat-lady certification a few years and a few cats early."

"Sugar Spoon."

"Don't Sugar Spoon me. I won't be lectured by imaginary book boyfriends."

"I'm real," he roars. "What do I have to do to prove it to you?"

"Okay," I say, grabbing a pair of jeans. I pull them on and throw my bunny slippers at him—the only footwear that will fit him. "You want to prove you're real? Let's see if somebody else can see you."

"What do you mean?"

"Let's go to the coffee shop downstairs. If you can order a cappuccino, I'll shut up."

"I'm not going out of the house dressed like this."

"Don't worry, you don't exist. No one will actually see you."

His jaw sets. Features etched with determination, Killian pulls on the bunny slippers and gestures to the front door.

From my apartment building, the coffee shop is right across the street. I grab my bag and keys on the way out and precede Killian down the hall.

He keeps sulking for the entire elevator ride down.

The streets below are still mostly deserted. I check the time on my phone and confirm it's only 6.45 a.m. on Sunday morning.

My hair is still wet, making me shiver in the chilly morning breeze as we cross the street.

I stop in front of the coffee shop, silently daring Killian to pull the door open.

To my astonishment, he does, making the overhead bell chime as well.

The shop is predictably empty at this hour. There's only the young barista behind the cash register.

"Morning, what can I get for you?"

"A cappuccino, please," Killian says in that rough but velvety voice of his.

Nonplussed, the cashier taps in the order. "Anything else, sir?"

"You can see him?" I interrupt. "You can actually see him?"

The barista raises an eyebrow at me. "The hairy dude in a floral kimono and bunny slippers?" He clicks his tongue. "Yes, ma'am. Don't think I'm going to forget the sight any time soon."

I swallow, concentrating on the light tuft of hair on Killian's chest. Calling him a hairy dude seems like an exaggeration. When my gaze rises to his face, Killian glares at me.

This can't be real, it can't be happening.

"Ma'am, are you alright?"

Not even a little.

"Sure. So, we'll take a cappuccino and..." I stare at Killian interrogatively.

"An Americano, black."

Long. Dark. With just a splash of sugar.

"And a cinnamon bun, please," Killian adds.

I pay with money I can't spend, and we wait in silence at the end of the counter for our order.

When our drinks arrive, I ask Killian if he wants to stay or go.

He leans in to hiss in my ear. "I'm not staying in a coffee shop wearing bunny slippers and a kimono."

Fair enough.

We walk back to my place in silence, nursing our cups of coffee.

As we re-enter the apartment, I suddenly feel embarrassed at how drab the open space looks.

There's a bed in front of the built-in wardrobe that I used to share with Ivy and that now sits more than half empty thanks to my recent purge. A small dresser with a tiny TV on top. No couch or living room or even a table, only a tiny desk pushed underneath the window. And my bookshelf. The kitchen in one corner with a bar and two stools. And the only room with a door, the bathroom, has a broken lock.

Killian steps in after me, closing the door. He looks undecided on where to go. I'm sure he's taking in the scarcity of seating options and assessing the penury of the apartment.

He settles for one of the stools at the bar, and I join him, still nursing my coffee cup.

"So..." I start and stop unsure what to say.

"So..." Killian echoes me, and it's the first time I've seen him slightly unsure of himself. "Care to explain what's going on?"

"As if I knew! I was reading a romance novel that had half

blank pages and started dreaming about having a cowboy billionaire book boyfriend." I fidget with the coffee cup in my hands, tracing the plastic lid nervously. "And with every new dream, a new chapter would appear in the book. I didn't believe that was possible. I thought I was having some kind of nervous breakdown. But then you materialized out of my sex dreams. And now I'm pretty sure I should check myself into a mental institution."

"Are you saying I'm a book character come to life?"

"Pretty much." I avoid his gaze, opening my cup and staring into my coffee as if it held answers.

"But you weren't in the book?"

"Not initially. But then the story stopped and I imagined a continuation. Then the new chapters started writing themselves just as I dreamed them, with me in them." I finally look up at him, meeting his penetrating gaze.

"Ah, the supposed *sex* dreams." His eyes darken.

"I mean, not that we actually had sex. At least I was never there for *that*."

Killian raises an eyebrow. "Interesting. So, how did I end up here?"

"I've no idea. Maybe my subconscious conjured you up because I was feeling lonely and needed someone to talk to."

Killian leans forward, resting his elbow on the counter. "Just talk?"

He manages to be extra sexy even in a kimono and bunny slippers.

I hold up my hand. "Whoa, hold your horses, cowboy. We're not an item in this world."

"How come?"

"You can't just waltz in here and expect everything to be the same as it was in..." I flap my hands wildly. "Wherever you came from."

Killian's face falls, and he looks genuinely hurt. "Why not?" he demands, crossing his arms over his chest. "I just told you I love you, and this is all you have to say back?"

Sighing, I run my fingers through my hair, trying to find the right words to explain myself. "Look, Killian, the person you think you love doesn't actually exist. I'm not her."

"Of course you are," he insists, his eyes searching mine, determined to find a glimpse of the woman he fell for.

"Really? Well, newsflash: I've never been on a horse, wouldn't know the first thing about baking, and can't drive a stick shift." I tick off each point on my fingers, watching his expression change with each revelation. "I'm not a put-together business owner with a house and a car. And I don't wear shorty-shorts all the time or heels or flannel shirts knotted over my belly. I'm no Daisy Duke and I have cellulite. So, no, Killian, you don't actually know me."

"Sugar Spoon," he says softly, reaching out to touch my arm. I resist the urge to pull away. "I may not know those specific details, but I know the core of the woman I fell in love with is the same."

I shake my head, still unconvinced. "You can't possibly—"

"You have the same dark, curly hair." He gently pulls on a lock and lets it bounce back.

"I might look the same but—"

"And you get the same deep crease over your nose when you're displeased with me." He smooths over the wrinkle with his thumb.

Even a simple brush is enough to sear my skin. He might be a fictional man, but his touch feels all too real. So does the pull of the connection between us. Maybe there is some merit to what he's saying, maybe the core of who I am is the same person he fell in love with. And maybe he is the same man that has consumed my thoughts for the past ten days.

But I can't trust that what I felt in the book world is real. Despite the reality check at the coffee shop, I can't even trust that Killian is real. Or that he is here to stay.

I swat his hand away. "Can you just not go into full seduction mode right away?"

The grin that curls his lips is devilish. "Why, are you seduced?"

"Can we just not?"

"Fine," he interrupts, holding up his hands in surrender. "Let's table the discussion for now. What do you want to talk about?"

His expression is too angelic, giving me a hint that the topics he'd like to discuss are all but holy.

I scowl, then remember what he just told me about the crease over my nose and rearrange my features before he thinks of smoothing it again.

"Are you sure you're real?"

"I can't tell you how I went from falling into a lake hundreds of miles away to being in this—" he stares at the open space— "apartment in a blink. But I can tell you I'm real, Spoon, 100 per cent. As real as the heat of this cup." He lifts his coffee. "As real as the spicy-sweet smell of this cinnamon bun. Or as the sound of that dog barking out your window."

An incessant yapping has been drifting in from the road below.

"And for the record, I still don't believe I'm an imaginary book character," he says stubbornly.

"Okay, how old are you?"

"Twenty-seven."

"Where did you go to school?"

"Lakeville High."

"What was the name of your first horse?"

Killian opens his mouth to reply, but shuts it back, confused. "I can't seem to remember."

"Isn't that something you should know?"

"And what's your theory for me not knowing?"

"That maybe it's a missing detail of your back story the author didn't bother with, and that's why you don't know."

Killian shakes his head. "I'm not an imaginary man."

"Okay, fine." I stand, grab my laptop from the small desk, and bring it over to the kitchen bar. "Let's settle this once and for all." I open a web browser and type his name into the search bar. The anticipation of proving him wrong bubbles inside me like champagne.

"See?" I say triumphantly when the search doesn't produce any results. "You don't exist in this world."

"I have a team of cyber experts making sure no one can just *google* me," Killian retorts, sipping his coffee with a raised eyebrow.

I type some more and turn the screen toward him triumphantly. "Did your team also erase Lakeville Hills from the map?"

He doesn't even flinch. "You know navigators are always iffy around town."

"Fine," I huff. "What's your phone number?"

"Ooh, asking for my number already?" He smirks playfully. "I didn't know we were moving so fast, Sugar Spoon."

"Ugh, just give it to me." I scowl, rolling my eyes at his flirtatious tone and ignoring the shiver that hearing my nickname sent down my spine.

"Alright, alright." He gives me a number starting with a Kansas area code.

"Thanks." I dial the number and put the phone on speaker,

hoping for the call to go through. The line connects, at least the number exists.

It takes a few rings before someone picks up: a nice-sounding old lady. "Hello?"

"Hi! Is Killian St. Clair there, by any chance?"

"Who, darling?" the woman asks, clearly confused.

"Killian St. Clair," I repeat, glancing at him with a smug smile.

"Sorry, dear, there's no one by that name here."

"Apologies for bothering you. I must've had the wrong number," I say before hanging up. I turn to Killian, my grin widening. "Well, what do you have to say for yourself now?"

"Fine, you win," he concedes, finishing his coffee. "I'll hand it to you that something strange is going on, but it still doesn't mean I'm imaginary. Maybe I just..." He trails off, searching for answers that don't exist.

"Maybe you just what?" I prompt, genuinely curious about his explanation.

"Maybe I'm from a parallel universe," he says with a mischievous glint in his eye.

I roll my eyes at his response, but can't help the small smile that tugs at the corner of my lips. "Sure, Killian. A parallel universe."

"You never know." He shrugs. "It's a more plausible explanation than me being a book character come to life."

"Can't argue with that," I say, raising my coffee cup in a mock toast.

Killian takes the cinnamon bun out of its paper bag and bites down on it, the sweet icing clinging to his lips as he chews thoughtfully. "So, what now?"

I don't know what to tell him. "I need a minute."

He takes another bite out of the bun. "Take all the time you need."

"I'm going for a walk," I say on instinct, hopping off my stool.

Killian polishes the last of the pastry. "Okay, I'll come with you."

"No!" I say a bit too forcefully.

He raises an eyebrow at me in a silent question.

At a loss for what to say, I eye the tuft of hair that's coming out of the deep V of my kimono. "You can't walk around in a robe and bunny slippers, I'll go buy you some more suitable clothes."

Killian gives me a long stare, as if he knows the shopping is just an excuse to get out of the house alone. "Thank you." He nods eventually.

We stay in a sort of silent standoff until Killian licks stray icing off his lips, attracting my gaze to his mouth. My heart flutters, and the corners of his mouth turn up in a knowing smirk.

"How are the shops in town?" he asks, too nonchalantly. "I prefer organic fabrics."

"Of course you do." I sigh, rolling my eyes. "Well, let's see what we can find on a grad student budget."

I finish my coffee and go to the bathroom to dry my hair, still damp from our unexpected dip into the book world's lake.

When I come out, I find Killian sprawled on my bed, reading one of my romance novels.

"Please, make yourself at home," I taunt.

"I meant to ask." He pulls the book shut with a loud bang, seemingly unaffected by my barbs. "Where is this famous book I supposedly come from?"

I blush, self-conscious about how I've been hugging the novel to my chest every night. "Should be there on the bed, check the floor, maybe it fell off."

Killian starts searching, lifting the sheets and throwing aside the pillows. "It's not here."

I pull on my coat. "Look under the bed."

He gets on all fours, and the sight of his buttocks sticking up in the air under my flowery kimono wrings another smile out of me. "Not here."

"Well, you keep looking while I go shopping."

I grab my keys and wave goodbye. Maybe he won't be here when I get back.

18

THE ROMANCE RACK

The cool morning air feels nice on my skin, I tilt my head up to catch the sun. Have I gone mad? Am I still dreaming?

Just as I'm soaking up the morning sunshine, a herd of joggers barrels down the sidewalk like they own it. Before I know it, one of them clips my shoulder, sending me staggering against a trash bin. They don't even pause, not a single sorry thrown over a shoulder. Instead, what I get as I try to steady myself on the curb is a chorus of chuckles and a "Watch where you're standing, sweetheart!"

Definitely not dreaming. I roll my eyes, check my coat for stains, and keep walking toward the consignment store where I put some of my old clothes on sale last week, Organic fabrics, my ass. Killian will be lucky if I can afford to buy him outfits from this century.

Oh my gosh, am I seriously buying clothes for a person who doesn't exist? He probably won't even be there when I get back home and I will only have wasted money I should save.

Still shaking my head, I push my way into the secondhand store and its treasure trove of fashion relics. The shop is divided into the women's and men's sections, and the racks of clothes are separated by size. Each item on the hangers is unique.

I forgot to ask Killian his size, so I'll have to guess. I'll get only a couple of essential items so when I come home and he's vanished at least I won't have wasted too much money. And if by some weird cosmic happening there's still a naked cowboy in my apartment, then he can come shop for himself. Still, I should ask if they do refunds.

Before I start browsing, I check at the counter if some of my things sold. Thankfully, some clothes I brought in last week have already been purchased. I swap the petty cash I made for store credit and start digging through the racks.

I find a pair of jeans. They're worn, but the wear could pass for an intentional fashion statement. I get two newer-looking flannel shirts that seem to fit Killian's country aesthetic, a couple of plain T-shirts, and black boots. Unfortunately, the only wool sweater available is an ugly Christmas sweater. But I can't afford to buy him a coat and the cold season is coming so he'll have to lower his airs.

On the way home, I stop at a regular store to buy him new underwear because nobody should have to wear used underwear.

When I make it back to my apartment, I pause for the longest time outside my door, chanting, "Please be gone, please be gone."

But when I step into the apartment, Killian is sprawled on the bed, waiting for me with a foxy expression. "Welcome back, Sugar Spoon."

So a hyper-realistic hallucinatory state is the new normal. "Why do you look so pleased with yourself?"

"Found the book." He hops off the bed, tapping the cover.

"Oh, great." I drop the store bag on the kitchen bar. "Did

some kind of explanation on why you're here write itself by magic?"

"No, but I found a lot of other interesting info."

I prop my hand on a hip. "Such as?"

"Such as how, according to you, I smell like lust and ruin, am the dark angel of smut incarnate, and have a sinful mouth that just begs to be kissed."

I gape, and his lips twist in a smug grin.

"Those were private, inner monologue thoughts you have no place reading," I say, indignant, making a grab for the book. But he snatches it up over his head, where, no matter how much I stretch myself, I can't reach. But that doesn't mean I stop fighting. "Give that back."

"I don't know, Spoon," Killian muses. "I'm quite enjoying you trying to climb me like a tree."

That's when I realize how close we're standing. In my attempt to reach the book, I've pressed my front to his chest. And he's still only wearing a flimsy satin kimono and nothing else underneath.

I immediately take a step back, scowling.

Killian ignores my glares and peeks inside the shopping bag, holding up the ugly Christmas sweater with a mix of disbelief and amusement.

"Hey, beggars can't be choosers," I scold him. "This is the best I can do on my limited budget. I'm surviving on my grad student's wage. I don't have a rich family bankrolling me."

Killian frowns, looking concerned—all mocking gone from his face. "How bad is your financial situation?"

"Well, I wouldn't say I'm exactly poor," I reply, feeling my cheeks flush. "But I do have to pinch pennies, especially with all my friends getting married lately. Weddings are so expensive!" I gesture broadly, becoming worked up. "There's the dress, and shoes, not to mention all the events leading up to them like showers and bachelorette parties. On top of that, you have to buy a gift, and hotels are never cheap..."

I trail off, realizing I'm rambling. Killian is watching me with an amused smile.

"Anyway," I say, regaining my composure. "Let's just say supporting you is going to be a stretch for me financially. So make the most of what we've got here."

This time, Killian's smile is almost fond. "I can rock any clothes, Sugar."

He grabs the bag and makes to hand me the book, but when I go to grab it, he snatches it back once before actually giving it to me. Then he heads into the tiny bathroom to change.

"The door doesn't lock," I call after him.

"Should I worry about you barging in to get a peek at my *perfectly sculpted body*?"

I press the heels of my palms over my eyes. "How much did you read, exactly?"

"Only enough to know you've become pretty fond of my coffee order."

Long. Dark. With just a splash of sugar.

A shameful groan rips out of my throat, making him chuckle in response.

After that, I wait nervously outside, trying not to imagine him naked in there. But flashes of what I saw of him earlier this morning come unbidden—his powerful arms, broad chest, washboard abs... I stare daggers at the book in my hand.

"Don't you dare to write any of this," I hiss.

My cheeks flush at the idea of Killian reading even more of my inner thoughts. I should probably hide the book.

I drop it in my underwear drawer, camouflaging it under a layer of bras, and I take out my nervous energy biting down on a few cuticles as I wait for him to change. I'm still chewing when the bathroom door swings open and Killian steps out, looking unfairly sexy even in his cheap secondhand clothes. The flannel shirt may be a little small, but I won't complain about the way it strains against his muscular frame. The jeans are a perfect fit. They hug his thighs in all the right places.

"Not bad," he says appraisingly.

I just stare, pulse racing. *Focus*, I tell myself.

I shake myself out of my daze and nod approvingly. "Yeah. Not bad, cowboy."

"Wait until I put on the *pièce de résistance*." He spools the ugly Christmas sweater and pulls it on. "Ta-dah." He flashes me the goofiest smile.

I chuckle. No matter how sexy the man is, even he can't make a dirty-gray merry moose sweater look hot.

"That sweater really brings out your eyes," I tease.

Killian rolls a finger within the collar. "Is this polyester? It's dreadfully itchy."

"A hundred per cent wool, I checked." I roll my eyes.

"Guess I'm more used to cashmere."

"Seriously? You're lucky to have clothes at all, buddy. Maybe next time, don't splash out of magical books into unsuspecting women's apartments."

Killian grins, holding his hands up in surrender. "Fair enough. And I do appreciate it, truly. It's just a bit of an adjustment from bespoke Italian suits to... well, this." He tugs at the sweater distastefully.

"I would've thought switching worlds would be more distressing than cheap clothes."

"What can I say? I'm a practical man."

I move closer, pulling the collar of the flannel shirt out so that the sweater won't chafe his neck. "There, ugly Christmas fashion shouldn't have to hurt." His intoxicating scent envelops me and I have to resist the urge to run my hands over his broad chest. I go for an understated pat.

Killian's eyes lock with mine, his voice lowering. "You know, I could just take all this off if it's so offensive..."

My breath catches, but I manage to extricate myself and take a step back. "Nice try."

He winks and walks past me, brushing my shoulder and lingering the extra second. "I'm always here if you change your mind."

I wheel round to face him. "Isn't there anything you'd rather do other than riling me up?"

He smiles his real smile, no taunting. "Still my favorite thing, Sugar. But if you're not down for the fun stuff, we should probably come up with a plan?"

"A plan for what? To get you back to Lakeville Hills?" Typical man, a few hours in the real world and he already wants to leave me.

"No, Sugar." He beckons for me to come closer. I stubbornly stand my ground. Killian rolls his eyes but continues speaking. "A plan for me to fit into your world."

I can't control the warmth that spreads through my belly and keeps traveling over my chest, up my neck... Please tell me I'm not blushing. Trying to keep a steady voice, I ask, "You're staying?"

"Do you want me to stay?"

"Do you always answer a question with another question?"

"Do you?"

I throw my hands in the air. "You're still impossible."

"A beautiful bastard, right?"

When I don't respond, he tilts his head and gives me a long stare. "Come on, boss girl, let's figure some stuff."

"What stuff?"

"If you're in a financial bind, I should probably start by finding a job."

I cross my arms over my chest. "You can't have a job without identification papers."

"Then we should get me papers."

"How?" I sit at the kitchen bar.

"Let's figure it out together." He pulls up the stool next to mine and sits. "Smile, Sugar, I'm not going anywhere."

His words land in my belly like a small punch. I've no idea what we are, friends, lovers, strangers, but I know never seeing him again would cut deep at this point.

I clear my throat, trying to regain composure. "How do you propose to get papers?"

He shrugs. "A fake ID?"

I ponder for a second. "I'm not sure getting you a fake ID is the best choice."

"Why not?"

"First off, I wouldn't know where to go to get one that could pass any real security checks. And you don't just need an ID but an entire identity with a social security number and stuff."

"What would you suggest instead?"

"What if we go to the hospital and claim you're a John Doe with amnesia?"

"What? I just go in with no injury and claim I don't know who I am? They'd probably send me to a mental facility."

I tilt my head. "I could hit you on the head if you think that'd help to make the story more credible."

"You sounded a little too willing there, Sugar Spoon."

I suppress a smile, my heartbeat quickening. "Wouldn't dream of it."

"What else wouldn't you dream of?"

According to how I woke up naked next to him in my fantasy,

my dreams are pretty liberal. But I think it's best not to comment on it. "Let's concentrate on reality here. It's a definite no to the John Doe approach?"

"Yep, we should go with the fake ID."

"I already told you I don't know where to get one."

"You never had one made? Not even before you turned twenty-one?"

"Me, personally, no." I drum my fingers on the bar. "But when I was in college, there was this guy who made pretty legit fake IDs for underage students."

Killian slaps the counter. "Let's call him."

"Forged papers are not something you can ask for over the phone."

He stands up. "Let's go see him, then."

"We can't. Not right away, at least. He operated out of South Bend, where I went to undergrad."

Killian leans forward eagerly. "Isn't South Bend just a couple of hours away? We should hop in the car and get the ID."

"Not so easy, cowboy." I shake my head with a wry smile. "We have to make the request and then wait for him to make the ID. It's not an express service. We'll have to stay at least a couple of days in town, and I can't afford that. I also don't have a car."

Killian's face falls. "Oh. Right." He grabs his chin, lost in thought.

"Unless..." I trail off, an idea slowly forming.

Killian looks at me expectantly. "What is it?"

"Well, my friend Maggie—one of the ones soon to be getting married—lives in South Bend, and has asked me to come visit for a Notre Dame football game. We could go next weekend, stay at her place, and get your ID sorted."

"Would she be okay with you showing up with a random plus one?"

"If I told her you were my boyfriend, probably yes." I flush head to toe even as I say it.

Killian smirks. "Fake dating, huh? This another one of your romance thingies?"

"What do you mean?"

He turns his mouth down, nonplussed. "Like the cinnamon rolls."

"Yeah, sure. Okay with the fake dating, then?"

"I think we should cut the crap and real date from the start, but if that's the way you want to go. We already nailed the enemies-to-lovers, so I don't see why fake dating shouldn't work for us."

I throw my hands in the air. "How do you even talk in romance tropes?"

"According to you, I'm a hero from a romance novel. Some of my heritage must be showing through."

I check on my phone that Notre Dame has a home game next weekend. "We're lucky the Irish are playing next Saturday. Let me call Maggie."

My friend is enthusiastic about the idea. She credits her coupled human's wisdom for the fact that I found a boyfriend so quickly after our call, and agrees to host us for the weekend.

Killian's eyes are twinkling when I hang up. "Do I take it I'm officially your fake boyfriend?"

Oh, boy.

19

ALL THE PINING

My stomach grumbles, reminding me of the fact that it's almost lunchtime and I've only had coffee for breakfast. Killian glances at me with a smirk.

"Sounds like someone's hungry," he teases. "Why don't we make some lunch?"

"Sorry." I snort. "I'm no chef in this world. Unless you're in the mood for burned toast."

"Ah, but lucky for you, I'm a pro in the kitchen," Killian replies with a wink.

"Is there anything you *can't* do?" I ask skeptically, my eyes narrowing playfully.

"I'm sure there must be. But cooking is not part of that list." He feigns innocence, placing a hand over his heart. "But trust me, your taste buds are in very capable hands."

I don't know what else his hands are very capable of. I have my suspicions.

"*Mi kitchen es tu kitchen.*" I gesture toward the tiny stove.

Killian steps behind the counter and rummages through the

cabinets, his brow furrowing as he realizes my pantry is woefully understocked. He turns to me with a raised eyebrow.

"Sugar Spoon, what on earth do you usually eat?"

"Um, well." I blush, embarrassed. "Lately, it's been mostly instant ramen or white rice."

"Ramen and rice?" Killian shakes his head. "That won't do. We need to expand your culinary horizons."

With determination etched on his face, Killian scours the cabinets and fridge for any ingredients he can use. Eventually, he gathers a small assortment of items and lines them on the counter before starting the stove. I'm curious to see what grand recipe he's going to pull off with spaghetti, tuna, and canned tomatoes.

Killian sets a pot of water to boil and, as the room heats, he pulls his ugly Christmas sweater over his shoulders. The simple gesture is sexy as hell. Add the sliver of skin that briefly becomes visible over the waistband of his jeans, and my mouth waters.

Because I'm starving, that's all. And that dehydrated garlic he's frying smells divine. I quickly avert my eyes.

"Alright," Killian announces, clapping his hands together. "Time to work some magic."

As I watch him expertly stir and season the canned tomatoes, I admit that a man at the stove has an unfair advantage. And Killian St. Clair doesn't need the extra leg-up to be irresistible.

Gradually, the scent of the sauce fills the air, making my stomach grumble even louder. I'm getting hungrier by the second, only I'm not sure if it's for the food or the chef himself. I try not to get lost in his movements, but it's hard not to be drawn in by his confidence and skill.

"Almost ready," Killian says, flashing me a grin as he plates our pasta. "I hope you're prepared for a taste sensation, Sugar Spoon."

"Color me impressed," I admit, eyeing the spaghetti hungrily. I fill my Brita with tap water and bring two glasses to the bar.

"Let's dig in," Killian says, handing me a fork.

As I take my first bite, I can't help but moan with delight, savoring the delicious flavors as they dance across my tongue. "Mmm, are you sure these are canned tomatoes?"

He rolls a handful of spaghetti around his fork. "I take it the dish is to your satisfaction?"

I've just stuffed my mouth with another huge forkful, so I have to chew before I can answer him. "This is the most delicious thing I've eaten in forever. Maybe you should be a chef in this world."

"Nah, I've got a few handy tricks, but I'm not sure I could pull it off long-term."

He winks at me, and my stomach flip-flops on itself. Also robbing me of the ability to speak, it seems.

"Alright," Killian says, flashing me that charming grin of his. "If not a pastry chef, what do you do in this world? You mentioned grad school?"

"Ah, well." I'm a little self-conscious under his intense gaze. "I'm a computer science major. My research focuses on artificial intelligence and language models."

"Wow," Killian responds, clearly impressed. "Why language models?"

"It helps combine my passion for coding with my love of reading."

"Ah, so you're not just a bookworm with a penchant for romance novels."

"Hey!" I laugh, swatting his arm playfully. "There's nothing wrong with being a bookworm, thank you very much."

"I'm the prince of bookworms, no judging here," he says, smirking as he takes a bite of pasta.

"So, what about you?" I ask, still chewing. "How did you become a billionaire, anyway?"

"Ah, that's a bit... foggy," Killian admits, looking genuinely perplexed. "I'm not entirely sure, to be honest."

"See?" I tease, pointing my fork at him. "You do have amnesia!"

"Perhaps." He chuckles. "Or as you said, the author of the book didn't bother too much with my back story. The story opens with me already rich."

"And you have no other memories of your past?"

"Recent past." He stares at me intently. "I'm stark clear on everything. Distant past? It's a bit hazy."

I twirl spaghetti over my fork, staring down at my plate. "I'm sorry."

"Hey." The softness in his voice forces me to look up again. "What for?"

"Killian," I murmur, tracing the rim of my glass with my finger, "this transition, from your life to... this. It's my fault." My gaze locks with his, searching for any sign of struggle or discontent he's too kind to voice. "How can you be so calm?"

A hint of vulnerability flickers in his eyes. "It's a bit surreal, to be honest." He leans back, his eyes searching mine as if I could give him answers. "And I know I should probably be more freaked out. It's strange, but having you here is grounding me. Everything else"—he gestures at the surroundings—"is second fiddle."

My heart skips a beat at his words. "So, you won't miss your old life?" I probe gently, curious about his feelings.

His gaze on me is steady. "There are aspects I will miss, sure." Killian pauses, collecting his thoughts before responding. "And it is unsettling to be here, but almost exciting in a way."

"Exciting how?"

"It feels like getting a clean slate, a chance to redefine myself."
There's a determined glint in his eyes. "So, yes, there will be challenges, but also the freedom to explore, to be someone new. And that's exhilarating."

"But you were super successful before, what if you can't replicate making billions?"

"You want in on a little secret, Spoon?"

"Sure."

"When you have so much money you don't know how to spend it, it almost stops meaning anything."

"Ah." I roll my eyes. "Said every rich person who never had to worry about making it to the end of the month."

"I'm just saying you might get more satisfaction from saving thirty bucks for buying a new hardback from your favorite author than I would've gotten from buying a new champion Arabian stallion for two million dollars."

I choke on a mouthful of pasta. "Two million dollars for a *horse*?"

Killian shrugs. "Not even close to being the most expensive."

"And you're fine not being able to make extravagant equine purchases anymore?"

"I told you, it all becomes meaningless after a while. It'll be fun to build it all up again."

I roll the fork between my fingers, contemplating. I'm not sure why, but I believe him. Maybe because I want what he's saying to be true more than I'm ready to admit.

We finish our lunch in silence, both lost in our own reflections.

"Let me do the dishes," Killian offers after we've polished off the last of the meal.

I raise an eyebrow skeptically. "Aren't you used to having servants and staff do these things for you?"

"Spoon," he says, rolling his eyes playfully, "I might not know much about my past, but I'm not a stuck-up prick. Of that, I'm certain."

"If you insist," I relent, watching as he collects our dishes and heads over to the sink.

Then he does the unthinkable.

Killian unbuttons his cuffs and rolls up his sleeves. All the while staring at me with a self-satisfied smirk.

"Something caught your interest, Sugar?"

Okay, now. Everyone knows rolled-up sleeves and sexy forearms on display are a major pitfall in romance novels. Even the strongest heroine in the most heated enemies-to-lovers is powerless before the sight of wrist-to-elbow bare skin. But does *he* know?

If the cocky smile on his face is any sign, he's well aware.

"Nope, nothing," I squeak, swallowing hard and tearing my eyes away from those veiny hazards.

Killian winks and finally turns toward the sink. But I still seem to be hypnotized because I keep following his every movement. The way he swiftly grabs the soap dispenser and effortlessly pumps out a dollop of foam onto a dish sponge. He turns on the faucet with a graceful twist and starts scrubbing the frying pan he used to make the pasta sauce.

I can't help but watch, captivated by his every action. The way he massages the soap into a lather, his hands moving in rhythmic circles, is oddly enchanting. He has a knack for turning mundane tasks into seduction rituals. Now I wish I needed to be cleaned as well.

"Stop staring, or you're going to make me blush," Killian teases without turning.

"Who says I'm staring?" I feign innocence.

"Oh, I just have a sixth sense for these things," he replies with a shrug.

"Well, this time your radar is off."

The jerk dares to laugh. "Sure is."

To save what little face I have left, I reluctantly pull myself away from the Killian show. "Thanks again for lunch and for taking care of the cleaning, too." I head over to my tiny desk, determined not to fall behind on my research and classwork. "I really need to get some work done," I explain, trying to ignore the magnetic pull I feel toward him.

"Of course," he says.

I power up my laptop and settle on the task that requires the least mental bandwidth, namely grading homework assignments. Still, as I begin to sort through papers, I remain hyper-aware of Killian's presence. In fact, I know exactly when he's finished doing the dishes and can sense him hovering near the counter, probably unsure of what he should do with himself.

As I turn, I find him staring at the room, a little lost.

"Hey, why don't you go for a walk, explore the neighborhood a bit? I'd go with you, but I can't fall behind, especially if we're going to be gone all of next weekend."

Killian scowls at the window. "I don't think that weather calls for a stroll around the neighborhood."

I follow his gaze to the window and note for the first time the battering rain. Oh, so I could tell the exact moment he turned the faucet off, but the storm an inch away from my nose completely escaped my notice.

"Or you can enjoy our last days of streaming TV. I can put noise-canceling headphones on. You won't disturb me."

He gazes at me. "What's behind door number three?"

I try not to let my eyes linger on him for too long as I think. "Or maybe start figuring out what you want to do in this world.

There aren't many ranches or cowboys in Chicago." My cheeks heat up as I add, "That is if you plan on staying here with me once you get your papers sorted out." I hate the dread that pools into my stomach that he's going to say no.

Killian stares at me intently, making it difficult to breathe. "Sugar Spoon," he says softly, "I intend to stay with you for however long you'll have me."

I chuckle. "That's cheesy, even for a romance novel hero. You have many of those lines in your repertoire?"

"Guess you'll have to find out."

"Here." I toss him my phone. "Start researching possible career pivots."

He catches it, showing impressive reflexes.

"The passcode is 1234," I add, trying to sound casual, even though my heart is doing somersaults in my chest for no reason at all. Maybe the fact that I'm handing a perfect stranger the key to my most personal possession. Or maybe it's the way those gray eyes are fixed on me.

"Seriously—1234? Your security is extremely lacking."

"Hey, we don't all have a team of cyber experts at our beck and call."

"Aren't *you* supposed to be the cyber expert?"

"Yes, but since I've nothing to hide, I don't need my phone to be inexpugnable. No secrets there," I conclude, glad I deleted the half a million dating apps on it a while ago.

The corner of Killian's mouth tilts upward, and he gives me a mock military salute before plonking on the bed with my phone in his hands. I turn back to my work, doing my best to ignore the occasional prickle on my scalp when I can't shake the feeling he's looking at me.

The afternoon passes like that, Killian researching potential careers while I mostly focus on my work. We make it through the day like two people who are somehow both new and familiar to each other.

We eat leftover pasta from lunch for dinner that Killian insists on reheating in the oven—not the microwave—as it'll taste ten times better. It does, I admit reluctantly.

This time, though, I refuse to let Killian clean up. "It's only fair," I insist, grabbing the dishes before he has a chance to argue. Also, I'm not sure I could withstand another display of forearms without swooning past the point of no return.

When I finish washing everything and turn around, I find Killian already under the covers in my bed.

"Excuse me," I say, trying to keep my voice steady, "what do you think you're doing in my bed?"

"Going to sleep, of course," he replies nonchalantly. "Or were you planning on going out?"

"Uh, no. But you're sleeping on the floor."

"Why would I sleep on the floor?"

"Because I don't know you. We're not sharing a bed."

Raised skeptical eyebrow. "You know what I smell like, what it's like to kiss me, how I prefer my *coffee*—"

I struggle to keep a straight face while blood rushes to my cheeks. "None of that happened in this reality. You should stay on the floor."

Killian makes a show of looking down to the hardwood. "Nah, doesn't look too comfy." He flashes me a grin, lacing his hands behind his head—elbows wide, biceps bulging. "I prefer the bed."

"We're not sleeping in the same bed, period."

"You can have the floor if you'd like."

"Shouldn't you be a gentleman about this?" I huff, putting my hands on my hips.

"Ah, not a cinnamon roll, remember? You should consider

yourself lucky I've kept my underwear on since I usually sleep naked."

"Ugh!" I groan, exasperated and intrigued all at once. "Cinnamon roll or not, that's not how romance heroes handle themselves in only-one-bed situations, you know?"

"Maybe I'm a romance villain." He smirks, his eyes sparkling with mischief.

I roll my eyes but can't help smiling as I decide this is not a hill worth dying on.

Resigned to sharing my bed with the beautiful bastard, I slip into the most unsexy flannel pajamas I own, brush my teeth—noting how Killian already helped himself to my spare toothbrush—and crawl under the covers next to him. I'm hyperaware of the warmth radiating from his side, and I try not to let it distract me as I mentally prepare for a night of awkwardness. Or to even tempt me into removing any of my flannel protective layers.

I kill the lights with a curt, "Goodnight."

"Night, Sugar," he purrs.

I keep quiet on my side of the bed, but I'm far from falling asleep. True, I've gotten used to going to bed early, wanting to join him in Lakeville Hills. But now that he's here... I can't rest.

"Sugar Spoon," Killian says, his voice low in the darkness. Looks like he can't sleep either. "Can I ask you a question?"

"Will you ask even if I say no?" I counter, trying to keep my tone light despite the nervous flutter in my stomach.

"Probably," he admits with a chuckle.

"Fine, ask away."

"Okay." He clears his throat, and I can practically hear the mischievous grin on his face. "Why don't you want to date me in this world? Is it only because we don't really know each other—or is it because you don't like this version of me?"

I sigh inwardly, thinking that I might actually like the real him more than the fictional adaptation. But I don't tell him that. Instead, I choose my words carefully, letting the truth spill out while still keeping a playful tone. "Well, that we don't know each other is definitely a major factor. But I'm also scared you're not here to stay. You could vanish at any moment, just as fast as you appeared."

"Ah," he murmurs, and I can feel him shifting under the covers, turning toward me. "So what you're saying is you're afraid of falling for a figment of your imagination?"

"Exactly," I reply, relieved that he gets it. And in the darkness, it's easier to be honest. "I'm not saying I feel nothing for you, because I was there at the bakery and the first time you brought me to the lake and at the barn and when we kissed after escaping those thugs. But I don't know if I could stand it if I let things progress between us and then you, poof, disappeared."

He doesn't respond, so I continue. "It's best if we just stay friends for now."

"Friends," he repeats, and there's a hint of *something* in his voice that makes my heart ache. "Alright, friends it is." I'm about to apologize for hurting him when he adds, "Even if I have to say that's going to be the hard road for you."

So much for hurting him. I can hear the teasing in his tone, loud and clear. "Hard road? Road to where?"

"To happily ever after, friends-to-lovers is always the hardest for the woman."

My turn to shift and face him. "Why?"

"Here's how it goes. You say now you want to be friends, but you'll soon realize how truly madly deeply in love you are with me."

"Confident much?" I interrupt.

"Factual. And then you'll want to confess how you feel, but

since I won't have made a move on you in ages to respect your request, you'll doubt if I'm still interested." Pause. "I will always be interested in you, by the way."

Those last whispered words are an electric shock to the spine. I don't know what to say.

"Then, when other women will inevitably get into me, the jealousy will begin. And the pining, oh, sooo much pining. I'm almost sorry for how lovesick you're going to turn—"

I whack him with a pillow before he can continue. "You're a jerk."

He chuckles, completely unfazed by my pillow assault. "I'm just saying, friends-to-lovers is a bumpy road."

I roll onto my back and let out a heavy sigh. "I can handle a bumpy road."

What I can't handle is a broken heart.

20

ELEVATED STAKES

I wake up in a cocoon of warmth, a sensation so foreign in my normally chilly apartment that it momentarily confuses my sleep-fogged brain. As consciousness seeps in, my eyes flutter open to the sight of a broad, bare chest mere inches from my nose—*Killian's bare chest.*

We're tangled together on his side of the bed, evidence of my accidental trespassing during the night. I must've rolled over in my sleep and am now shamelessly cuddling him. My arm is draped possessively across him, our legs entwined. I risk a glance upward, hoping he's still asleep and that I can retreat without being busted, but find him already awake, looking down at me with a playful glint in his eyes.

"Morning, Sugar," he rumbles, his voice still gravelly with sleep. It sounds like a secret shared in the dark. It's a voice that suggests late nights and whispered confessions. The kind that makes the heart trip over on itself and cuts rational thinking off at the knees.

I yearn to ignore the alarm bells and sink back into his embrace. Into the promise that I'm safe in his arms. But I resist.

My cheeks flush as I extricate myself, murmuring a flustered, "Oh, uh, good morning."

After that awkward awakening, we have a rushed, stilted breakfast together. Again, Killian isn't impressed by my pantry's selection of cheap coffee, barely unexpired milk, and white yogurt.

If nothing else, the ordeal is over quickly as it's already eight thirty and I have to rush to campus for my weekly meeting with my grad advisor. After how frustrating the last session turned, I'm dreading a repeat. I hope at least Dr. Hammond won't be almost an hour late this time.

Killian refuses to stay home and comes to campus with me, following me to the computer science building. We pause outside Dr. Hammond's office, a knot slowly tying in my stomach. "Wait for me here."

Killian must pick up on my discomfort because he says, "No need to be nervous." He gently squeezes my shoulder. "You rock."

"Thanks," I reply, taking a deep breath before knocking on the door.

"Come in," Dr. Hammond's bored voice comes from the other side. He motions for me to sit before his desk, and I brace myself for another round of constant interruptions and undercutting comments.

"Good morning, Dr. Hammond."

"Morning, Leighton," he greets me while scrolling emails on his PC. "What updates do you have for me?"

"I've tinkered with the algorithm parameters like you suggested, and the language model is showing improved syntactic parsing."

Without looking up, he tsks. "Ah, 'improved,' is a rather vague term for such a complex task, don't you think?"

I grit my teeth, trying to maintain my composure. "Yes, well, the precision rates have gone up by 5 per cent since we integrated the new contextual embeddings." I place a graph on his desk.

Finally, he tears his eyes from the screen and peers at the printout. "Hmm, but what about the model's ability to discern nuanced language, idioms, or humor? There's more to language than structure. Have you considered that?"

Only as the entire core of my language model, as I've told him countless times already. "Of course. I've been fine-tuning the model on datasets rich in figurative language to enhance its understanding to—"

"That's all good, but let's try to think more critically, shall we? A model's ability to mimic understanding through pattern recognition isn't the same as true comprehension."

"I am aware. That's why I'm also exploring reinforcement learning techniques to enable the model to ask clarifying questions when it encounters ambiguity."

Dr. Hammond has the guts to actually sigh at my response, and then he talks as if he is trying to explain basic concepts to a three-year-old. "Asking questions is a feature, not evidence of genuine intelligence or an understanding of pragmatics. We need to dig deeper, Leighton."

My cheeks flush. I'm bringing him excellent progress, and he's dismissing it like it's nothing. "My coding digs deep enough," I say, a bit too loudly.

"Now, now, no need to get emotional." Oh, flipping hell. He lasted a whole twenty minutes before calling me emotional. Maybe I should drop a Tampax on his desk and watch as he jumps back as if it were a snake. "Let's stay focused on checking the biases encoded in your training data, okay?"

The irony of him talking to me about biases.

"Absolutely." I struggle to keep my tone even. "That's why I've already implanted several audits of the training datasets for biases as part of my methodology. Like I told you two weeks ago?"

"Ah, yes, yes."

But I doubt he listens to anything I say unless it is to find something wrong with it. I clench my jaw, biting back a retort. He's implying yet again that my work lacks depth and insight. I know he's only being this hard on me because I'm a woman.

The rest of the meeting continues along the same lines, with Dr. Hammond repeatedly second-guessing and undermining me. By the time I leave his office, I feel completely deflated. Some advisor he is.

In the hall just out of his door, I take a deep breath, trying to shake off the negativity, and blink back tears of frustration that threaten to spill. I'm not going to cry. Not here where I can be labeled as a hysterical wreck. I plaster a smile on my face as I spot Killian waiting for me around the corner.

"Hey," he breathes, his eyes searching mine. "Rough meeting?"

I sigh. "That obvious, huh?"

His jaw clenches, but he forces a smile through. "Well, you look like you want to karate chop someone, so I took a guess."

I can't help but laugh at the visual. I'd like to karate chop a very specific, pompous someone.

"Ah, there's that smile," Killian says, nudging me playfully. "Your advisor isn't cool?"

"Ugh, he's impossible," I say. "He treats me like I know nothing just because I'm a woman."

Killian shakes his head, looking genuinely indignant on my behalf. "What a jackass. His loss for not recognizing your brilliance."

I roll my eyes, but his outrage and faith in me make me feel lighter.

"How do you deal with all the patriarchy?" Killian asks.

"With plenty of coffee and a lot of internal screaming," I reply, attempting a genuine smile.

Killian grins, reaching out to lightly tug a lock of my hair. He pulls the curl and lets it bounce back. The gesture is too intimate. I step a little further away but still grin at him.

His playful banter is a reminder that not everything has to be as serious and draining. By the time we reach my classroom, I'm smiling again and some of the weight has been lifted from my shoulders.

Killian gives my hand a quick supportive squeeze before following me inside. "Go teach those bright young minds. I'll be at the back of the room if you need me to rough up some inattentive student."

I can't help but laugh at his ridiculousness, the sound bubbling up from my chest.

In an out-of-body experience, I watch as cowboy billionaire Killian St. Clair takes a seat at the back of the classroom.

His striking, larger-than-life presence causes a few murmurs and distracted glances from my students—especially the female student body. But I don't mind. Knowing he's here, supporting me, gives me a renewed sense of confidence.

Once class is over, Killian follows me out of the lecture hall.

"You were great," he tells me as we head toward the elevator. "I couldn't understand half the things you said, but you sounded really competent."

I shrug the compliment off. "It was just Introduction to Computer Systems, but thanks." I push the call button, and the downward arrow dings red at once.

The old elevator groans in protest as we step inside, the doors sluggishly closing behind us—we're the only two people inside. I press the button for the ground floor and lean back against the faux wood paneling as the elevator lurches into motion. It's not long before the familiar shudder through the cables halts, leaving us suspended between floors in an uneasy quiet.

Killian shifts, checks the cabin, then starts pacing the confined space with an energy that seems too large for it.

I stay put, trying to project calm. "Happens all the time," I assure him. "It'll start up again."

"Are you sure?" he asks, his brow furrowed. Despite his tough exterior, I can see the unease underneath the surface.

"Trust me," I say with a smile, hoping to ease his tension. "I've been stuck in this thing more times than I can count. It's practically part of my routine."

But a minute passes, and then another, and the elevator remains motionless. Killian keeps pacing the three steps the narrow space allows, running a hand through his hair. He stops in front of the panel and pushes the call button.

There's no reply from the other side.

"Spoon, this thing is not moving."

Killian's impatience bristles in the cramped air. He pushes the button again, still to no effect.

"Okay, that's it," he declares, hands on his hips. "I can't take this anymore."

"Killian, really, it'll start up any second," I try to reassure him, but my words seem to have the opposite effect.

"Nope. Can't wait. Time for Plan B," he announces with sudden determination.

"Plan B?" I ask, raising an eyebrow as I watch him inspect the elevator's ceiling.

"Heroic rescue." He grins, his eyes sparkling with mischief. "Watch and learn, Spoon."

"Are you serious?" My eyes bulge as he jumps, reaching for the overhead latch. His fingers just barely graze it, and I stifle a giggle at his frustrated expression. But then he somehow manages to perch on the narrow railing and remove the top panel, revealing the endless dark tunnel of the shaft above.

Cold air rushes in as Killian, with an impressive display of arm strength, hoists himself up.

"What are you doing?" I hiss. "That's dangerous."

"Oh, pffff, this is nothing."

"Killian, this is not a book, it's real life! You can't pull stunts like that."

"Watch me."

Moments later, however, it becomes apparent that Killian's escape plan isn't going as smoothly as he'd hoped. I hear him grunt and curse above me, the sound echoing eerily through the shaft.

"Killian!" I call after him. "You can't go anywhere up there. Just wait, the elevator will—"

A shrill alarm cuts me off, and a red light starts flashing on the panel.

"Killian!" I shout, covering my ears. "What did you do?"

"Nothing! I swear!" he yells back, his voice strained as just his face reappears in the hatch, looking sheepish. "I just... may have set off some kind of alarm."

"Great." I sigh, as the siren continues to wail. "Now we're definitely stuck."

That's when the speaker finally crackles to life, and a disembodied voice asks, "Uh, everything okay in there?"

"Yes, we're just stuck."

"Are you sure, miss? Because I'm getting an alarm that the overhead hatch has been opened."

I bite my lip, watching Killian's legs dangling from the open ceiling panel. "Yeah, my friend got a little claustrophobic and tried to escape that way."

Static—that almost sounds incredulous—sizzles through the speaker.

"Wait a second, miss."

"I've got nowhere to go..." I trill back, starting to feel nervous.

"I'm sorry, miss, but since you opened the hatch and triggered the alarm, we're unable to restart the elevator remotely. Please remain calm; firefighters are on their way to assist you."

"Firefighters?"

"Yes, you and your friend just have to be patient." The line fizzles out.

That's when Killian drops from the ceiling with the grace of a cat, landing lightly on his feet barely two inches in front of me. "Insisting with your friends philosophy, Spoon?"

We're standing so close that if I breathed a little deeper, my chest would touch his. I look into his gray eyes, then can't help myself, and luxuriate in the perfection of his mouth that I could touch now. Kiss for real.

"Those are not friendly looks, Sugar." His voice is a soft murmur, close and personal, as if weaving his words directly into my thoughts.

The elevator jolts suddenly, jostling us together. My back hits the wooden panels, and Killian's body squishes me against it.

"Sorry," the metallic voice crinkles from the panel. "That was me, making a last attempt. But it didn't work. Help is on the way."

Neither of us pays the guy any attention. With Killian's hard body pressed down on mine—for real this time, no dreams—I can only function as far as keeping on breathing.

Killian is making no move to back away, nor am I nudging him. My gaze drops to his mouth again, and his eyes darken in response. Killian places a hand on the panel next to my face, and the small space suddenly feels even more confined. The red light continues to pulse like a heartbeat gone out of control.

"Sugar," he murmurs, his breath fanning across my face, "if you keep looking at me like that, I can't be held responsible for my actions."

I swallow hard. "What sort of actions?" I wonder aloud, the question half-teasing, half-serious.

"Well," he begins, his voice coming down another octave, "the kind that involves less talking and more... doing."

His other hand moves to my waist and his thumb just skims under my sweater, over the bare skin of my belly, just above the waistband of my jeans.

I swallow hard, the sound embarrassingly loud in the silent space between alarms.

Killian's eyes are now a stormy sea, and I'm an inexperienced sailor lost in the waves. "More doing?" I echo, my voice barely more than a breath.

"Yeah," he says, his thumb making small circles now, sending electric impulses straight through my nervous system.

I'm acutely aware of how this should be the most anxiety-inducing moment of my life—stuck in an elevator with alarms blaring and the fire department on their way. Yet here I am, more focused on the sensation of Killian's thumb circling a patch of skin like he's drawing a spell right into me.

"And what if..." My voice wavers with daring and desire despite my words. "I said I wasn't down for doing anything?"

His eyes search mine, mischief sparkling within them. "Then I'd say you're a terrible liar, Sugar," he teases, his thumb pausing its bewitching journey.

I arch into him in response, wanting the motion to resume.

He restarts, probably satisfied he's called my bluff.

His lips twitch into a knowing smile, and I'm more aware than ever of the proximity of those lips to mine—so close yet infuriatingly not close enough.

"Killian," I breathe out, half-warning, half-invitation.

He tilts his head, our noses almost brushing. "Yes?" The tease in his voice is maddeningly irresistible.

Just as I'm about to close the gap between us and finally get a taste of those lips that have been haunting my dreams since the day we met, someone clears his throat from above. "Err... sorry to interrupt."

I peek past Killian to stare shamefacedly at a firefighter peering down at us from the open hatch.

The firefighter's brows are raised in a silently amused question, and it's clear that he's trying to keep a professional demeanor while witnessing our little elevator escapade. Killian steps back, his hands dropping from me as if they've been scalded, and I can't help but miss the warmth.

"Hello, officer," I say in a too-shrill voice. Are firefighters even officers? I don't know.

He doesn't seem to mind the appellative, wrong as it may be, and smiles. "Just a heads up that I'm going to reset the shaft safety and close the hatch. The elevator should restart shortly after."

I just nod.

"Thank you," Killian says.

"No problem." The fireman nods back. "But next time maybe leave the *Mission Impossible* antics to movies, uh?"

Killian scratches the back of his head, embarrassed. "Will do."

"And just so you know. All the campus elevators have cameras."

I'm going to die of shame.

21

DOMESTIC DISASTERS

After the elevator debacle, which has me seriously wondering if Killian will ever fit in a world where there are no grand gestures or over-the-top heroics, I have to focus on my research. I send Killian to explore the town, begging him not to get into trouble before I give him a spare key to my apartment.

"Alright, Sugar," he says with a wink, leaving me alone in the computer science lab.

And I swear I do not ogle his retreating butt as he departs. Once he's gone, I try to concentrate on my work, but my thoughts keep drifting back to Killian. Where did he come from? Who is he? Is he really here to stay? And if he is, can he adapt to the toned-down, practical, mundane life of real people? There are no answers...

As the afternoon wears on, I force myself to push my distractions aside. I need to prove to Dr. Hammond—and to myself—that I am more than capable of succeeding in this field, no matter the obstacles thrown in my way.

When I finally make it back to my apartment that evening, I'm surprised to find Killian already there. The rich, comforting scent of something delicious fills the small space, and I can't help but smile as I take in the busy kitchen.

"Hey, Sugar," Killian greets me, looking up from where he's stirring a pot on the stove. "Thought I'd surprise you with dinner."

"Wow," I say, dropping my bag on the floor and approaching the counter. "What are you making? It smells amazing."

"Your boxed mac and cheese," he replies. "But I've added some special touches to make it extra delicious."

He's looking extra delicious, too. I sit down at the bar, where the warmth of the oven mixes with the enticing aromas of herbs and spices, and a different cozy heat that has nothing to do with cooking wraps around me.

As we eat dinner, we talk about our day—studiously avoiding the almost kiss in the elevator. Killian asks me why I was so upset that morning, and I explain the situation with my advisor more in depth. He listens intently, his expression growing concerned.

"Why can't you just change advisors?" he asks. "You shouldn't have to put up with that kind of treatment."

"Because, as much of a chauvinist as he is, Dr. Hammond is the best in his field," I reply, sighing. "Plus, it's never a good look to be a complainer, especially for a woman."

Killian nods, understanding but clearly not happy about it. We finish our meal and clean up the kitchen together. Then it's time to get ready for bed. I head toward the bathroom, determined to beat him to it tonight, but when I reach for the knob, my hand closes on empty space.

I frown down at the hole in the door where the handle used to be. "Killian?" I ask. "Did something happen to the door?"

"Ah, yes." He flashes me a self-conscious grin. "I was trying to fix the lock but the handle sort of fell off instead."

I fight not to pinch my nose. "What did I say about no more heroic rescues?"

"Fixing a lock hardly seemed heroic."

I shake my head and go look for some duct tape to patch the hole. By the time I find it, Killian has already finished in the bathroom and is under the covers.

"Are you sure you don't want the floor?" I ask, almost hopelessly, after brushing my teeth. "Aren't cowboys supposed to enjoy the firm ground as a mattress and a hard rock as their pillow?"

"What's up, Sugar Spoon? You didn't seem to mind me too much last night?" The jerk waggles his eyebrows.

I blush. "I just get cold during the night and naturally gravitate toward heat sources."

"Then I'm happy to be your personal heated blanket."

The way he says it, the teasing curl of his lips, and how he keeps his gaze trained on me. If those eyes get any more suggestive, he might turn into a one-man bonfire, and I into a marshmallow, ready to burn and melt. The smolder in his gray irises could set off smoke alarms—but we've had enough red alerts for today, right? I don't suppose Evanston FD would tolerate a second call from the two of us in the span of twelve hours.

I swallow, slipping under the covers on my side of the bed and inevitably ending up sprawled on him during the night. We both politely ignore the fact the next morning.

Tuesday is a research day for me. I go to the lab alone, leaving Killian to explore more of the campus. When night arrives and I return home, I find a surprise waiting for me.

"Guess what, Sugar?" Killian says, eyes sparkling. "I got a job bartending at a sports bar."

"Really? Which one?"

"The Blackhawk."

"That's great!" I exclaim, genuinely happy for him. "They didn't ask for any ID?"

"The owner is not too scrupulous about paperwork. I did a trial shift, and they hired me on the spot." He sounds proud. For someone used to handling millions of dollars, I'm impressed he'd take on an ordinary bartending gig without complaint. Then I remember his words of the other day about reinventing himself and hope he'll enjoy working at a sports bar. "I got some groceries with my share of the day's tips."

As Killian moves around the kitchen, crafting yet another sure-to-be-delicious meal, I'm struck once again by a warmth that has nothing to do with the stove's heat. It's a dangerous comfort, one that wraps around me like a soft blanket, tempting me to snuggle in deeper. A part of me knows I should maintain some emotional distance, but the way Killian tastes a spoonful of sauce and then grins at me makes resistance seem like a lost cause.

After dinner, we curl up in bed together, as is now the norm. And to celebrate the last day of my Netflix subscription, we pick a late-night comedy, laughing our heads off the entire time. I'm watching a movie with a book character I conjured out of my head. It should be the weirdest thing in the world, but for whatever reason, it feels just right.

In fact, as Wednesday evening creeps in, and Killian is not here because he's working, it's his absence that feels wrong. The air is heavy with silence. I hadn't realized how accustomed I've become to the sound of his laughter, the warmth of his voice filling every corner of the room, until now. With him gone for his night shift, the emptiness carves a hollow space inside me.

"Get a grip, Leighton," I mutter to myself as I wander into the kitchen. But even as I chastise myself, my heart flip-flops when I open the fridge and find a pre-made meal waiting for me. There, on top of a neatly wrapped plate, is a handwritten note:

Microwave for three minutes, even you can't screw that up—
K.

My cheeks warm at Killian's playful jab, but it's the tenderness woven into his gesture that sends a flutter through my heart. Killian, with his effortless charm and disarming smiles, seems like an impossible man not to fall for hard and fast. But is he just a dream that slips away at dawn? The thought of him staying, really staying, spins a web of hope and fear inside me. Will he still want the real me—the one with morning breath and a cranky attitude before coffee—when the novelty fades? Doubts nag at me. No one's ever wanted me before. Why would he, with a world of options at his feet, choose to stay with someone as unremarkably real as me?

I shake off the fears swirling in my mind and focus on heating dinner. He's right, even I can operate a microwave without incidents and get to enjoy another delicious meal.

After I've eaten, I head to bed alone. No more Netflix. I'm too tired to work, and reading feels almost dangerous now, after what happened the last time I picked up a book. I'm in the mood for a steamy romantasy novel with dragons. But what if I get too immersed in the story and a fire-breathing dragon pops into my apartment uninvited? One book character to contend with is more than enough. I should just sleep.

Still, I take the mysterious book out of my underwear drawer to check if more chapters have appeared. And indeed, they have. I re-live the elevator incident as I read it. And the sexually charged chapter does nothing to ease my nerves. Makes things worse if possible.

I toss and turn; the sheets tangle around me as I try to find a comfortable position. The bed feels too big without Killian next to me. My thoughts run wild, spinning out endless questions that I can't answer.

The clock ticks away the minutes, and still, Killian isn't back. I didn't even think to ask what time he gets off. How has he become such an integral part of my routine in just a few days? Life has turned infinitely more interesting since he stepped out of the pages of that book and into my world. And as scary as it might be to admit it, I'm not ready for this story to end just yet.

22

COLD SEATS AND WARM PASTRIES

The morning sunlight filters through the blinds, casting a warm glow across the bedroom. I stretch my arms above my head and sigh, feeling well-rested—if not a bit cold—despite my fitful sleep last night. Eventually, exhaustion pulled me under, and I drifted into a restless slumber before Killian came back.

Realizing that with a jolt, I turn to Killian's side of the bed. My heart sinks when I find it empty. My first thought is that I'm waking from some kind of crazily vivid dream, and that Killian was never here. But then I have to use the bathroom, and the door still has no handle.

I shuffle into the small room, half asleep, and lower myself onto the toilet without looking—big mistake. The shock of the cold, unwelcoming ceramic sends me springing up, wide awake now. "Seriously?" I mutter, glaring at the raised toilet seat.

I must have words with Killian, apparently not even book boyfriends are so perfect that they don't leave the toilet seat up.

Killian. Where are you?

At once, my mind races with thoughts of him spending the night in some random woman's house, and I can't help but feel a pang of jealousy and disappointment. Looks like our story is over before it even started.

"Morning, Sugar Spoon," Killian's voice startles me as I exit the bathroom. He's standing in the doorway with a pastry box in his hands. "Breakfast in bed?"

I try hard not to blush. The toilet seat offense already forgotten. "What do you have there?" Heart thundering in my chest, I'm impressed at the casual tone I pull off.

"Cinnamon buns." He sits on his side of the bed and opens the box. The sticky, fragrant treats immediately make my mouth water. Killian's grin widens as he sets the pastries down on the comforter, coaxing a smile in response. Okay, maybe we have another page or two million to write.

"These smell amazing. Where did you get them?" I ask, joining him in bed and reaching for one of the still-warm buns.

"Fancy bakery at the corner."

His eyes twinkle as he watches me take a bite and moan appreciatively.

"Gosh, these are incredible," I say between bites. "You're going to spoil me with all this delicious food."

"That's the plan," he teases, taking a cinnamon bun for himself. "Get you spoiled every day until you can't live without me."

The words hit a little too close to home, but I brush them off with a joke. "Without you or without your culinary treats? And that place is too expensive. You can't get breakfast there every morning."

"Don't worry, my tips from last night were great."

I finish my bun and eye the remaining two dubiously. They're fantastic, but I don't think I can eat another entire one. I pick off the outer swirl of the second one, but then I'm too stuffed and I have to give up. Killian doesn't share the same limits. He finishes his second bun and then polishes off the rest of mine, too.

Cinnamon buns become our unspoken breakfast ritual. Even if he's out working until late, I wake up with freshly baked buns delivered to me in bed both on Thursday and Friday.

In this short time, our interactions grow beyond those quiet, early-morning exchanges. We share more—stories, laughter, even comfortable silences.

On Friday morning, I leave the apartment to go to class early unable to wipe a smile from my face. In a blink, my lecture is over, and it's time to go back home and pack for our trip to South Bend. I don't have any classes to teach or attend in the afternoon, so we're able to get an early start.

As I get home after my only morning lecture, Killian astonishes me by emerging from the bathroom dressed almost exactly like the first night we kissed. He is in full cowboy attire, looking like he's about to attend a Western-themed party rather than going on a trip. The oversized belt buckle catches the light, almost blinding me. The hat on his head is so big it'd put John Wayne to shame. And the cowboy boots are stamped with intricate designs. He's only missing a lasso to complete the picture.

The ensemble is so over the top, I'm not sure if I should laugh or cry.

He smiles and widens his arms. "What do you think?"

I sidestep the question. "Did you go on a secret shopping spree without me?"

"Ah, yes." A hint of sheepishness laces his voice. "I thought it was time to upgrade my wardrobe a bit. I didn't want you to be embarrassed of me in front of your friends."

"Killian," I say with a lump in my throat. "I wouldn't have cared."

But how do I tell him he can absolutely not show up at Maggie's place dressed up like this?

"You don't like it." He blinks, taking in my expression. Then looks down at himself with a self-deprecating smile. "I had wondered if maybe this was a bit too much, but you liked these clothes in Lakeville Hills."

"It's not that I don't like them." I try to be diplomatic. And, honestly, he looks hot as hell in his cowboy costume. But that's what it feels like in this reality, *a costume.* "But we don't live in Texas or on a ranch in Montana." I step closer, placing a gentle hand on his arm. "Killian, I appreciate the effort you put into this. It's incredibly sweet that you wanted to dress up for me and my friends. But the thing is, in this world, dressing like a cowboy for a casual get-together might come across as a bit... eccentric," I finish gently, giving his arm a reassuring squeeze. "Did you keep a receipt, by any chance?"

Killian's face falls slightly, but then his usual wicked smile curls his lips. "Are you sure we shouldn't keep the clothes just for us? Last time you saw me dressed like this, you stole my hat and took advantage of me against a barn wall all night."

Electric shocks sizzle down my spine. "Oh, I was the one taking advantage?"

"You might have forgotten the way you bit my—"

I stop him putting a hand over his mouth. "I remember," I say, now slightly out of breath. That night I got so carried away I almost drew blood from his luscious lower lip. But nothing good can come of reminiscing.

In response, Killian nibbles on my hand. I drop it as fast as if it were on fire.

Killian laughs. "Don't worry, Sugar, I don't mind a little bite."

I scowl. "We should get going if we want to return your

clothes and catch the bus to South Bend in time." I shoo him
back into the bathroom to change.

* * *

The bell above the door jingles as Killian and I step back into the
department store where he bought his cowboy clothes. The
familiar scent of leather and fabric fills my nostrils as we begin to
search for more understated clothes for him.

"Alright, let's start with some basics." I steer him toward the
men's section. "A few sweaters, jeans, sneakers. That kind of
thing."

Killian rolls his eyes but grins in agreement. "Alright, fashion
expert, lead the way," he teases as we stroll through the aisles.

I spot some cozy sweaters and immediately pick out a few for
Killian to try on. One is a soft beige knit, while another has
stripes of muted blues and greens. "How about these?" I ask,
holding them up against his chest.

He shrugs. "Pretty boring."

"But perfect to blend in." I drop the clothes in his arms to go
try on later.

He already has those black boots from the consignment shop,
so I grab a pair of simple white sneakers and some straight-leg
jeans to go with them. Killian stands there stiffly as I drape a light
winter jacket over his arms.

As I'm sorting through more racks for him, a flash of lavender
catches my eye from the women's section. I glance over to see the
most adorable oversized sweater—soft, fluffy, with a cowl neck
that looks perfect for snuggling into, and a unique pattern woven
into the fabric. I barely resist the urge to run my hands over the
plush fabric, but I quickly shake off the thought and refocus on
helping Killian.

"Alright, I think we've got a solid wardrobe for you now," I say as I hand him the last item, a stylish button-down to alternate with the flannels. "Go try everything on, and let's see how it all looks."

As I stand outside the dressing room, I can't help but feel a little nervous about how Killian will take the wardrobe restrictions. Am I being a bitch for forcing him to change clothes? If a man told me what I could or *couldn't* wear, he'd get a boot to the behind in no time. But does that apply also to Killian? I'm not being mean, or controlling. I'm just trying to help him transition. And if, after he's been here a while, he still wants to dress as a cowboy, that will be his decision. I won't stop him.

My heart skips a beat when the door creaks open and he emerges.

"Alright, what do you think?" Killian gives me a little twirl in a cozy sweater and jeans. He looks totally huggable. I have to physically restrain myself not to go snuggle.

"You look great!" I squeak.

He smiles and ducks back into the fitting room. The rest of the outfits are similarly successful. Once he's tried on all of them, Killian disappears into the dressing room one last time to change into his original clothes. But when he re-emerges, he surprises me by handing over the lavender sweater I'd been eyeing earlier. "Here, try it on," he encourages, winking at me.

"You noticed?" I ask, surprised he picked up on my interest without me saying anything.

He grins, bending down so that his mouth is almost grazing my ear. "The way you were eyeing it, Sugar... it got me a little jealous."

Ignoring the goosebumps, I step inside his now-empty dressing room—more to take advantage of the full-wall mirror than for any real need for privacy. I remove my hoodie and swiftly pull the sweater over my head. It feels soft and luxurious against my skin, making me feel warm and fuzzy inside. However, as I attempt to close the small clasp at the back of my neck, I struggle to secure it.

"Umm, Killian," I call out sheepishly, "could you help me with this clasp?"

"Sure thing." He steps into the dressing room, dropping his new clothes on a stool and pulling the door closed behind him.

The air suddenly feels charged with electricity.

"Turn around," Killian instructs softly, and I comply, lifting my hair out of the way and exposing the back of my neck to him.

Our eyes lock in the mirror. I don't know what I see in his stormy gaze, but it's enough to have my knees go weak. And that's even before his fingers brush against my skin as he fastens the clasp, sending shivers down my spine.

His hands don't leave my neck when he's done. Instead, his fingers wrap around the front of my throat. "Last time I had you in front of me like this, Spoon, your fashion didn't fare too well."

His eyes never leave mine as he talks, which is even worse than the scene in my fictional kitchen when he ripped my shirt. At least there, I didn't have to sustain eye contact.

Heat blooms across my cheeks, and I laugh to hide the sudden onslaught of butterflies in my stomach. "Well, let's hope this sweater is luckier than my shirt," I retort. "Because I can't afford to buy it."

Killian's lips quirk up. "I'd buy it only to rip it off you."

His words send a fresh wave of heat through my body and I swallow hard, unable to look away from the intensity in his eyes. The air between us crackles with tension, and I'm acutely aware of every point where his skin touches mine—his fingers still wrapped around my throat, his thumb on my nape, his chest brushing my back.

A shop assistant clears her throat just outside the dressing room. "Do you need help in there?"

I practically buckle away from Killian and launch myself at the door, opening it. "No, we're fine, thank you."

She regards us with a stern look. "Changing rooms are strictly for one person at a time."

I smile embarrassedly. "He was just helping me with the clasp."

The shop assistant doesn't reply, she just pointedly waits for Killian to step outside. I don't look at him as he grabs his clothes and exits. And I've already closed the door when the clerk says, "I'll start ringing these up for you. Did you need anything else?"

"We'll take the sweater, too," Killian declares with an air of finality.

23

COWBOY CONFESSIONS

"Thank you for the sweater," I say, as we head back home laden with shopping bags. I didn't expect Killian to pay for it. The gesture caught me off guard, turning me way too emotional—ah! Dr. Hammond would be vindicated if he could see me now, having a semi-meltdown over a sweater. "You didn't have to, but the gift is much appreciated."

Swinging his shopping bag in one hand, he gives me a heated stare. "The gift might've been self-interested, Spoon. You just looked too gorgeous in it."

He waits until we're at my door and I'm fumbling with the keys to let us in to press into me lightly from behind. "I can't stop imagining you wearing that sweater and nothing else." I drop my forehead on the door, no longer trying to fit the key into the lock. "How I'd slowly drag it over your thighs..." He's not touching me, but I can still feel phantom fingers trailing over my legs.

"Miss Witherspoon, is this young man bothering you?"

I turn around to find Mr. Calvin, my ninety-year-old neighbor from upstairs, in the hall—he makes a point of keeping healthy by taking the stairs.

"No, Mr. Calvin, thank you."

The old man gives us a foxy grin. "Then, by all means, carry on. Enjoy being young."

I die of mortification for the second time in less than an hour and hand my keys to Killian. "You open the door."

"You fluster too easily, Spoon." Killian chuckles.

"And you'll be out of a place to live if you keep that attitude up."

He's still smiling as he gets behind the stove to make us a quick lunch before we have to leave.

We eat simple grilled cheese sandwiches that Killian elevates to a gourmet treat. With a satisfying crunch, I take the last bite of my toast and drop my plate in the sink. "Ready to head to the bus station?"

"Yep." He wipes his mouth with a paper napkin before quickly rinsing our dishes.

We grab our bags and head out the door, making our way toward the bus station on foot under a bright afternoon sun.

As we approach the parking lot, I notice Killian eyeing the Greyhound buses with a hint of skepticism. He wrinkles his nose ever so slightly, and I can't help but tease him about it.

"Aw, what's the matter, St. Clair? Is this not up to your billionaire standards?" I playfully nudge him with my elbow.

He looks mildly embarrassed, but chuckles. "I suppose I'm still adjusting to this new lifestyle. But I hope you don't think I'm ungrateful for everything you're doing for me, Spoon. I truly appreciate it."

"Of course not." I reassure him with a warm smile. "And don't worry, bus rides can be charming."

"Charming?" he repeats, raising an eyebrow. "That's one way to put it."

We join the line to board the bus, and I have to give it to him, the smell of old upholstery and stale coffee that greets us inside isn't exactly pleasant. Killian follows closely behind me, taking in the narrow aisle and cramped seats.

"Welcome to the glamorous world of affordable transportation." I grin as I motion for him to pick a seat. "You get used to it after a while."

Killian insists on me having the window seat. I sink into it with a silent "oof," grateful to have a view. "Thanks, cowboy," I quip, the corners of my mouth hitching up into a teasing smile.

Killian, showcasing more the air of a chivalrous knight than a cowboy, nods and parks himself in the aisle seat. Despite his body being too large for a cheap bus service, he still displays that effortless grace of his. The way he adapts to the tiny strip of Greyhound real estate is impressive.

The bus leaves soon afterward. Just as I'm about to nap in the comforting drone of the engine, a chatty stranger takes the seat on the opposite side of the aisle to Killian. The newcomer greets us with a cheerful hello that is threateningly friendly.

I snuggle closer to the window while Killian gives me a brief, helpless glance before he's sucked into a conversational vortex.

"So what do you do for a living?" the stranger asks after a while.

"I'm a rancher," Killian replies on reflex. The fact that he is actually a bartender in this world hasn't sunk in yet, apparently.

"A rancher? Wow, like those cowboys you see on TV?"

"Something like that," Killian deflects, his tone even, patient.

But the guy's off with a never-ending stream of questions about ranch life, horses, and the price of beef per pound—things Killian can answer but looks increasingly desperate not to. I bite my lip, torn between rescuing him and continuing to enjoy the comedy gold unfolding before me.

Killian catches my eye between the barrage of cowboy-related inquiries, and I can't help it; I grin.

"Any funny stories on the ranch?" the man asks at one point.

"Well, there was that time that my neighbor stole my prize rooster, Sir Clucks-a-Lot," Killian responds as if this were a story he's told a million times before.

The man's eyes bulge. "You had a rooster called Sir Clucks-a-Lot?"

Killian shrugs. "Sure. He was a crowing champion three years in a row," he says without a hint of sarcasm. I have to fight hard not to laugh at the shocked expression on the nosy man's face. "That's why my rival rancher chicken-napped him. When I confronted him, he denied it, of course. But I could recognize my rooster's clucks coming from his henhouse. So I went back, in the dead of night, on a stealth mission to retrieve him."

I'm fully aware this anecdote must be from some kind of made-up back story, but I'd be lying if I said I'm not sitting on the edge of my seat to learn the fate of Sir Clucks-a-Lot. I look around, and see half the passengers on the bus are doing the same.

"I snuck past their guard dog, an old German Shepherd with a nasty temper. But turns out, he was more bark than bite—or more accurately, more snores than chomps because the old boy was asleep by the chicken coop. Quiet as a cat, I tiptoed up to where Sir Clucks-a-Lot was stashed and—wouldn't you know it—the darned bird recognized me and started up one of his serenades. That woke up the dog, alright."

"Did you make it out in one piece?" the man asks.

Now the entire bus is waiting for Killian's answer.

"Sure did." He leans back in his seat with a self-satisfied smirk. "But my jeans weren't half as lucky. The old shepherd managed to latch onto them just as I was hoisting Sir Clucks-a-

Lot over the fence. Ripped them right down the backside. So there I am, in the moonlight, with a squawking rooster under one arm and my dignity flapping in the wind."

The bus erupts into laughter, and even the driver glances at us in the rearview mirror, his lips twitching into an amused smile.

I can't help but join in; Killian's story is just too absurd, too vividly painted not to find it utterly hilarious. And if something like that comes up while we're at Maggie's, we can always claim Killian grew up on a farm.

But a tiny part of me still wonders how much of his personality is part of a fictional construct. Even now that he is here with me, are his thoughts his own or pre-programmed into him? Is that why he likes me? Because I was the heroine in his story? I squash the disturbing thoughts aside, and before the chatty stranger has a chance to ask Killian for another story, like he's clearly dying to, I take pity on him and take advantage of his neighbor having to take a breath to ask him if he wants to listen to a playlist with me.

Killian gratefully agrees, taking one of my earbuds—the old, corded kind—from me like a literal lifeline.

The moment I open the music app, my favorite playlist starts playing automatically, Taylor Swift blaring out of the earbuds at top volume.

I glance at Killian, whose expression is a mix of bemusement and mild panic. "Uh, interesting choice," he mutters, and I laugh, my finger already skipping to the next track.

The playlist mellows into a soft acoustic number, and Killian's shoulders sag against the seat. He gives me a grateful look, his hand finding mine and squeezing it gently.

With the music pounding in my ears—*ear singular*—and

Killian's reassuring presence next to me, I relax and close my eyes.

I wake up an hour or so later as the bus comes to a stop. Unsurprisingly, I've once again used Killian as my personal pillow. I look up, and he gives me a wink.

My spine straightens up in response as if I'd just been electrocuted. I touch my mouth. Dry. At least I didn't drool on him.

"Sorry," I say.

"No need to apologize, Sugar Spoon. You needed the rest."

"Why?"

He swipes a thumb over my knuckles as he draws near, his breath warm against my neck, speaking in hushed tones only I'm meant to hear. "It's going to be a long weekend of fake dating."

24

GHOSTS OF UNDERGRAD PAST

A black Lexus SUV pulls into the station just as Killian and I get off the bus. Maggie hops out of the car from the passenger side before it's even fully parked. Excitement and nerves war within me at seeing her after such a long hiatus. It's been an entire year since our last rendezvous, and I'm thrilled to catch up with her. Yet there's a twist in my gut, a cocktail of anticipation and anxiety, as I prepare to introduce her to my fake boyfriend—who might also be an imaginary person.

Killian wrapping his arm firmly around my waist doesn't help, nor does the kiss he just dropped on top of my head. My scalp tingles where his lips touched me, and I have to resist the urge to scratch.

Get it together, Leighton.

I tuck an errant strand of hair behind my ear to give my hands something to do and plaster a smile on my face as Maggie approaches.

"Leigh!" she squeals, barreling toward me for a hug. I extricate myself from Killian's grip to return it.

"Maggie, I've missed you!" I say into her shoulder.

She pulls back, grinning ear to ear. "Me too! Oh my gosh, you look amazing!"

I laugh. "Thanks, so do you! Love the new hair." Her formerly straight brown locks are now vibrant waves with caramel and honey highlights.

"And you must be Killian," she says, turning to him with an outstretched hand. "I'm Maggie, Leighton's better half."

Killian shakes her hand, giving her a friendly grin. "It's lovely to meet you. I've heard so much about you."

His gravelly voice makes the words sound almost carnal, causing Maggie to look as dazzled as I feel every time he speaks.

Corey, Maggie's fiancé—a tall, sandy-haired guy—climbs out of the car. "Babe, need any help with the bags?"

"Nope, I think we've got it covered!"

A quick round of introductions and soon we're all piled into the car, heading to Maggie's place in a nice residential neighborhood. In the backseat, Killian's thigh presses against mine and he has absent-mindedly dropped a hand on my knee. The gesture is casual, intimate. Exactly what a boyfriend would do. Except we're not really dating, and it's not like he has to pretend back here.

Not that I wouldn't mind climbing into his lap right now. Which is probably why I should keep some distance.

I'm considering shuffling toward the opposite side of the seat when Maggie turns back with a conspiratorial grin. Her gaze drops to Killian's hand on my leg, and she winks at me. Okay then, maybe it's wiser to keep up a modicum of pretense at all times. Looks like I'm staying put.

Killian squeezes my knee gently and lowers his voice to a tender rumble, intimate and meant for me alone. "Relax, we've already done much worse."

I glare at him, hissing, "I don't remember any of it."

"You don't remember when we kissed after I rescued you?"

His fingers dig a little more firmly into my flesh. "Let me remind you, Sugar Spoon." His voice drops to an even lower hum. "I had you on the hard ground underneath me, your hands pinned over your head in the dirt, your legs wrapped around my waist as we—"

"I remember," I admit.

"Good." Killian smirks.

I keep my gaze trained forward, trying to ignore the wave of heat that is spreading from my knee to all over my body. I have to remind myself this is all pretend, that Killian will probably poof out of existence at any time. All rational arguments, but the tingling doesn't go away. This weekend is going to be pure torture.

We pull up in front of a cute red-brick house with a big front porch. Vines crawl up the outer walls and flowers bloom in window boxes. It's everything I imagined adult life would be like back in our dorm days. Maggie has the whole grownups thing nailed down. Me? Not so much.

"Home sweet home!" my friend announces.

We grab our bags and head inside. The living room is cozy but stylish, with immaculate cream-colored couches that wouldn't last a day in my care, potted plants that *all* seem to be alive, and a giant marble fireplace at the back of the room.

"You two are in the guestroom upstairs," Maggie says.

By now, I'm the queen of only-one-beds-shared-with-impossibly-sexy-men. I'm not at all fazed by the news that Killian and I will bunk together.

Killian winks at me. "That'll be perfect, won't it, Sugar?"

"Yep! Just great, *Bun*."

Killian raises an eyebrow at the new nickname, prompting a viciously sweet smile from me.

Maggie gives us a quick tour of the house, just before Corey

—a surgeon, obviously—has to head back to the hospital for an emergency. She shoos us upstairs to settle in while she finishes prepping dinner.

Once we're alone, I turn to Killian. "So there's only one bed..."

He grins. "Nothing we haven't handled before."

True. But the bed in Maggie's guest room looks tinier than the one at home. Maybe I am just a little fazed.

I take a deep breath. "Okay, well, at least Maggie bought our story."

"Was there any doubt?" Killian moves closer. "We make quite the convincing couple, don't you think?"

My heart races as his eyes lock onto mine.

Focus.

"Uh, right! Anyway, we should check how much time we have before dinner and see if we can sneak away and go look for the fake ID guy."

Killian nods, the moment broken. "I'll be there in a second."

I head down to the kitchen without looking back. This weekend is going to be the death of me.

I find Maggie working at the island, her sleeves rolled up, hair up in a ponytail, as she chops away at a colorful array of vegetables. The knife hits the cutting board at a precise tempo.

"Need any help?" I offer, leaning against the counter.

Maggie shakes her head, ponytail swishing. "And let my guest cook? What kind of host would I be?"

"An efficient one," I joke. I watch her work for a moment, nostalgia washing over me. "Remember sophomore year, when we tried to make pad Thai from scratch? What a disaster that was."

Maggie laughs. "We nearly burned down the dorm!"

"Worth it for the look on the RA's face alone." I grin at the memory, watching her expertly dice an onion. "And remember that time we thought it was a cool idea to play *Sex and the City* and make Cosmos?"

Maggie laughs, nodding vigorously. "Gosh, we got the whole floor drunk! I still remember the hangover."

"But it was an epic party," I remind her.

"Agreed." She grins as she tosses some chopped peppers into a bowl.

"You'd gotten the fake ID to buy all the alcohol here in South Bend, right?" I ask casually.

"Yeah, from Spotty, bless his heart." Maggie shakes her head. "I think he still has the operation running down in the Rum Village."

My heart beats faster, but before I can respond, a pair of familiar arms wrap around me from behind. Killian pulls me in close, dropping a soft kiss on my neck that makes my knees weak. Judging from the heat marking the spot, I'm pretty sure I'm going to have a blister tomorrow.

"What are you ladies up to?" he asks, resting his chin on my shoulder.

"Reminiscing about college," Maggie replies, giving us a knowing look. "Have you ever been to South Bend, Killian?"

"No, I haven't," he admits.

"Then Leighton has to bring you to campus and show you around!" Maggie exclaims, her eyes twinkling. "Corey won't be back until late evening, so you two should go have fun."

"Don't you want to join us?" I ask just to be polite, hoping she'll say no.

"No, you go, guys. I'll just finish prepping everything and then I have a couple of house showings this afternoon. I hope you don't mind?"

"Not at all," I say. "Is there a bus we can take to campus?"

I've never lived in this neighborhood, so I'm not familiar with the public transportation here.

"No need." Maggie dusts her hands on her apron and fetches a set of keys from a bowl, dangling them in front of us. "Take my car."

"Won't you need it for your showings?"

"No, both houses are just a couple of streets over. I can walk. You take the car. It's the cherry-red Lexus out front."

They're really into grownup cars in this house.

"Thanks, Mags." I grab the keys and almost drop them immediately as Killian's fingers start tracing little circles on my waist.

"Sounds like a plan," he says.

"Alright then, it's settled!" Maggie claps her hands together. "Go enjoy yourselves. I've got this under control."

Moving out of the kitchen allows me to unwrap my unbearably sexy fake boyfriend from my back.

"Aren't you taking your part a little too seriously?" I glare as I shove on my coat in the entryway.

That too-perfect mouth curls at the corners. "I never do things half-heartedly, Sugar."

"Thanks again, Maggie!" I call out as Killian and I exit the house. "We'll be back before dinner!"

"Have fun!"

Killian makes a beeline for the driver's side, but I point out that he doesn't have a license in this world and take the wheel.

As I study the control panel, I feel like I'm borrowing my mother's car—not that we could ever afford a Lexus—as opposed to a vehicle that it's normal for someone my age to possess.

"Alright," I say, after fastening my seatbelt, "time to find this ID guy." I pull up the last-known address for Spotty on my phone and start navigating us through South Bend.

"Is it just me, or is this part of town a bit sketchy?" Killian asks, eyeing the surroundings with a hint of unease.

"Definitely sketchy," I agree, feeling a little tense myself. "But I don't suppose criminals set their lairs in the most respectable parts of town."

"Right," he says, not entirely convinced.

I take advantage of a red light to flick his arm. "What's happened to you? Did you eat grouchy pie?"

"Sorry if I'm still smarting from the last time you tangled with criminals."

He has to be talking about the kidnapping. "That was clearly an exaggerated fictional scenario. And what's life without a little adventure?"

"You don't have to put yourself in danger just to get me an ID. We can find another way."

"There is no danger. Spotty is a local legend, I promise." I turn stations until I find a country-pop song that I'm sure even Killian knows the lyrics to and start singing my heart out.

Killian raises an eyebrow at me. "Are you seriously singing your way out of the argument?"

"Isn't that what princesses do in fairy tales?" I tease and double my vocal efforts.

Killian tries to keep a stern face, but I can still see the twitch at the corners of his mouth.

I sing the rest of the way until the map app informs us we've arrived. I pull up outside a ramshackle house with a dirty siding and a boarded window that scream drug den. The yard is overgrown and half-filled with trash.

But if eighteen-year-old freshmen come here alone to get fake IDs and get away unscathed, we'll be fine.

I knock on the door, and a second later, it swings open to reveal a thin man who wouldn't look out of place as a cast member of *Breaking Bad*. He has a beanie covering light brown hair and is dressed in layered, loose-fitting clothing—a graphic tee under an open, boldly colored hoodie paired with baggy jeans.

He leans against the doorframe, giving us a once-over.

"Whaddup, you two lost?" he asks, as loud hip-hop music blasts from inside the house, making it hard to hear.

"Uh, hi," I say, trying to sound casual. "You're Spotty, right?"

The dude crosses his arms over his chest. "Who wants to know?"

"We're looking to get a fake ID?"

"Yo, lady, hush. Not outside," he says, opening the door further and welcoming us into the house.

The interior is no better than the front yard. Stained carpet, battered furniture, and rubble everywhere—pizza boxes, a bong, empty beer bottles. The only brand-new fixtures are the giant TV mounted on the back wall and a set of stacked speakers from where the music comes with an incessant beat. A joint smolders away in an ashtray on a nearby table. The place reeks of weed and dirty laundry.

Spotty meanders down a corridor and leads us into a room that's contrastingly sterile compared to the rest of the house. White clean walls. Clean floors. There's a fancy printer on a table and in the corner, a professional camera sitting between two soft-boxes. A computer setup that looks powerful enough to launch missiles at NASA takes over another table along with other various tech equipment.

"Who's the ID for?" Spotty asks.

"That'd be me." Killian steps forward, trying to shield me with his body.

I find the gesture absurd. Spotty looks as threatening as an overcooked noodle.

"Sure thing," Spotty replies, unfazed. "Standard ID takes twenty-four hours, costs two hundred and fifty bucks, cash upfront. No refunds."

"Actually," I interject, stepping forward from the wall of over-protective man, "we were kind of hoping you could provide us something a little more... uhm... sophisticated."

"Alright, whatcha looking for exactly?" he asks.

"An ID tied to a social security number that can withstand security checks."

"Ah, I see," Spotty says, stroking his chin thoughtfully. "That's gonna cost you extra and it'll take forty-eight hours at least."

"How much extra?" I ask.

"That kind of work. Two grand at least."

"Two thousand dollars?" I exclaim, my heart dropping. I don't have a dime to spare. Killian has already assured me he'll repay me every single penny as soon as he makes the money back at the bar. But I live paycheck to paycheck. I don't have two thousand dollars sitting in my bank account. "Are you kidding me?"

"Hey, quality ain't cheap, lady," Spotty says with a shrug.

"Please, there must be something else we can do, or pay you with?" I plead. "A favor? A service? Anything, really?"

"Yo, lady, you're cute, but I've never paid for sex and I ain't gonna start now."

"Excuse me? That's not what I meant!" I splutter.

My face turns beet red, but I'm distracted by a feral growl to my left. Does Spotty have a dog or something? I turn but only see Killian in the room.

Oh my gosh, he's the one *growling*.

"What are you doing?" I hiss, bewildered.

He doesn't reply, still snarling at Spotty.

"Killian, stop," I plead, trying to keep my voice steady.

"But he was being disrespectful," Killian answers, his tone protective.

And I know we all love it when men growl possessively in romance novels, but trust me, in real life, it's beyond ridiculous. "Stop it," I tell him firmly. "You sound like a lawnmower with indigestion."

"Fine," he mutters, taking a step back.

"Look," I say, turning back to Spotty, "we're desperate. There has to be something we can do for you."

"For two grand? Yo, lady, that'd have to be pretty big."

"Go big or go home, right?" I cheer nervously. "Isn't there really anything that you need? We could clean your house or mow the lawn..." He's not looking impressed, I think harder. "I'm a computer expert. I could up your security, lock down your IP, make you totally untraceable, whatever you need..."

"You're a computer whizz?"

I nod enthusiastically.

Spotty eyes us skeptically before finally relenting. "I'll tell you what, I'll take the standard two-fifty bucks, the cyber upgrade, and there's something else you could do for me..."

25

THE HEIST

I stare at Spotty, mouth agape. "You want us to do *what*?"

"Steal the leprechaun costume before the big game tomorrow," he repeats casually as if asking me to grab him a soda.

"Why?"

"I hate the Fighting Irish, and that mascot is creepy, yo."

Killian jumps in before I can respond. "Dude, that's insane. How would we even pull that off?"

Spotty leans back in his gaming chair, steepling his fingers like a supervillain. "Yo, easy. There's an event at the stadium tonight. I can whip up some fake press badges to get you inside."

My mind reels at the absurdity of it all. "They'll obviously just use the backup costume," I argue. "What's the point?"

"The point," Spotty says, eyes glinting, "is that it will curse them. Jinx the game, lady."

Killian and I exchange bewildered looks.

"Jinx?" Killian chimes in, raising an eyebrow. "I'm sorry, but why do you hate the Fighting Irish so much?"

Spotty chuckles, but it's hollow. "Cuz I'm originally from Ann Arbor. My family's been Michigan fans for generations. When you grow up in that house, hating Notre Dame isn't a choice, man, it's a birthright."

Whoa. Who knew college football hatred could run two thousand dollars deep? I mean, good for us. But stealing the costume... that's next-level crazy. But we have no choice.

Killian seems to read my mind. "We'll do it," he says, locking eyes with me, "but we can't bring the costume back tonight."

Spotty nods. "Yo, fine. I won't have your fake IDs ready until Sunday, anyway. I'll just watch the local news for reports about the heist." He grins wickedly.

"Now, let's get your pictures taken for those press badges."

He snaps photos of us and swiftly prints out the fake badges. "These should get you into the event at the football stadium," he says, handing them over alongside a professional video camera and a mic. "Good luck."

"Thanks," Killian replies, pocketing the badges and dropping the camera over his shoulder. I take the microphone. "We'll be in touch."

If anyone had told me a week ago that I'd be engaging in a mascot abduction, I would've snorted coffee through my nose. But here I am, with Killian, my cowboy turned counterfeit crew member, plotting to purloin a leprechaun. Sabotaging my college team for the greater good.

The sun is sinking low, casting an orange glow over the car dashboard as we drive toward campus. My hands are tight on the wheel, and I can feel Killian's eyes on me, his presence an oddly grounding force.

"So, Bonnie, what's the plan?" Killian's voice is light, but I can hear the undercurrent of pissed-offness. Guess fictional world or not, me dealing with criminals always puts his panties in a bunch.

I let out a breath I didn't know I was holding. "Well, *Clyde*, I guess we pretend to be the most enthusiastic sports journalists ever. You got your camera skills ready?"

He laughs, a rich sound that eases the knots in my stomach a bit. "Always. But are you ready to channel your inner Erin Andrews?"

I snort. "More like her bumbling, clueless cousin, twice removed. I wouldn't know a touchdown from a field goal."

Killian reaches over, giving my shoulder a squeeze. "Just follow my lead. I'll be the charming cameraman. You be the distractingly beautiful reporter. We'll be out before they even notice anything's amiss."

Did he say distractingly beautiful? I turn to him only to get chided. "Eyes on the road, Spoon."

The campus looms ahead, the buildings already dark against the twilight sky.

We pull into the parking lot and I take a deep breath.

Killian grins. "Let's go catch ourselves a leprechaun."

We head toward the gym, our fake press badges displayed prominently.

"Remember," I whisper as we approach the security guard, "we're here for an exclusive interview with the mascot about his pre-game rituals."

We stride toward the gym entrance as if we have every right to be here. "Press," I say with a nonchalant wave of our badges to the campus guard at the door.

"Hold up, where do you think you're going?" The security guard is a fortress, blocking our path with a skeptical frown as he checks his clipboard. "I have nothing about an interview."

I flash my best smile. "Special feature with the beloved mascot," I say, voice steady, heart not so much.

The guard eyes us suspiciously, but Killian steps forward, all confidence and easy smiles. "We're a bit early, I know. But it's Friday night. We just want to get home after a long week."

Somehow, it works. The guard's eyes flick from me to Killian, then back again before he waves us through with a grumble.

Close call.

We slip past him and into the belly of the gym, where the air is stuffy from limited ventilation and smells like rubber. The mascot, in full leprechaun regalia, is taking photos with fans.

Showtime.

Killian slings the camera up and nods at me. I stride over to the mascot, pulling out my best reporter's voice and the microphone prop Spotty provided that I'm not sure what he uses for. Karaoke night with his thug friends? "Mr. Leprechaun, sir! Your fans are dying to know, tell us about a typical day in the life of a college mascot..."

After bullshitting my way through an endless stream of questions, the mascot is called away to meet with more fans. Checking that no one is looking our way, Killian and I discreetly disappear behind a door opposite to the one we used to enter. While interviewing the guy playing the leprechaun, I asked him where the precious costume was stored, and the guy pointed me in the direction of the locker rooms. Hence where Killian and I are headed right now.

The corridor on this side is mostly dark. I'm nervous again as we don't have a proper reason to be here, or even a plausible one. I've barely had a look down the hall when Killian pulls me into a random storage room. It's a dark, tiny room filled with sports equipment where there's barely enough space for us to stand toe to toe.

"What are you doing?" I hiss as Killian clicks the slatted door shut behind us.

His eyes twinkle in the scarce light filtering through the slats, a mischievous glint that I'm starting to recognize. "Hiding," he whispers back, his breath warm against my ear. "Unless you want to explain to the janitor coming our way why we're snooping around."

I hadn't seen anyone. "You know, for a guy who's used to the high life, you're pretty good at slumming it."

Killian chuckles, shifting a basketball so it doesn't dig into his back. "I'm full of surprises, Sugar Spoon. Besides," he adds, his voice lowering, "it's not the worst thing, being this close to you."

My heartbeat still drums in my ears, but I scoff playfully, "Focus, Romeo. We're on a mission."

"The event is still going. It'll be at least another half an hour before everyone leaves. How should we kill time while we wait?"

I bite my lip as I think of how to answer that question. We kept the lights off to avoid detection from the outside and Killian's proximity is already driving me wild, my imagination running rampant with possibilities.

"Well, we could... play a game," I suggest, trying to keep my tone light.

"What game?"

"How about 'Two Truths and a Lie'?" I propose, hoping my voice doesn't betray the flutter in my stomach. "I'll start. I can't ride a bike, but I can play the piano. And I'm terrified of clowns."

"Mmm... That you are terrified of clowns seems like the most easy truth. You don't have a piano at home, but that doesn't mean you can't play. And I find it hard to believe you can't ride a bike... but you might also have planted that option as a trap?"

He's so flipping hot when he rationalizes. "But did I?"

"Something so impossible to believe I'd pick it without

thinking? You could have. But you said you don't have a rich family bankrolling you. If you grew up with little money, maybe your parents never got you a bike and you never learned."

Killian's deduction hits closer to home than I expect, stinging a little, but also warming me. It's not just his charm or his looks; it's this—every word he speaks, every little detail he notices and remembers, only adds to the attraction. I listen, almost bewitched, as he finishes his reasoning.

"So, is the lie the piano or the clowns? Clowns are easily believable and the piano is not as easily unbelievable as the bike, but still less common than clown phobia. And if your parents could never afford a bike, it'd seem odd they could afford piano lessons. I call bullshit on the piano."

"Almost, cowboy." My voice is raw. "My parents could never afford to buy me a bike, true. But they also couldn't afford a babysitter when they had to work a double shift. So I spent countless afternoons and evenings with the old lady living next door to us, and *she* had a piano. She taught me how to play."

I wait, heart beating, for Killian's reply.

He gently pulls a curl and lets it bounce back into shape. "I'll teach you how to ride a bike if you teach me how to play the piano."

I love that he didn't make my confession that I don't know how to ride a bike awkward. That I just basically told him I grew up in poverty, and he didn't even flinch. He's still being himself, still being kind and charming and insanely attractive.

"Don't all billionaires learn how to play the piano at a young age?"

"I picked up the violin instead."

"Really?"

"You tell me." His grin is devastating even in the semi-darkness. "My turn. I can play the violin. I've read every book by Jane Austen. And I've traveled to all five continents."

"Uuuh." I pop my knuckles. "Let's see. The Jane Austen thing seems like the most obvious lie. But it could also be your booby trap."

I poke his chest with my index finger.

Grin. "But is it?"

"Let's see. You were a billionaire until I pulled you into this riches-to-rags reality, so it'd make sense that you've traveled to every continent. But it could also be a too-obvious truth. And then there's the violin."

"What about the violin?"

"It seems hard to believe, but you also answered me on instinct, saying you could play the violin and then rolled with it, so you didn't plant it. And I'm pretty sure you're trying to reverse-psychologize me on the Jane Austen thing, hiding the lie in plain sight. I call bullshit on Jane."

"Almost, Sugar Spoon. I've never been to Africa or Australia."

So far, the only places I'm sure he's actually been are Evanston and South Bend, but I don't point that out. I don't want to hurt his feelings, reminding him none of his memories are real.

"Me neither." I don't know why my words come out on a ragged breath.

"Then we'll go together one day..."

I deflect. "Let's hope Spotty is so good at what he does that he can get you a passport."

"Speaking of Spotty, if Mission Leprechaun is still a go, we should probably steal the darn costume."

We hear footsteps outside.

"Let's give it another ten minutes," I say. "How come you can play the violin?"

He smiles. "I'm a cowboy, Sugar, country fiddle is my jam."

"Oh, is it?" I mock-scowl. "And don't think I'm not going to test you on the Jane Austen novels. Which one is your favorite?"

"It's a hard call between *Pride and Prejudice* and *Northanger Abbey*."

"Not *Emma*?"

"Oh, please, I loathed *Emma*."

"Oh my gosh, me too." I lean into him. "I don't think I've ever confessed that out loud to anyone."

"I like that you told me." His voice is a low whisper that spears right through my heart.

"Do you remember your childhood?" I ask, changing the subject so fast I might get motion sickness.

I can't properly see his face, but I know he's squinting. "Not really. I have a general feeling it was bright and happy except for a dark stain under the surface."

"Uh, that's probably your character arc. The scar in your past you have to overcome before you can truly heal and love."

"I can love alright, Sugar."

I'm not just swooning. I'm puddling. If I didn't have a supply rack pressing against my back and a book boyfriend to my front, I'd be a puddle on the floor.

"What's your character scar?" Killian asks in a whisper.

"I don't know, almost twenty-five years of being single? Dating apps? All the bullshit I had to take over the years from my coupled friends? You pick."

He lets out a low chuckle. "Don't worry, you have me now."

Do I? I don't ask the question aloud.

"You want to play another round of Two Truths and a Lie?"

I shake my head. "I don't think we have time if we don't want to be late for dinner at Maggie's."

"We could always change games?" His voice sounds suspiciously teasing.

"Oh, yeah? And what would you have in mind?"

Killian's mouth drops to within a sliver of my ear. "We've got time for a round of Seven Minutes in Heaven…"

The tension hangs heavy between us, electric and undeniable. We lean in, so close that our breaths mingle. Just as the air we're sharing thins to breaking point, someone calls outside, "That was the last one, Joe. Everybody's gone. I'm gonna close up now."

A voice in the distance yells a reply, and in response, the first man lets out a resounding burp, effectively killing the magic.

I squish backward as far as the rack at my back will allow me. The realization that I was about to let Killian kiss me is hot in my belly. He stares at me in the semi-darkness of the storage room, his intense eyes promising a rematch.

We wait for another heartbeat before Killian grabs my hand. "Let's go steal a mascot."

26

BACKWARD CAPS AND BORROWED IDENTITIES

Killian and I burst through the front door of Maggie's house, practically vibrating with adrenaline. He's donned the leprechaun hat we swiped while I've draped the stolen jacket over Spotty's video camera as camouflage before I can hide it in our room. The rest of the loot? Tossed into a bin outside Notre Dame's campus—the main costume and the two spares as well. If I don't make a career for myself in AI, I'll always have a life of crime as backup.

"Well, don't you two look spirited!" Maggie says with a laugh, taking in our appearance. "You guys are all in for the Fighting Irish, huh?"

If only she knew we're actually saboteurs.

"Did you enjoy visiting the campus, Killian?" she asks, trying to hide her amusement.

"Absolutely. It was... enlightening." He grins, and we exchange a knowing glance.

Dinner that night is filled with laughter and good-natured teasing. I don't know Maggie's fiancé well, but he seems like a gracious, kind man who adores her. And I'm genuinely happy they're getting married.

My gaze drifts to Killian, and a pang of *something* pulls in my heart. He makes it really hard not to like him, but how can I give in to the attraction when he doesn't even know who he is? Can he ever truly love me if he remembers nothing about his past? If he *doesn't have* a past? Maybe not even a future.

I need to dust off a few amnesia romances and check what the protocol is. How long does someone with a blank past take to rediscover themselves? When can I trust Killian will be ready to explore a relationship? Will he ever?

I have this inexplicable premonition that the moment I let myself truly believe he's here to stay, the joke will be on me and he'll disappear.

That night in bed, those thoughts are still swimming in my head when he calls me out. "You're especially pensive tonight, Spoon."

I turn to him. "How aren't you more freaked out by this whole situation? Your entire life has been turned upside down, you lost everything, and you act like it's nothing."

There's a beat of silence and a sigh. "Would worrying or obsessing over it change anything?"

"Probably not."

"Then the best I can do is take it one day at a time and enjoy what I have instead of complaining about what I lost."

"That is such a collected answer." I shift under the covers and turn to him. "But if you get moody about me pulling you into my world, know that you can bitch about it as much as you want."

The low laugh he gives me in response coils around my spine. "Noted, Sugar Spoon. Thanks for giving me free bitching rein. Goodnight."

"Night."

I keep quiet after that and completely still, but I don't fall asleep. It takes a while, but my lids finally become heavy. I'm about to be pulled under when Killian whispers into the night, "I didn't lose everything. I still have you."

Like the coward I am, I pretend not to hear. To be sleeping. Even if, once again, sleep is the furthest thing from my mind.

* * *

The next morning dawns sunny and crisp, a perfect fall day for a football game. South Bend comes alive with the tradition of tail-gating outside the stadium. The scent of grilled food fills the air as fans gather in the parking lot, their excitement palpable.

Maggie, Corey, and a few of their friends have set up a tent with foldable tables and a professional portable grill. The men have been grilling meat since ten in the morning.

Killian mans the barbecue like a pro, charring sausages and acrobatically flipping burgers as the crowd cheers him on. I hang back with the excuse of catching up with Maggie and other old friends. But mostly I just watch him. Someone has given him a baseball cap that he's wearing backward, melting the few sane brain cells I had left after spending half an hour locked in a closet with him yesterday and another night in the same bed.

The tufts of hair escaping the cap on the sides shine in the sunlight. His cheeks are flushed from being behind the grill for so long. And he has a warm smile for everyone. He's the most gorgeous man I've ever seen. I could spend all eternity just watching him and be happy.

Maggie sidles up next to me and follows my gaze. "You've got it bad, don't you?" she says knowingly. "I've never seen you look at someone like that. And to think you only went on a first date last week."

For simplicity, I told her that Killian was my date of Friday night, the one I'd told her about over the phone, keeping vague about the details.

"He's a keeper," Maggie adds. "I can tell."

My cheeks flush, but I don't argue. Because what can I say? She's right. I've got it bad, no matter how hard I try to deny it. And when I watch him blend in like that, I can almost see a future. At least until one of Corey's friends asks him if he's into college football, and Killian replies he follows more the high school league.

"Oh, which team?" the dude asks.

"Lakeville," Killian replies on instinct.

The guy frowns. "You mean the Lake Travis Cavaliers?"

Killian is quick to recover. "Yeah, man, sorry, me and my buddies call them Lakevaliers."

Only he has no buddies. Corey's friend leaves with a face as perplexed as I feel. Every time I think Killian might just fit into my life, something like this happens.

As the morning progresses with no more slip-ups, we eat, drink, and revel in the camaraderie of fellow fans. The anticipation for the game grows, and soon enough, it's time to head inside the stadium.

A guy bumps into me from behind, sending my Coke sloshing over the rim of my glass. Thankfully missing my shoes. When I lift my eyes from checking for potential damage, I see the guy who bumped into me dangling one foot above the ground, being held by the collar of his jersey by a furious Killian. "Apologize to the lady," he growls.

The skimpy kid looks at me with a terrorized face. "I-I'm sorry, miss, I didn't mean to—to—" Words fail him.

"It's okay." I smile tensely. "Killian, please put him down."

Killian must hear the note of displeasure in my tone because he sets the poor kid down and turns to me, eyebrows raised.

The moment his feet touch the ground, the kid skedaddles, getting lost in the crowd.

"He was rude to you."

"So what? People are rude. It's a fact of life. You can't rough up everyone who isn't a perfect gentleman to me. And I can take care of myself."

I push ahead of him, perhaps angrier than I should be. But it's just these over-the-top behaviors of his that set me on edge.

Killian catches up with me. "I'm sorry."

I look at him and I can't stay mad. It's not his fault if someone wrote him up as a headstrong alpha male. I just hope that aspect of his personality will tone down once he's been living in the real world for some time.

"It's okay." I take his hand and guide him to the stands, joining in the chants of "Let's go, Irish!" along with the crowd. I feel a bit of a hypocrite after sabotaging the team yesterday. But Killian and I agreed last night to keep our escapades incognito and make up for jinxing the game with relentless cheering.

As we take our seats, a blaring announcement echoes through the stadium. "Ladies and gentlemen, we regret to inform you that our beloved Fighting Irish mascot costume has been stolen. Our leprechaun will be... improvising today."

Killian and I lock eyes with an "oops" expression—the tiff about his excessive alpha-ness already forgotten—as the poor guy we interviewed yesterday steps onto the field dressed in nothing but clover-print boxer briefs, a bright green top hat, and leprechaun shoes.

The entire stadium cheers the mascot on. The spirit of the Fighting Irish is very much alive. Killian and I share a complicit shrug and add our voices to the roar, our cheers and whistles echoing louder than those around us.

As the game kicks off, the energy in the stadium is palpable. Notre Dame plays hard, fueled by the indignation of their mascot's misfortune. The action on the field is fast and furious, keeping everyone on the edge of their seats. Despite the close score and the mounting tension, Killian and I can't help but share occasional smirks, silently acknowledging our little secret.

Just as the clock runs out, Notre Dame pulls off a miraculous win, sending the crowd into a frenzy. I'm glad our jinx didn't make them actually lose. I just hope Spotty won't hold the home team's victory against us. We completed our part of the bargain.

* * *

On Sunday, I hug Maggie goodbye as Killian loads our bags into her car.

She drives us to the bus station where we say one last farewell.

"Thanks again for having us, Maggie." I squeeze her tight. "We had a blast."

"Anytime," she replies, stepping back and giving Killian a hug as well. "You two take care of each other, okay?"

"Will do," Killian promises.

She reaches out and gives my upper arm a last squeeze. "We'll catch up at the bachelorette party. And Killian," Maggie adds, stepping back and adjusting her sunglasses atop her head, "Corey is sorry he had to rush to the hospital this morning, but you're invited to his bachelor party as well. And of course, we'll see you both at the wedding."

As Maggie drives away, we idle on a bench, waiting for her to be safely out of sight before we hail a taxi to head back to Spotty's place and retrieve Killian's fake ID.

Spotty leads us into his house, and we follow him to the now-familiar "white" room where all his illicit businesses take place—if you don't count the pot smoking in the living room, I suppose.

"Here you go," Spotty says, handing Killian the fake ID with a flourish. "Meet your new alias: Oswald Finch."

"Oswald Finch?" Killian does a double take, staring at the card in disbelief. "Seriously, man? That sounds like the name of an old man who feeds pigeons in the park."

"Yo, don't knock it," Spotty retorts, looking mildly offended. "I had to steal an identity from a cemetery to get you a social security number, and South Bend's graveyards aren't exactly teeming with cool names like Killian."

"But Oswald?" Killian shudders dramatically, still eyeing the ID with distaste.

"Yo, it's not my fault all the cool kids are still alive in this town. And I picked a guy who would've been about your age, with no surviving family, or social profiles. Oswald Finch is your golden ticket, man."

While the two of them continue to bicker about the merits of the name Oswald Finch, I turn my attention to Spotty's computer system. I sit in his gaming chair and figuratively crack my knuckles and get to work tweaking his firewall and encrypting his data. It takes a minute. For being a notorious criminal, his security is surprisingly basic.

A few more keystrokes and... done. Spotty's network is now ironclad.

I swivel around in the chair. "Ready to blow this joint, Oswald?"

Killian scowls, shoving the ID into his pocket. "Keep it up, I dare you."

I laugh as we head out of Spotty's house, our dabble into a life of crime hopefully over.

"Come on. Oswald isn't that bad," I tease, trying to lighten the mood as we finally sit on the bus. "It has a certain... flair?"

"Flair?" Killian huffs, rolling his eyes. "If by 'flair' you mean 'makes me want to take up knitting and start complaining about my arthritis,' then sure."

"Exactly." I grin, nudging him playfully. "You'll fit right in with all the other elderly gentlemen at the retirement home."

"Ha, hilarious," Killian says, but I can see the hint of a smile tugging at the corner of his mouth.

And why does making him smile fill me with a rush that feels like the first drop on a rollercoaster, thrilling and a bit terrifying?

* * *

Back in Illinois, the bus station is a madhouse. The bus doors hiss open and a surge of passengers pours out onto the platform. People pushing, shoving, everyone trying to grab their bags at once. In the chaos, I lose sight of Killian. I crane my neck, scanning the crowd, and spot him not far away.

He's crouched low, a hand outstretched toward... is that a dog? It's hard to tell beneath the dull, matted fur. The mangy stray animal is cowering before him, as Killian whispers gentle words I can't make out, trying to coax the shaking creature into being petted.

"We have to take him with us!" Killian declares as he notices me approach.

I eye the snarling mess skeptically. "Um, I'm pretty sure that thing is rabid. Or at least completely feral."

Killian blinks, genuinely confused. "But what do normal

people do when they find a lost pet? Shouldn't we give him shelter?"

"Normal people call animal control to pick them up. I don't think taking Cujo home is the best idea."

Killian frowns. I know he wants to argue, but the dog snaps viciously at his reaching hand.

"Okay, you win." He sighs.

I fish my phone out of my pocket. "I'll call the city to come get him."

We wait together until a CACC van arrives, and the animal control officers secure the frightened pup into a cage.

Killian watches the cage being loaded onto the van, a forlorn look on his face. I know he's just trying to help, but this world has different rules.

"I'm sorry," I say, placing a hand on his shoulder. "It's great you wanted to rescue him. But we can't save every stray, you know?"

He nods, but I can tell he's still disappointed. Impulsively, he turns and starts heading toward the van.

"Killian, wait!" I call after him. "Where are you going?"

"I just want to make sure he's okay," he shouts back.

I hurry to catch up as he steps into the road. A bus barrels by, blaring its horn. Killian stumbles back in shock.

"You can't just run into traffic!" I cry, grabbing his arm. "You're not invincible here."

Killian blinks, chastened. "You're right. I'm sorry."

He allows me to lead him back to the curb.

I shake my head. "Just no more heroics, please."

27

OSWALD AND GERTRUDE

FROM OLIVER

FYI. Last night I brought you to the North Pond near Lincoln Park and we had a blast

TO OLIVER

Uh-huh, what's the vibe of the place? I've never been

FROM OLIVER

Great views of the Chicago skyline and even better farm-to-table food

TO OLIVER

Tell me again why aren't we real dating?

"Something funny?" Killian's voice makes me jump.

I lower my phone and stare up at him from where I'm sitting on the bed. As part of his new wardrobe, Killian has also bought gray sweatpants, which should be banned from hot men's closets all over the world. They just don't give us poor ladies a fair chance. Killian gives off professional athlete vibes in his white T-shirt, gray pants, and crew socks. Leaning against the wall in a macho pose, he looks like he belongs on a billboard sports ad, not in my living room.

He arches an eyebrow at me.

"What?" I ask.

Am I ogling too hard?

"I asked if you were looking at something funny?"

"Oh, that, no, I'm just texting."

"Who?" The single-word question comes off a little territorial.

"Err, my other fake boyfriend," I reply, feeling slightly guilty for no good reason.

Killian tilts his head with a wry twist of his lips. "You have a *second* fake boyfriend?"

"Technically, I was fake dating him first! I'm very in demand as a fake girlfriend. It's the real thing that I'm not good at."

Killian gives me such an intense look but doesn't comment. "Why are you fake dating him?"

"Relax, I'm just doing him a favor."

"What kind of favor?"

My phone vibrates again, but I don't look at the screen. "It's basically so his family will stop sending him on random blind dates."

"That all?" Killian asks, unconvinced.

"Not the whole reason. But I can't tell you everything because it's personal to him. And he's asked me not to share."

"Mmmph."

"It's nothing romantic, don't worry."

Killian's eyes narrow, a shadow crossing his face before he smooths it into a nonchalant expression, heading into the kitchen.

And am I horrible for relishing the fact that Killian is a little jealous?

I stare down at the last text Oliver sent, replying to my question about why we're not real dating, and laugh my head off.

FROM OLIVER

> Because then I'd have to share my desserts, and I'm not ready for that kind of commitment

I reply with one of the most vicious "coupled humans' wisdom" pearls.

TO OLIVER

> Aww, Oliver, I think it's so great you're happy being alone! I really don't know how you do it...

FROM OLIVER

> *eye rolling emoji*

> Walked right into that one, didn't I?

I can't stop smiling as I reply.

TO OLIVER

> Yep

As I look up from the screen, I find Killian's gray eyes of steel locked on me.

"You like this dude?" he asks. "Because if I'm wasting my time here, I'd rather know."

And he's gone alphahole on me again. But in all fairness, if he was texting some other woman—a fake girlfriend—and laughing his head off, I'd be pretty jealous, too.

"It's completely innocent, I swear," I reassure him.

Killian doesn't look reassured. He crosses his arms over his chest and stares me down. "So, nothing ever happened between you two?"

"We kissed once, but there was no spark."

The frown deepens. "When was this?"

"Last weekend?"

If this were a romantasy novel, shadows would be pooling around Killian for how pissed he looks. "You mean the same weekend you were kissing me?"

Technically, he's right. But in my defense, I still thought he was an imaginary book boyfriend. "Killian." I sigh. "A week ago, I was convinced you weren't real." I tap my temple. "You were just a fantasy in my head. A dream."

He surprises me by letting go of the possessive attitude as he comes crouching down on the floor next to the bed in front of me. He places his big hands on my thighs and all the air leaves my lungs.

"What about your feelings for me?" he asks, only open sincerity on his face. "Did you ever think those weren't real?"

And the way he's looking at me, like an open book—pun intended—I can't give him anything but the honest truth. "No, my feelings have always been real. That was what scared me so much, that I was falling for someone who didn't exist. And also why I went on a date with him, to sort of get over you."

"And now that I'm here?" Killian's voice is soft, his eyes searching mine for an answer as his hands gently squeeze my thighs, a reassuring pressure that sends a jolt through me.

"Now that you're here... it's complicated," I confess, my gaze drifting to where his hands rest on my thighs, feeling the warmth of his touch seep through the fabric of my leggings.

"Why?"

"This is all so new for you. You have to find your footing in this world, discover who you really are before you can decide I'm someone you'd like to share the journey with."

"Okay, and what about you?"

"Same. I only know Killian St. Clair, the cowboy billionaire, but I want to get to know Oswald Finch, the bartender and mascot stealer."

He arches that flawless eyebrow again. "You're really getting a kick out of using my fake name."

"Wouldn't you? If I suddenly had to be called Gertrude Quagmire?"

"All right, Gertrude. Can I make only one request?"

I tilt my head. "What request?"

"That if you don't date me, you also don't date anyone else? Or at least that if you start dating someone you tell me because—"

I silence him, pressing a finger over his perfect mouth. "I don't want to date anyone else."

Even under my finger, he smiles. He reaches for my hand and pulls it away from his mouth, kissing the tip of my finger first. "I don't want to date anyone else either."

"So we're non-dating exclusively?" I smile, trying to control the racing of my pulse. "That's new."

Killian grins now. "I'm doing it only to save you all that friends-to-lovers pining."

I laugh now. "Sure you are."

As our laughter subsides, Killian's expression turns serious. His eyes lock with mine, and I can see the intensity in his gaze.

"Gertrude," he breathes, his voice filled with a mix of vulnerability and determination. "This is definitely complicated and there's a lot we don't know, but I'm all in. I'm here for you, no matter what it takes. And more than anything, I want to learn about the real you."

A lump forms in my throat, threatening to choke me as his words sink in. "Same here, Oswald, same here."

* * *

Monday is another all-too-real day. Frustrating meeting with my advisor, check. Teaching a pack of half-asleep students in class, check. An afternoon of research in the CS lab, also check. The only thing keeping me sane is that Killian will be home tonight. He worked a day shift today, so we're going to have dinner together.

I get to the apartment before him and sit at my desk to work some more as I wait for him to get home. He arrives after an hour. The door opens. I hear fabric shuffling as he removes his jacket, then the tumble of boots on the hardwood.

"Hey, you," he says.

I turn to find Killian casually leaning against the column at the end of the kitchen bar. His body is slightly turned to one side. Right arm bent at the elbow, with his hand resting on the back of his head, while his left hand is coolly sunk into his jeans pocket. He's gazing directly at me.

I swallow. "Hey."

His mouth curls up at the corners. "Just hey? Shouldn't you at least swoon a little?"

"Why?"

He beams at me, raising both eyebrows in an impossibly cute frown. "I'm leaning against a wall."

If I snapped a picture and posted it on BookTok, I'm pretty sure it'd go viral. He's the epitome of every hot book boyfriend ever leaning on random surfaces.

I narrow my eyes at him. "Have you been reading my smut?"

He jerks his chin toward my bookshelf. "You have quite the selection. Lots of inspiring ideas."

I blush because some books on that shelf are level five spicy. Then, before I get some ideas to test exactly how good Killian would be at level five spicy stuff, I deflect. "You have your fly open."

He looks down at his jeans. "Yeah, about that. I think the dryer in the basement is a bit too aggressive. My clothes are shrinking."

"Or maybe eating three cinnamon buns for breakfast every day is catching up with you, and you're gaining weight."

"Nah, impossible. I never worked out a day in my life and always stayed in perfect shape."

I throw my head back and laugh at that. "Yeah, maybe in the fictional world. But in the cruel real world, if you eat your weight in pastries and never exercise, you can kiss your six-pack goodbye."

"Oh, so you've noticed my six-pack?" He grabs the only other folding chair in the house and drags it next to my desk. He opens it with a flick and sits on it backward, his elbows resting on the backrest.

Have I noticed his six-pack? I pretend to mull the question over, drumming my fingers on the table. "Hmm, I might have."

Killian raises an eyebrow, a mischievous glint dancing in his eyes. "How come you're so fit, then? You eat the buns as well."

I lean back in my chair, crossing my arms. My body is average by any definition, nothing to do with his statuesqueness.

"I only eat *one* cinnamon bun for breakfast, not three. I walk a lot to and around campus and back. And I go to the gym three times a week."

"You go to the gym? When?"

"In the morning, between work and classes." I swivel slightly in my chair to face him more directly.

"Then you have to bring me. I have to try this exercise thing."

"Are you sure? I have a body pump class tomorrow morning if you want to join, or do you just want to use the treadmill?"

"Nah, the treadmill seems boring." He dismisses the suggestion with a wave of his hand. "I'll go with the body pump."

"It can be really intense for a beginner."

"I think I can handle it."

* * *

Fast forward twelve hours, and Killian is lying down on the gym floor panting, utterly destroyed.

As the other patrons of the class slowly file out of the room, I sit in butterfly pose next to him and offer him my water bottle.

He takes it, still chuffing. "I should've gone on the treadmill. Exercising sucks."

I smile. "It's an acquired taste. But you'll feel so much better after."

Killian groans, pulling up on his elbows. "I hope so. Right now I feel like I've been through a spin cycle on a washing machine except I ended up the opposite of clean." He dries his face on his T-shirt and I do my best to ignore the still very much present washboard abs.

"If you don't like training, maybe you don't even like sex in this world."

Why did I just say that?

Killian tilts his head toward me, eyes twinkling. "Want to help test that theory?"

The way my heart was pumping blood at top speed during the workout is nothing compared to the way it hammers in my chest now. "Did we have sex in your world? You never told me."

He smiles mysteriously. "Wouldn't you like to know?"

"Yes, I would."

Killian hops up on his feet. "I think I need a shower."

"Why aren't you answering me?"

As Killian makes his way toward the locker rooms, his

mischievous grin still intact, I scramble to my feet and follow closely behind him.

"This is the way to the men's locker rooms," he chides me.

"Why are you refusing to answer me about the sex stuff?" I ask again.

He shrugs and disappears where I can't follow.

28

LEASE ON LOVE

When Oliver texts me a couple of weeks later, inviting me out for drinks, I know something is up. I text him back, asking if it's okay to meet in Evanston. He says yes, so I give him the name of the bar where Killian works. Mostly because I still haven't been and I'm curious to see my roommate, who I'm exclusively non-dating, bartending.

I suspect the sight won't be good for my ovaries. But what can I say? I'm weak. I should already get a medal for sleeping next to the man every night without jumping his bones. As long as I keep my hands to myself, my eyes are free to gorge.

Our time since coming back from South Bend has gone surprisingly smoothly. Killian works, we exercise together regularly, and we eat together when our schedules allow it like a proper couple. The Evanston Fire Department hasn't heard a peep from us, and Killian hasn't tried to adopt any more strays, or damaged house property, or attempted heroic gestures. He still leaves the toilet seat up most times, but I'm afraid the occasional encounter with the ceramic ring is almost a prerequisite of cohabitation with any man.

Speaking of the devil, I'm working at my tiny desk when Killian walks into the apartment, holding an envelope in his hands and sporting a serious expression.

"What's with the long face?" I ask.

"I got my first paycheck. The official, on-the-books one."

"That bad?" I try to keep my tone light but worry that for someone used to handling billions, a regular paycheck might seem a pittance.

Before answering, he does that thing again, where he drags a chair next to my desk and sits on it backward. I should've gotten used to the sight by now, but instead of becoming immune, my heart thrashes uncontrolled in my chest every time he does it. I force myself to focus on his words rather than his ever-seductive presence.

"No, it's not *that* bad," he says, a small smile tugging at the corners of his lips. "Pay's good, at least once you add in the tips." He drags a hand through his hair which has gotten longer in the month since he's popped into my life. He looks even sexier, more rugged. And I might need an oxygen mask because I'm having trouble breathing.

"So? That's good, right?"

"Yeah." His chin dips. "I wanted to ask you how much my half of the rent is."

"Oh, that would be four hundred and fifty dollars; I mean, if you made enough."

"I made plenty."

"Like how much?"

"With the tips, thirty-one hundred."

"Three thousand dollars?" My eyes bulge. "Academia was clearly the poorest career choice *ever*."

Killian smiles, but it's not a serene smile. He's nervous.

"What else?" I prompt.

He drags his hand through his hair again; the gesture revealing a new vulnerability and threatening to strip away my self-control. "Well, now that I have a job and an identity, do you want me to move out?"

My spine turns to ice. I swallow and turn in my chair to face him fully, clasping my hands in my lap to keep them from trembling. "Do *you* want to move out?"

"Honest truth?"

"Always."

"I don't, but I think it might be best."

My mouth is suddenly cotton-dry. "Sure." I'm tempted to just leave things hanging. In all my past relationships, I would have. But with Killian, everything is different. I can be more honest. More myself. "Why do you think it'd be best? Do I snore too loud or something?"

He flashes me a lopsided grin that threatens to melt the last of my self-restraint not to jump his bones STAT. "No, Sugar Spoon, you're the cutest teddy to hug in bed..."

"But?"

"But you refuse to even kiss me before"—he makes air quotes—"I find myself. And I thought living alone would be a good step in that direction."

I'm a stupid cow and no one should ever listen to a word I say. "That actually makes sense." I force a smile. "Do you want my help house hunting?"

"Sure, Sugar."

"Then come here." I revive my laptop and open a real-estate website.

Killian takes my invitation to move closer literally. He stands and, instead of bringing his chair next to mine, he lifts a leg and wedges himself between me and the back of my seat.

This fold-up chair wasn't built to bear the weight of two

people, especially not when one of them is a six-foot-four moun-
tain of a man like Killian. I brace myself for the inevitable topple,
but one of his big hands glides over my stomach to secure me in
place while the other casually rests on my thigh.

His scent wraps around me, a familiar blanket of spice that
just feels right.

"How many bedrooms and baths are you looking for, sir?" I
struggle to keep an even tone.

"Just one?" Killian drops his chin on my shoulder.

My skin tingles with a sudden warmth and my ability to think
is lost in the haze of all the places where our bodies are touching.
For goodness' sake, I use the man as my personal pillow every
night. I should be used to the close proximity. But I'm not. So I
check all the wrong boxes and pull up million-dollar mansions
for sale instead of studio apartments to rent.

"Those might be slightly out of my budget in this world,
Sugar Spoon," Killian whispers against the shell of my ear.

Then he reaches over to cover my hand over the mouse with
his, guiding my movements to pull up the right section of the
website.

With every accidental brush of his hand, the idea of him
moving out becomes a less bearable thought. House listings
scroll by, but it's the unlisted feelings between us that seem to be
on the market now.

* * *

On Thursday night, I'm supposed to meet with Oliver at eight.
But I arrive at the Blackhawk, the bar where Killian works, early.
Besides checking him out while he bartends, I also want to give
Killian a heads up that I'm meeting a friend here.

I push open the heavy glass door of the posh sports bar,

taking in the sleek black leather booths and gleaming wood floors. The rich mahogany and brass fixtures scream elegance, but the rowdy cheers and clinking glasses keep the place grounded in its purpose. The large flat-screen TVs remind me this is still a space where sports reign supreme.

I spot Killian immediately. He's working his magic behind the counter, muscles flexing under the fabric of his black T-shirt as he vigorously shakes a cocktail mixer, and I can't help but think that jeans have never looked so good on a man. The warm air of the heating system kisses my cheeks, but it does nothing to stop a shiver from running down my spine.

Killian lifts his gaze and spots me as I'm still standing on the doorstep, fighting to remove my scarf without getting strangled. His entire face lights up with a smile that has no right being that devastating—it should come with a warning label.

"Spoon!" Killian's voice booms from behind the counter as he pours the drink into a glass, garnishing it with a twist of lime.

"Hey," I say, heading toward the bar, slightly out of breath from rushing to get here early or from the sight of him—both are equally probable.

"To what do I owe the pleasure?" He grabs a bottle of gin and casually flips it behind his back, catching it with his other hand.

Showoff.

"I'm meeting with a friend here tonight, just wanted to give you a heads up."

He puts away the bottle and leans his elbows on the counter, eyes twinkling with unspoken things. "No problem! Grab a table, and I'll bring you a cocktail."

"Thanks, Oswald," I reply, unable to keep a grin off my face.

As I walk away, I can feel the weight of his gaze on my back. It's like a physical touch, and I fight the urge to peek behind me.

Instead, I choose a high table with a view of the bar, giving me a perfect vantage point to observe Killian in his element.

I finally get rid of my outer layers, dropping them on an empty stool, just as Killian arrives with my cocktail.

"Here you are." He slides a tequila soda in front of me—the same drink that was my go-to in the book world but that I've actually never tasted in real life. "Your favorite."

I abstain from correcting him and take a sip, keeping an open mind. And it's divine—same citrusy sweet taste from my dreams. "Amazing," I tell him, and I'm not even sure I'm talking about the cocktail.

"Enjoy your drink!" Killian says, giving me a wink before returning to work.

I watch him, mesmerized.

With each shake, pour, and garnish, he commands the attention of the room—and not just women. Every person with a pulse in this bar seems to be as drawn to him as I am. The men exchange friendly banter and sports commentary with him, while the women bat their lashes at him, slipping him outrageous tips. I spot more than one twenty-dollar bill being sultrily pushed his way and at one point, even a fifty. No wonder his paycheck is better than mine.

Another part of me notices how he makes no faux pas, no slip-ups that reveal him for anything other than a regular hot dude behind the bar with charm to spare. He fits. And if he blends in so well in a crowded bar interacting with all sorts of people, could he also fit into my life on a permanent basis? Is it time I gave us a chance?

My thoughts are interrupted by the door chiming. I swivel in my seat, waving when Oliver swings inside. He crosses the threshold with the effortless grace I remember from our blind date. A smile lights up his face when he spots me.

"Leighton!" He wraps me in a hug that smells like fresh laundry and cold air.

"Hey, you," I say, squeezing back before we part. He flags down a server with the kind of casual charm that could win wars or at least bar tabs. "A beer for me, please," he tells the server, who nods in response and scurries off.

"Okay, spill. Why are we meeting?" I say. "You've got that 'I've just adopted a puppy' glow, which is either alarming or adorable." I prop my chin on one hand, watching him.

"Please don't hate me, but..." he trails off, fidgeting with the edge of the menu, "but I met someone."

Instead of feeling left out, as I would have in the past, I can't help but smile. My eyes wander over to the bar, and for the first time, I don't squish down the hope; I let it blossom in my chest, warming me from the inside out. Because for once in my life I, too, have met someone. More made him up in my head and then somehow conjured him into existence—but that's irrelevant. Also Killian has changed a lot since splashing into my life. He's still stubborn and a little overprotective, but he's less impulsive, less exaggerated... he's becoming less of a fabricated romance hero and more of a man I could really give my heart to every day.

"Are you kidding?" I laugh. "I'm so happy for you! Tell me everything. Boyfriend or girlfriend?"

"Boyfriend."

"Oh, that's amazing, Oliver. So, how did you meet him? It must've been something ridiculously romantic, I assume?" I tease, leaning forward, elbows on the table.

"Actually, he crashed into me with his bike." He chuckles, rubbing the back of his neck. "Literally swept me off my feet, into a bush."

"Awww," I deadpan. "Romantic much, uh?"

"Leighton, I'm really happy." He gives me a sheepish grin.

"Me too, Oliver. For you." I squeeze his hand across the table. "But you know what this means?"

"Time for us to fake break up," he quips, dropping his gaze to our joined hands as if mourning our staged love story.

"George and Ivy are going to flip," I muse, feeling only the tiniest twinge of guilt. "But how do we play it? Sudden but amicable split? Or should we have a pretend blowout?"

"Knowing George, he'll want to mediate our non-existent problems. And Ivy will bring you ice cream and rom-coms." Oliver shakes his head in mock sorrow.

I'd welcome the ice cream and rom-coms even without a real reason, but then I'd have to explain to Ivy my roommate situation, and I'm not sure I'm ready to go there. I wouldn't even know what to say. Better make it clear this breakup doesn't warrant support sweets and a girlfriends' movie night. "Can't we just go with the truth for once?" I suggest. "Say we realized we're just friends and met other people."

"Lady, you've been holding out on me. Who did you meet?"

I'm about to reply when a shadow falls over our table.

"Here's your beer," Killian growls, not quite slamming the glass onto the wooden surface, but close enough. His jaw is set, eyes flashing with a possessive glint that, while misplaced, I don't really mind. Except for the fact that he's growling. Maybe he's still a bit exaggerated at times.

"Killian, please stop snarling."

"Then stop holding a random dude's hand. I thought we'd agreed—"

"This is Oliver," I interrupt. "My fake boyfriend who's invited me out to tell me he's met someone else and ask if we can fake break up."

Oliver casually disentangles his hand from mine and waves

sheepishly. "Hey, man." My friend looks half amused, half worried.

Killian is still staring murder at him.

I grab Killian's arm and make him face me. "This," I say, flipping a finger between us, "is not a 'touch her and you'll die' kind of deal."

"I don't know," Oliver says, tilting his head. "The handbook on 'touch her and you'll die' could've been written on his face right now." Then he sticks out his hand in that irresistible, friendly manner of his. "I'm Oliver, the ex-fake boyfriend."

Killian's face relaxes only slightly as he takes Oliver's offered hand. "Killian."

I have to admit *that* sounds more intimidating than if he'd gone with Oswald.

Someone calls him from behind the bar. Killian acknowledges the request with a curt nod, then looks at me with such burning heat, his gaze could make the sun seem like an amateur heating source. "I have to go," then, lowering his voice, he leans in to add, "I'm sorry if I overreacted. Seeing you with someone else just—" He runs a hand through his hair, a clear sign of frustration I've learned to recognize. "It does things to me, okay? Talk later?"

He pulls away, giving Oliver a quick nod before throwing me one last heated glance and returning to the fray behind the bar. I watch him go, my heart doing erratic somersaults in my chest.

Oliver tsks, mock fanning himself. "My, my. Is it just me, or did the temperature rise a few degrees with that look he gave you?"

I roll my eyes, but I can't entirely hide the flush creeping up my cheeks. "Shut up, Oliver."

He chuckles, his gaze softening. "How did you and Mr. Alpha meet?"

"Oh, you know," I say, glossing over the question. "One day I woke up, and he was warming my bed..."

29

THE UNFOLDING OF US

That night, I wait up for Killian to get home.

The moment he steps into the apartment, I attack him with a request. "We need to come up with a great story for our meet-cute." I'm kneeling on the bed like an eager puppy.

He shuffles out of his jacket, kicks off his boots, then melts my flannel pajamas with a single stare—the usual, in short. His head is tilted down, locks of hair falling over his forehead as he looks sideways at me. "Do we have to do it now, or can it wait until another time?"

I wet my lips. "It can wait."

I shuffle to my side of the bed and watch him as he approaches, but he deviates for the bathroom at the last minute. When he comes out, he's still dressed.

I watch as he yanks his T-shirt off, two hands at the back, tugging it over his head. I can't blink or look away. My eyes are glued to the mouthwatering cut of muscles that arches down from his hips toward the top of his low-cut jeans.

As he reveals the smooth, hard planes of his stomach, I

remember to breathe. My gaze drifts up to the broad expanse of his pecs and collarbones that I suddenly yearn to kiss.

He unbuttons his pants next, and I simply can't handle it. I turn away, pretending to fiddle with my phone charger on the nightstand until I feel the dip of the mattress and Killian shuffling under the covers next to me. I switch off the lights and finally feel safe enough to face him again.

"Any pointers for how you want the meet-cute to be?" His voice cuts through the night.

"We—err—I mean..." Words. I know how to use them. Put vocables in a coherent sequence to form a phrase. It's simple. "It should be something revoltingly romantic."

I sense the smile more than see it. "Revoltingly romantic, gotcha."

"Great. Goodnight."

A beat of silence and then, "Are you going to pretend you'll keep to your side of the bed, or will you just come over now?"

The air shifts. He's opened his arms to welcome me. "I suppose I could be persuaded to venture over," I tease, not needing any real persuasion at all.

I slide across the sheets and into the safety and warmth of his embrace.

Once I'm settled, Killian drops a soft kiss on top of my head. "I'm sorry about earlier. I didn't mean to be rude to your friend. It's just when you said you were meeting a friend, I assumed it was going to be a woman, and you looked so cozy with him."

I sigh. "Just no more growling, please." I feel like a total hypocrite. If I'd seen him holding hands with a gorgeous woman, I would've probably snarled louder than a famished lioness. Or scratched her eyes out in my imagination, at least. But I'm not about to admit that.

Killian's chest vibrates with a chuckle, his arms tightening around me. "I can't make any promises, but I'll do my best to behave."

* * *

The following night, Friday, I'm alone at home. Oliver and I agreed to wait until Monday to break the news of our fake breakup so that Ivy and George won't feel compelled to check on us over the weekend. Meaning that even if I felt like going out, which I don't, I couldn't call my best friend tonight. But it's okay, I'm ready to just relax at home. And for once, I don't feel pathetic about it. I'm content instead. I no longer feel like there's a missing piece in my life.

I shower and change for a quiet night in. I make a quick book unboxing video of a surprise book mail I received for my BookTok account that I've neglected even more than usual lately. Then I curl up in bed for what has become one of my favorite pastimes when I'm alone: reading about Killian and me in our magical book, which now is almost written to the end. I wonder what will happen when the book runs out of blank pages.

Part of me doesn't want to know. Part of me is still scared Killian will disappear, even if he seems more real with every day that passes. At least if our argument of this morning about his stray socks on the floor is an indication.

I pick up the book from the drawer in my nightstand and frown. Something feels weird. I flip the pages and the book lands open over the leprechaun heist chapter in South Bend. It's not by chance because the top right corner of the page is folded into a little neat triangle.

My pulse picks up. Did Killian dog-ear my magical book?

I live with a monster. A book maimer.

I'm half tempted to shoot a picture and ask BookTok if dog-earing should be a deal breaker, but then an even graver suspicion takes over. I go to my shelf and check a few books. And sure enough, some bear the scars of dog-ears.

Oh my gosh. I'm going to kill him. Perfect book boyfriend, my ass. Killian has just gotten his name in red underlined at the top of my shit list.

Fuming, I go back to bed, pointedly undoing Killian's mutilation and shoving a proper bookmark between the pages. That he would even read this behind my back is baffling. I never expressly asked him not to read this book, but he's been sneaky about it.

Still huffing and puffing with indignation, I flip to the last chapter I haven't read. I find it pretty insightful, too. Soon frustration gives way to soft mellowness.

Through the book's eyes, I read about how my relationship with Killian is evolving, deepening in ways neither of us could have predicted. It's funny how the book nails the subtle shift from playful antagonism to something richer, more profound. It captures the essence of our growing bond, noting the moments we start to lean on each other, not just for laughs, but for support, for solace.

Our story speaks of evenings spent in comfortable silence, the easy exchanges that come when you truly know someone. This progression of us, from nemeses to lovers back to strangers and then to being the core of each other's days, it's written in the spaces between our words, the looks we share.

The magic of the book isn't just in its recounting of our adventures, but in its acknowledgment of the quiet moments that truly define us. This narrative, in its whimsical wisdom, charts these changes with a tender accuracy, highlighting the beauty in the mundane. It's in these chapters that I see how much we've grown together, not through grand gestures, but through the accumulation of small, shared experiences that form the bedrock of our connection.

The book doesn't need to spell out the depth of our feelings; it's there in every page, a subtext that's become our story. The way our arguments turn into discussions, and our challenges into opportunities to understand each other better. It's a testament to the slow, steady building of a bond that's as unexpected as it is inevitable.

As I absorb the words, I can't help but marvel at how the story of us, as told by this magical book, mirrors the real, imperfect, beautiful journey we're on together. At least until I reach the last sentence in the chapter:

Because Leighton still didn't know their entire relationship was based on a lie.

I frown. What?

I turn the page, but it's blank. The chapter ends on that nasty little cliffhanger like it's nothing. I scowl and drop the book on the bed. What lie? Did Killian lie to me? About what?

I rack my brain to find something, *anything*, he could've lied about, but I come up empty-handed.

I check the time, 10 p.m. Killian won't be home for at least another four hours. I'm bone tired, but there's no way I'm going to bed without asking him what the book is talking about.

One thing is for sure—I can't just lie here stewing in conspiracy theories. That's how you end up with a case of perennial insomnia, a dozen half-baked hypothesis, and a sudden, unexplainable fear of garden gnomes.

I decide on a distraction. So I do the only thing a half-crazed, love-stricken woman in pajamas can do: I start pacing. My bare feet pad across the floor as I chew on my lower lip, turning over every conversation, every look we've shared since the beginning. The pacing becomes so intense, I'm pretty sure I'm going to wear a path into the floor. I'm like Nancy Drew on a sugar rush, trying to crack a case with nothing but a hunch and an overactive imagination.

Three and a half hours into my one-woman stakeout of our living room, I've concocted approximately twenty-three possible scenarios involving secret second lives and illicit affairs. Is Killian secretly hooking up with someone else? He's the one who insisted on our exclusively non-dating agreement. But men lie. Real men especially.

Just as I'm about to dive into scenario twenty-four, which involves Killian potentially being an international spy (because why not?), the front door clicks open. I freeze mid-pace, and every hair on my body stands to attention.

30

BETWEEN THE LINES

The book-desecrating man I'm not dating walks in, the fatigue etched on his face still unable to overshadow his unfair good looks.

"Hey," he says casually, his only sign of surprise at finding me still up a raised eyebrow. He pauses when he sees my expression. "Is everything okay?"

Do I confront him with the whole "our relationship is a lie" thing? Do I ask him directly, or do I beat around the bush until he breaks?

Instead of coming up with wild theories, I should've locked in an interrogation strategy while I waited for him to get home. Read manuals on reverse psychologization and mental warfare.

Now, I decide on a mix of both because who says you can't have your confrontation cake and eat it too?

"Yeah," I say, but even to my own ears, it sounds more like a question than an affirmation. I cross my arms and lean against the kitchen bar.

Killian sets his keys down and takes off his jacket, a small furrow forming between his brows. He's gone into problem-solving mode; I can practically see the cogs turning in his head. "Why are you still up?"

"Couldn't sleep."

He sighs, coming closer. But he stops when I nearly recoil. "You're clearly upset about something. Want to tell me what it is?"

"I don't know." I mockingly tap my chin. "Is there anything I should be upset about?" I know I'm practically rewriting the book on how not to handle a mature discussion, but I can't help the pettiness.

"Spoon, it's late." Killian massages his forehead. "If I forgot to replace the toilet paper roll or squeezed the toothpaste wrong, just tell me."

I scoff.

"Is it my hairs in the sink again? Because I'm pretty sure I left it clean this morning after shaving."

"Don't try to be cute. I'm mad."

"About what?"

"You lied," I accuse, pointing a finger at him.

He frowns. "No, I didn't."

"Yes, you did."

"About what?"

"I don't know," I yell. I'm at my wits' end.

"Sugar, it's late, and you're not making any sense—"

"Don't Sugar me anything."

Killian holds up his hands in surrender. "Fine," he concedes with a dramatic sigh, taking a cautious step forward. "What did I do?"

"I already told you, you lied."

"I didn't."

"Yes, you did."

He tilts his head, still definitely trying to be cute. "Then tell me about what so I can explain."

"I already told you I don't know what you lied about."

"Then how do you know I lied?"

"Because the book says so," I snap, pointing at my bed.

"The book? You can't seriously be mad at me about something that thing said."

"Why not?"

"Because it's just a book."

"A magical book that you magically splashed out of that knows both me and you almost better than we know each other." I storm toward the bed and pick it up. "And this 'thing,' as you call it, is saying that our entire relationship is based on a lie."

"And I have no idea what it's talking about."

"So you never lied to me, not once since we met."

Killian thinks hard, and I can pinpoint the exact moment he figures out what the book is talking about from the way his eyes widen and a shadow crosses his face. "Okay," he admits, holding his hands out like a traffic cop halting cars. "I've never lied since coming here."

I cross my arms and tap my foot. "And before?"

Killian lets out a huff of frustration. "Does it really matter what happened in Lakeville Hills? You always say it wasn't real."

"And you always say our feelings were real, so if they're based on a lie, I'd like to know."

"There was no other investor, okay?" At my confused frown, Killian explains. "For your bakery. I bought it because I wanted to open an upscale wine bar."

I gape. "So that entire tale about you saving the day was made up? Why even bother?"

"Because by that point, I was in love with you and didn't want you to hate me."

"So you lied to me? Why? What made you think that was a

better option than just telling me you'd been an inconsiderate douchebag and had simply changed your mind?"

Killian gets a fazed look that I haven't seen since the first few days he was here. "I don't know."

"What do you mean, you don't know?"

"It's hard to explain." He starts to pace, passing a hand through his hair repeatedly. "It feels like I didn't have a choice."

That's when the hard truth dawns on me. "Of course, because it was scripted. You're scripted. You're not in control of how you act or what you feel. The only reason you want to be with me is because you can't help yourself. Someone pre-programmed it into your very essence, like a line straight out of a cheesy rom-com. You're the 'bad boy with a heart of gold' trope to the letter."

Killian stops pacing and looks at me, his eyes earnest. Then he comes over and grabs me gently by the biceps. "It might've been that way in Lakeville Hills, but I've been nothing but in control since I've come here. I'm staying with you because I want to, not because I'm programmed to. I like you because you're adorably cynical with a humor so dry it can absorb an ocean. And you're smart and funny and fierce. And I haven't lied to you once since that day you pulled me here. Do you believe me?"

I look at him and then stare down at the magical book still in my hands.

Killian squeezes my arms. "Don't look at that damn book for confirmation. In a real relationship you can't rely on a magical trinket to tell you if you trust your partner. You have to feel it in here." He punches his chest twice. "Do you trust me?"

I shrug free. "How can I trust you when I cannot even trust you're real?"

Killian's face hardens. Without another word, he turns and grabs his gym duffle bag, shoving his few possessions inside.

"What are you doing?"

"I'm going to give you space."

"What does that mean?"

"That I'm going to check myself into a motel and leave you time to figure out what you want." The way he zippers up the bag has a sense of finality that turns my insides cold.

"Are you trying to prove you're a real man by leaving like all real men do?"

Killian drops the bag to the floor and wheels on me. I take a step back because the expression on his face is truly frightening, only I have little room to travel backward as my shoulders hit the wall. And then he's on me, caging me in.

"I'm not leaving," he says, the softness of his voice a stark contrast to the fury on his face. "I'm giving you space to figure out what you want. You have to decide if you want this, me, us. I can't be with someone who doesn't trust me. If you're too scared to give us a chance, then, yes, I want out."

"Surprise, surprise," I spit bitterly.

Killian pinches his nose. "Spoon, I'm trying real hard to do the mature thing here."

"What exactly is mature about leaving?"

"Everything," he hisses. "I'm giving you time to think, decide what you want. The me in Lakeville Hills would've simply kept you pressed against this wall until I had my way." He pushes his hips into me for emphasis, causing all sorts of reactions in my body: heat that spreads through my belly, a flutter in my chest, and a tingling awareness to my lips of just how close our mouths are. All signs that yeah, he could probably get me to do whatever he wanted simply by pinning me to the wall. "But I won't do that or pull off some extravagant grand gesture." He eases the pressure of his lower body against mine and I almost cry out in protest. "What you see is what you get. I've been here for over a month. We've slept together every night of that time. I've been patient, understanding, but I'm done waiting for you to make up your mind about me. So figure out what you want, Spoon. Quickly. Because I can't do this dance forever."

He takes a step back, and all the heat leaves my body.

Without another half look my way, he pulls his jacket back on, grabs his bag from the floor, and leaves.

And I could've almost believed that collected, mature speech about him just giving me space if not for the loud, angry slam of the door.

"And you shouldn't dog-ear other people's books," I yell at the closed door.

31

MORNING MISERY

I wake up bleary-eyed and emotionally drained after crying myself to sleep. I have a pounding headache and the sunrays poking through the blinds are not helping, shouting their harsh morning cheer like a drill sergeant at dawn.

I pull the blankets over my head, trying to block out both the light and the reality of last night's fight with Killian.

But no amount of polyester cotton blend can shield me from the truth: Killian has left. To "give me space," I know, but I can't help but feel it's more permanent.

Can I even trust anything he says after he so openly lied to me? My heart jumps in my throat as I realize there's a super simple way for me to know without the shadow of a doubt. The book will know if he's being sincere. And since it writes itself overnight, the answer will be already there this morning, spelled in black on white, only waiting for me to read it.

I throw the blankets away and recover the book from where it's lying abandoned on the floor. I take it back to bed and open it to confirm a new chapter has arrived, and there it is, "The Unfolding of Us." But I hesitate before reading it, Killian's words from last night ringing in my ears, *"Don't look at that damn book for confirmation... Do you trust me?"*

After that, seeking the help of the book in making a decision feels wrong.

My heart beats like a war drum, my mind screaming at me to just do it. It's not betrayal if he was the one who betrayed me first, right? But still, I can't shake the guilt. I can't do it. I close the book and put it away. Do I really need it, anyway?

Killian is right. In a real relationship I wouldn't have a truth-teller amulet to guide me. Unless my partner and I decided to keep a polygraph machine at home. I sigh again, realizing he was even more right. Because if a couple needed a polygraph machine to trust each other then what would even be the point of staying together?

It all boils down to whether I want to be with him or not.

Do I trust him? The answer deep down in me is a simple yes. Cowboy, daredevil Killian might've lied. But I never had a reason to mistrust Oswald. My sweet, charming, still hot as hell, Oswald who loves me despite my imperfections and my cynicism. Who loves me *because* of them. The arrogant billionaire in Lakeville Hills didn't know any of those things about me. But the Killian of this world knows everything. Sees everything. Notices every little detail. And still wants me. And all I did was push him away.

A sob claws its way up my throat. I've been so stupid.

Yes, Killian could disappear any moment, but do I really want to waste any second I'm gifted with him worrying instead of living it to the fullest with him? No.

But how will I ever recover if I let myself fully fall in love with him and then he's gone? I wouldn't. My heart would be shattered forever. But isn't that true of any relationship or any marriage, even? Yes. A lot still end up in divorce and heartbreak. But if everyone thought that way, no one would ever take the risk. There'd be no more coupled wise humans.

Have my friends been right all this time? Is it my fault that I've been single so long for not being willing to risk my heart?

Is it time I changed?

I need to look into myself and find some answers. I'm ready for a morning of raw, profound introspection when my phone pings with a reminder.

I check the screen and my heart jolts at the notice that today Killian has his first house-hunting appointment. Oh, right, because even if we make peace, he's still moving out.

Unless I convince him not to. Or at least have him leave with us on good terms. I don't know what motel he's checked himself into, but I know exactly where he's going to be in half an hour. I shower at the speed of light and still manage to get there with ten minutes to spare.

Killian, looking impossibly tall and handsome in simple jeans and a heavy leather jacket, is also already there, waiting on the curb in front of an older building.

When he spots me crossing the street toward him, instead of the usual warm tingle in his eyes I get a set jaw and a tight expression.

"Hi," I say tensely.

He just nods.

"I'm sorry," I blurt. "About last night. I overreacted."

"Did the book tell you I was telling the truth and so now you're here?"

"I haven't read the new chapter."

Something swirls in his eyes. "Okay."

"I trust you, Killian, I don't need the book to confirm it, to know you were telling the truth last night." Some of the harshness on his face melts away, but not all. "And I'm sorry it's taking me so long to figure out how I feel. That's not even it—" I pause, staring at the curb, pressing my hands to my temples before looking up again. "I know how I feel about you."

"That makes one of us."

"I know. And I'm sorry. I'm not good at relationship stuff. I've no experience. Half the time, I've no idea what I'm doing."

He crosses his arms skeptically. "Meaning?"

"Take this appointment. Instinctively, I don't want you to move out. I hated that you weren't there last night. But I don't know if we should live together, maybe it's put too much pressure on us. Add that the way we met is not exactly conventional, and I think it's normal for me to have some doubts."

"*Some*, yes. What's not normal is for you to doubt everything. Even when I tell you that I'm in love with you and you reply by saying my feelings aren't real."

"I'm sorry." My lower lip wobbles. "I was wrong. Your feelings are real, mine are too. And I get it, you're mad at me, that's valid as well. Just please, come back home tonight so we can talk and figure it out."

Killian sighs. "I'm not mad, Spoon."

"You're not?"

He shakes his head. "I'm just tired."

"Of me?" I ask in a small voice.

"I'm tired of being the only one who fights for us. Of being the only one who believes in us—"

"I believe in us."

"Since when?"

"Since forever."

"Then why do you keep me at arm's length? Why do you refuse to admit how you feel? Why do you keep doubting me? I need to know you're all in, too, because you're asking me to come back, to take a leap of faith, and it's hard when you refuse to do the same."

"Because I'm scared, okay?" I yell. "I'm scared of everything. I'm scared of you disappearing. And I'm scared that even if you're here to stay, you'll tire of me. That you won't like me for long. That once I give in, you'll just leave, and I don't think I can handle that. I can't handle losing you, Killian." My voice cracks. "I'm scared that I'll fall into the same pattern as every other relationship I've had, where I fall too hard and then they're gone."

His face is unreadable. "That's what has kept you away all this time?"

I give a small nod. "There was also the fact that you were still acting like a romance trope when you first arrived, but you haven't in a while. You fit. We fit. Just last night, reading the book say our relationship was a lie almost confirmed all my fears about you playing me for dumb, you know?"

"Sugar, all this time I've been scared you didn't want me because this version of me with my simple clothes"—he tugs at his jacket—"and my humble job wasn't enough for you."

"What? No!" I shake my head. "Then we've been two scared idiots because that thought never even crossed my mind."

"Come here." He opens his arms wide for me. "I think you need a hug."

Before I can move, he's already wrapped me into his arms, tucking me into his chest.

He squeezes me, but I keep rigid in his embrace. Still too worked up by our fight.

"You can let go now," I assure him.

"Do you feel better?"

"No."

"Let's give it another minute."

Eventually, I succumb to the warmth. I let myself go limp and wrap my arms around his lean, solid waist.

"That's more like it," he declares, satisfied as he lets go just as a portly, bald man clears his throat next to us.

"Mr. Oswald Finch?"

I almost laugh at hearing Killian's fake name out loud, at least before I remember this man is here to show us houses for him to move out. That we might've hugged and hashed out some feelings, but the argument from last night isn't solved. There's still so much to unpack, so much more to say and do before we can truly move forward.

32

UNDER ONE ROOF

The first apartment the real-estate agent shows us is a total hovel. And I couldn't be happier.

The walls of the one-bedroom are yellowed with years of cigarette smoke, peeling and stained with marks that look suspiciously like mold. The floors are even worse. A patchwork of unidentifiable stains and worn spots marks the carpet, and the furniture looks like it was picked out of a dumpster. Over the small windows, the blinds are dusty and crooked, barely able to keep out the harsh sunlight.

And that's before the smell even hits us like a punch to the face, a mix of mildew and dirty laundry. The strong scent of industrial cleaners tries to mask the underlying odors but only adds to the sickening aroma.

The taste of dust fills my mouth as I breathe in the stale air.

There's no way Killian could live here. Guess I'll be stuck with him for a little longer.

I beam at the real-estate agent. "Absolutely not."

The next apartment is equally disappointing—*yay*—though in a very different way. It's clean, I'll give it that, but it might as well be a shoebox for all the space it offers. The kitchen—if you can even call it that—is shoved into what must've once been a closet, and the bathroom is separated by nothing more than a flimsy curtain that ripples every time the ancient heater system coughs to life. The bed is a fold-out couch with a thin mattress that takes up half the apartment, leaving little space for anything else. There's no room for more than one person to turn around, let alone live comfortably. It's like a claustrophobe's nightmare come to life.

Killian watches my reaction, his lips twitching. "Guess not."

"Well, you told me you were on a budget," the real-estate agent complains.

"How much is this place?" I ask.

"Eight hundred a month."

I look at Killian. "We can do better than that."

I hold off until we escape the dollhouse apartment before I address the agent. "Do you have any decent places to show us that don't smell, that have a bathroom with a door, and that don't require a contortionist to live in them?"

The real-estate agent pouts. "I might have something, but it's eleven hundred per month." He turns to Killian interrogatively.

"Yeah, I can manage that much."

We walk to the next location, a slick, modern building nestled between a quaint coffee shop with steam fogging its windows and a vintage-records shop. The entrance, flanked by welcoming potted plants, features wide, transparent glass doors that seem to invite visitors with open arms. As we enter, the airy lobby unfolds before us, its sleek furnishings and clean lines a refreshing change from the previous dingy settings we've encountered.

Killian's eyes roam over the high ceiling, the gleaming floors reflecting the light that cascades through an expansive skylight. "This is more like it," he mumbles, almost to himself.

The real-estate agent leads us to an elevator with mirrored walls, pushing the eighth-floor button.

I have a bad feeling about this place. Why didn't I keep my mouth shut? The real-estate agent would've kept showing us pigsties, and Killian would've had no other choice than to keep on living with me. I don't care what I said. Or that it'd be wiser for us to live apart. The idea of him moving out is gut-wrenching. It's like watching the last leaf fall from a tree, knowing that winter is coming and there's nothing I can do about it. A visceral, deep-seated fear clutches at my insides that if I let him go, he'll never want to come back.

There's still hope. Maybe the neighbors in this unit will be unbearably loud and we'll have to rule out this place, too.

But the neighbors are inaudible, and the apartment is, well, honestly, perfect. It's still small, but a small mansion compared to the matchbox one, and it's also clean and refurbished with all-white surfaces and cozy furniture.

My heart sinks.

"These windows are way too big," I offer tentatively. "All that natural light? It's going to be a nightmare trying to sleep past sunrise."

The real-estate agent rolls his eyes theatrically, while Killian shoves his hands in his pockets and tilts his head curiously, lips twitching. "And what do you think of the kitchen?"

"Well, it's a bit too... modern, don't you think? It'd feel like living inside a spaceship."

"Are you interested or not?" The agent chips in. "Because this place is going to go fast."

"I like it," Killian declares, cutting me a side stare. "Despite the too-bright windows and too-modern appliances."

He winks. I scowl.

It's like he's testing me.

"If you want it," the real-estate agent continues, "the deposit is the first and last month's rent plus an extra month for eventual damages to the property."

Eyes never leaving mine, Killian asks, "Mr. Gavino, could you give us a minute?"

"Sure, I'll wait downstairs."

The man leaves and Killian turns to me. "This place is cool, and it's not too far from yours."

It might as well be Australia. "Sure."

"If I have to move out, I'm taking it."

"If?"

With his hands still in his pockets, Killian studies me. "Do you want me to move out, Spoon?" When I hesitate, he adds, "Not what general dating wisdom suggests, or what you think you should be doing, just what you want. Do you want me to move out?"

I slowly shake my head.

"Good." He takes a step forward and I take one back. "What do you want?"

"Many things." Step forward. Step back.

"Like what?" Step forward. Step back.

The dance continues until I inexorably end with my back against a wall and Killian with the flat of his palms next to my face.

"I've asked you a question, Spoon."

Staring into his soulful gray eyes, I bare a little piece of my soul to him. "I want to wake up next to you every morning, and I want to be the reason you come home with that goofy grin on your face every night," I blurt out, my heart pounding like it's trying to break free.

Killian's eyes sparkle with mischief and something warmer,

something that sends a thrill down my spine. "Is that so? Anything else?"

"I want to argue about silly things like how to properly squeeze the toothpaste tube and what brand of coffee to buy. I want to share inside jokes that no one else gets and smile like idiots when we remember them at inappropriate times."

He's so close now, his breath is warm against my cheek. My gaze drops to his mouth. "And if we're being completely honest, the thing I want the most right now is for you to kiss me."

That too-perfect mouth curls up in a wicked smile, and Killian uses his free hand to tilt my chin up. "Oh, Sugar, I wish we could. But we can't."

"W-why not?"

"Because if I kiss you now, I don't know if I can stop. And that real-estate agent downstairs is already going to be pissed enough we're blowing him off with the apartment, we don't want to cause a scandal as well."

"Then what's your next move, cowboy?" I ask, my voice quivering with anticipation.

"Taking you home and making sure we're not interrupted when we pick up where we left off here."

33

BURNING DESIRES

Kissing Killian is still at the forefront of my mind when we step into my apartment ten minutes later. But I also have a more pressing matter I want to take care of first.

Killian must pick up on my nervousness because he asks, "What's on your mind, Spoon?"

"It's about the book."

His expression immediately clouds.

"I think we should get rid of it," I say.

At that, both his eyebrows rise in his forehead. "As in?"

"Burn it."

"Arson, Sugar, really?"

"Hear me out." I pick up the book from where I left it on the bed this morning. "I feel like we've been held hostages by this thing for the entire time we've known each other. I also think the book likes the drama, and I don't want it to stir it on purpose. I also don't want to live in dread it might suck you back in. Or to read about its interpretation of our feelings. I don't need it to know if you're telling me the truth, and I certainly don't need it to tell me how I feel about you." I'm pacing now, the book clutched in my hands.

Killian's watching me, and the corner of his lip quirks up in that way that I can't resist. "You want to do it now?"

I go to him. "Yes, before anything between us happens."

"Are you still afraid my feelings are controlled by that thing?" Before I can say no, he continues. "Because I fucking want you, Spoon, book or no book."

"I—" My pulse picks up at the declaration, but then I frown. "Did you just swear?" This is the first time ever I hear him drop an f-bomb.

"Yeah, why?"

"You never swore in the book."

"Is that bad?"

"No." I sigh. "The opposite of bad. And I want you—" He presses a finger to my mouth before I can finish.

"You don't have to tell me how you feel at the tail-end of a fight." He frees my mouth and rakes a hand through his hair. "I'm sorry about yesterday. I didn't want to rush you into anything you're not ready for. It's just that thing that gets me on edge."

I lift the book between us. "So we should definitely burn it?"

"Give me the gasoline."

"It's paper. We don't need fuel. It'll just burn. Just maybe not inside?"

"Yeah, we're probably still on the fire department shit list. Let's go on the fire escape."

Killian empties my metal paper bin, and we climb out on the metal grate platform of the fire escape.

The chill of the morning air bites at my skin as I watch Killian hold up the book like a sacrificial offering to the romance gods.

We exchange a nod and I strike a match, setting fire to the lower-end corner of the middle pages. The paper catches fire immediately, the orange glow casting dancing shadows over his intense face.

Killian's mouth twists, as if he were in pain, and he drops the book into the bin, bending over with a muffled cry.

Then he's screaming, "My skin, I'm burning." He claws at his face.

Panic seizes me as I watch him contort. The book is burning and he's burning too. I was a fool to think I could have one without the other. "Killian." I launch myself at the bin, ready to risk third-degree burns to save the book before they're both gone, when strong arms wrap around me from behind.

I can feel the shaking of his chest against my back as he murmurs, voice barely above a breath, "When will you learn not to fall for my tricks, Spoon?" The bastard is laughing.

I turn in his arms and start to punch his chest. "Your jokes suck." Punch. "I thought you were burning alive." Punch. "That you were going to leave me alone with a charred romance novel and a broken heart!" Punch.

Killian's laughter is contagious, though, and despite my best attempts at outrage, I start giggling, the punches turning into half-hearted hits. "You absolute jerk!"

He grins, those gray eyes shining, as he grabs my wrist before my next half-assed assault. "I'm sorry. But you should've seen the expression on your face."

Killian pulls me closer, the warmth of his body seeping through the fabric of my sweater, he spins me round again and holds me to his chest as we watch the last of the book turn into cinders.

"See? I'm still here," he says when the last flicker of flame dies out, leaving behind nothing but a curl of smoke and the faint smell of charred paper.

I shiver despite the warmth of his body. "Let's go back inside."

There's a moment of slight embarrassment as we face each other across my apartment. Now that the book is truly gone and the adrenaline has faded, we're left with the unknown before us.

I hug my arms to my chest, suddenly awkward. "So, did you want to talk more about yesterday?"

The smile he gives me in response is predatory. "The time for talking is done, Sugar, this is more one of those *doing* moments."

"Oh?"

"Unless you've changed your mind about me kissing you."

This time I stand my ground as he approaches.

"No, I haven't," I say in a hoarse voice. His eyes darken with a hint of longing and a spark of hope that warm me to my core. I thread one hand through the hair at the side of his head. "You should kiss me now."

Killian doesn't need any more encouragement.

His hands cup my face and draw me into a kiss that scatters any lingering doubts to the wind. The fears that he might change his mind or, worse, vanish like a shadow in the morning sun, evaporate like mist.

I embrace the present, revel in the intensity of a kiss that is finally real and no longer a dream. Killian is real, too. There's no more book to take him back or tell him what to feel. We're together because we want it. We want each other despite our flaws and insecurities. We're the same people we were when we first met and at the same time we're completely different. As is this kiss.

At first, it started just how I remember kissing him from my dreams: all-consuming and overwhelming.

His lips move over mine with reverence and a frenzied passion that speak louder than words ever could. The world around us dissolves until there's nothing but the sensation of being thoroughly, irrevocably kissed by Killian—the man who has carefully dismantled every wall I've ever built.

But then he pulls back just enough to look me in the eyes, his gray gaze ever so intense.

"Are you sure?" he asks, voice husky with emotion, as if he's afraid to fully hope, afraid this might be a momentary lapse in my judgment rather than the turning point he's been waiting for.

I nod, breathless, my heart pounding a fierce proclamation in my chest. "Never been more certain about anything in my entire life."

A grin—slow, infectious, hopeful—breaks across his face, the kind that reaches the eyes and lights up all the dark corners of the world.

His thumb brushes over my cheek, and his lips meet mine in a kiss that feels different, like the crossing of a threshold, the beginning of something real and tangible. It's a kiss that says, *"Here, now, us,"* and it seals a silent promise that I hope is enough for the universe to let him stay with me forever.

34

EMBRACING THE UNWRITTEN

We pull up for air after what seems simultaneously forever and not nearly enough time. His forehead rests against mine, and we're both gasping, as if we'd been submerged underwater and only just now broke through the surface. Which, considering how he arrived into my world after a splash in a lake, is almost poetic.

"Is this real?" I pant, still drowning in the depth of his gaze, the warmth of his breath mingling with mine.

"It's as real as you want it to be," Killian assures me, his voice steady but laced with vulnerability. "I'm here, Sugar, I'm not going anywhere."

"Can I just say?" I run my fingers through his hair because now that I've started, I can't stop. "How much I appreciate you being here with me?"

Killian grins as he drops a kiss on my temple. "I wouldn't want to be anywhere else, Spoon."

We stand there for a moment, lost in each other's gaze until the growl of my stomach interrupts our tender little bubble. This morning, in my haste to get to the house-showing appointment in time, I skipped breakfast.

"Someone's hungry." Killian chuckles.

Taking my hand, he leads me toward the kitchen.

Killian collects ingredients from the cupboards—which have never been better stocked. I can't help but salivate, not about the food, as I admire every ripple of muscles under the soft fabric of his sweater.

"If I ask you something..." I say in a casual tone. "Do you promise to give me an honest answer?"

"Of course," he replies, opening the fridge.

"Did we... you know"— I pause, trying not to lose my cool like I do every time I ask this question— "did we have sex in your world?"

Killian freezes, half bent over the fridge, before slowly turning to face me.

"You're obsessed with that question."

"And you're obsessed with not answering me."

He stares at me for a long beat. "No, we didn't."

I raise an eyebrow. "Then tell me how the kitchen scene ended without us having sex?"

"Easy." He stalks toward me, a feral glint in his eyes. Killian grabs me by the waist and sets me on the kitchen counter, wedging himself between my legs. "There's a lot of things a couple can do without having sex."

"Like what?"

"Like that night when I set you on the counter like this." His words are soft and deliberate. "And then I kissed you real good until you were ready to drag me to the bedroom and scream my name."

My heart hammers against my chest, a rapid drumbeat echoing his every word. At that moment, the world narrows down to the space between us, or lack thereof. And I curse again my stupid alarm clock for making me miss that night.

"You mean I was ready to scream, Oswald, oh, Oswald..."

He bites my earlobe in response. "You're such a tease, Gertrude."

I try to preserve some functioning brain cells as I ask, "And what happened afterward?"

"I left."

"Why would you leave?"

Killian trails featherlight kisses down my neck, shrugging. "Maybe because I like a slow burn."

"Are you talking to me in romance tropes again?"

More kisses and another small shrug. "Seems appropriate."

"So you just ripped my shirt for sport and then left me hot and bothered?"

"Yep."

"You're the worst, St. Clair. And you owe me buttons."

He throws his head back and roars with laughter. "Same words you yelled after me when I left your house. See?" He affectionately taps my nose. "Different world, same you."

"And that day at the lake, before I pulled you here?" I frown. "We were both naked."

"Just some innocent skinny dipping."

"So we've never..."

"Nope..."

"Why?"

Killian drops one last kiss on my collarbone and then takes a step back. "You're not the only one who likes to take things slow."

"But you're a guy."

"So?"

"So, in my experience, guys have been mostly interested in just having casual sex with me, to then disappear once they got what they wanted or ditch me the second I started wanting more. And before I met you, I made a promise to myself not to get naked with anyone again at least until I was engaged."

Killian raises his eyebrows, probably because I've just asked him about the last time we were together in his world at the lake when we both were very much naked.

"The lake thing doesn't count. I was behaving out of character in your world. Doing things I'd never do in real life."

"What things?"

"Taking risks, acting without thinking of the consequences."

"And you didn't like that version of yourself?"

"I did, but it's not sustainable. And I'm not saying you have to propose to me, but that's why I wanted us to take things slowly. I really wanted to get to know you, for you to get to know yourself and then me before you decided this is what you want."

Killian plants his palms firmly on either side of my hips and with a goofy smile, he asks, "I couldn't help but notice your use of the past tense there..."

I blink.

"*Wanted* to take things slow... you have a new pace in mind now, Sugar Spoon?"

"The way you're kissing me, Oswald, I *am* ready to drag you to my bedroom and scream your name."

His grin is teasing. "Not enough time for that now, Sugar, I have to be at work in less than an hour."

"That's plenty of time."

He flashes me a searing stare. "Not for what I have in mind."

My toes curl in my shoes. "Can't—" I swallow, mouth dry. "Can't your patrons wait an extra half an hour to be served their beers?"

"Not today. Mitch, the owner, has asked me to be there early. He says he needs to talk to me."

"About what?"

Killian shrugs. "I don't know."

"It'd better be good if it's making you skip first-time sex with your girlfriend."

"Girlfriend, uh?" He pulls one of my curls then sets it free like he always does. "When you put it like this, nothing he has to say will ever be *that* good. But I promised him I'd be there early, and I don't want to let him down."

I cup his cheek. "And you shouldn't. The way you always show up for those you care about is one of the things I love the most about you."

"Rain check?" The way he says it, he might've as well said, *"Undress for me, Sugar."*

I simply nod, mouth dry.

Smiling wickedly, he turns his face in my hand and kisses my palm before pulling back. "Now, if you could please move your pretty ass away from my counter, I could make both of us lunch and get to work on time."

Instead of complying, I wrap my ankles behind his knees. "I don't know." I suck in my lower lip. "I like where I am a bit too much."

He chuckles, the rumble in his throat vibrating against my skin. "Oh, is that so?" His hands find their way to my waist, fingers dancing just beneath the hem of my shirt. "Well, Sugar, as much as I appreciate your... dedication to this particular spot on my counter." He lifts me clear off it like I weighed nothing. "I can't let you starve."

With that, he sets me on my feet with a playful firmness that leaves no room for further protest, though his eyes sparkle with the silent promise of continuation at a later time.

35

BUSTED

Unfortunately, the later time is not the next day. On Sunday, I have a stupid conference all day that I can't miss, and he works a night shift. I try to stay awake and wait for him, but pass out shortly after midnight. Monday is the same. I work during the day and he at night. We barely see each other.

But Tuesday is our night. Killian has worked a day shift. So he should be home when I get back from campus. Before leaving the house this morning, I've scrubbed, shaved, moisturized, and I'm wearing pretty underwear just in case.

Only when I step into the apartment that night, Killian greets me at the door with a weird expression.

"We have company," he announces, uncertain.

I give him a blank look. "Company?"

"Hey, you." I hear Ivy's voice calling from behind Killian. "You've kept secrets." There's a hint of accusation in her voice. Oh my gosh, Oliver and I just announced the news of our fake breakup yesterday, so she must be thinking I've been cheating on her boyfriend's brother this entire time.

I lean sideways to peek past the six-foot-four wall of man in my entryway, and sure enough find my best friend seated at the kitchen counter sipping what looks like a fancy pink cocktail in one of our definitely not fancy IKEA glasses.

"Hey." I force a smile on my face before hiding back behind Killian and sending him a panicked look. Ivy is going to interrogate us, and, besides the Oliver thing that I'll have to come clean about now, Killian and I haven't gotten our stories straight. I completely forgot to come up with an appropriate meet-cute anecdote. Oh, gosh.

I hang my jacket on the rack behind the door and wipe my clammy palms on my jeans before I go to Ivy for a hug.

She squeezes me tight and then pulls back, giving me a once-over. "You look amazing," she declares, her eyes not so subtly shifting to Killian. "Have you changed your diet or something?"

"Ah, ah. Hilarious. You look fantastic too, as always." I scratch my head. "Err—how come you dropped by?"

Ivy takes a sip of her cocktail and gives me a sly smile. "I wanted to see how you were faring after the breakup with Oliver." She drops a hand on my forearm. "He told George he'd met someone else, a man, and that you'd also met someone else. But you hadn't mentioned anything in your text about meeting someone, so I thought you'd made up that last part to save face." Then, with a theatrical sigh and a little squeeze to my arm, she adds, "But I see my worries were unfounded." Her eyes flicker to Killian once again, who, in the meantime, has moved into the kitchen and is making dinner.

He looks devastatingly hot even with his back turned to us as he chops vegetables on a board.

"I—uh—yeah," I stammer. "It's been an interesting couple of weeks."

Ivy crosses her arms and stares at me expectantly. In a way that says, *"Fess up."*

Since Oliver has already told his family about being bisexual, I tell her everything. But still ask that she keeps the fake dating from George. I don't know if Oliver wants his brother to know. But, either way, I can't keep lying to my best friend.

I'm afraid she's going to get mad, but instead Ivy surprises me by apologizing. "I'm sorry, I totally went coupled wise human on you, didn't I?"

I smile because, yeah, she did. But then my gaze is drawn to Killian, and I whisper, "I might be a wise coupled human myself now."

Following my gaze, Ivy lowers her chin conspiratorially and mouths a *WOW*.

Yeah, because there are no other words to describe my boyfriend in all his chef glory.

Killian, probably sensing the silent communication between Ivy and me, turns around with a smirk, his hands still busy at work. "Hope you don't mind, I thought I'd make us dinner," he says casually, as though his presence was the most natural thing in the world.

Ivy's eyebrows arch up in a mixture of surprise and intrigue. "A gal could eat." As Ivy's gaze shifts from me to Killian, it's clear she's about to launch into a full-on analysis of us. I scowl at her, silently communicating that no boy talk should take place in front of Killian.

Killian, sensing the tension, wipes his hands on a dish towel and leans against the kitchen bar, all casual confidence and half smiles. "Leighton doesn't want to discuss me if I'm in the room," he says, a warm chuckle in his voice.

"Why?" Ivy asks, 100 per cent charmed.

"Because she'd have only good things to say, and she's afraid my ego will burst out of proportion." He looks at me, eyes holding a sparkle that suggests he's thoroughly enjoying this little game of cat-and-mouse. And I might be positively melting also because this is the first time I've heard him use my real name. No Spoon, no Gertrude. "But between us, she really thinks I'm quite the catch," he teases, with a wink thrown in my direction.

Ivy laughs, the sound rich and carefree. "Oh, I bet she does."

From a pitcher, Killian pours me a cocktail like the one Ivy's drinking.

"What's this?" I ask.

"New recipe I'm testing for the bar. Tell me if you like it."

With that, he knocks twice on the bar and goes back to his cooking.

I take a sip of the cocktail and it's the perfect combination of sweet and zesty with an aftertaste of spice that lingers just a moment on the tongue—a hint of mystery that Killian seems to infuse in everything he does.

Ivy watches me with an expectant expression, waiting for my verdict. "It's... fantastic," I admit, not sure if I'm talking about the drink or the barman.

"Noted, Spoon."

At the use of my pet name, Ivy's hand goes over her heart, and I swear she's this close to awwing.

I know I should enjoy this moment, when I finally get to introduce my boyfriend to the world, but I'm too nervous about Ivy stumbling onto impossible-to-explain truths, so I move the spotlight away from us. "How have things been with you and George?"

"Oh, great. He's fantastic. I cannot believe I would've never met him if not for a late-night craving. Sometimes I still wake up with a nightmare that I'm single and have to go on blind dates..." Before Killian magically turned real, this declaration would've sunk me. But now I can finally bear it and join Ivy in hoping our

Tinder days are behind us once and for all. "But then I wake up, and he's right there next to me, looking impossibly gorgeous as he sleeps, and I can take a breath of relief."

I feel the same way every morning that I wake up and Killian is in bed with me, or if he's not there, when he comes back from the bakery around the corner to deliver our cinnamon roll treat —he's cut down his indulging to a single bun per day.

I smile fondly. Oh my gosh, I must have the rainbow and unicorns look on my face. I really am a wise coupled human.

I silently make a vow that if I ever have to discuss my feelings for Killian with a friend who's still single, I'll try my best not to rub my happiness in their faces.

"We're spending so many nights at each other's places that we're considering moving in together," Ivy continues. That's when her eyes drift to the built-in closet, specifically to the open half that used to be hers and that is now filled with Killian's clothes.

Her jaw goes slightly slack, and she looks at me with a million questions on her face.

I'm already sweating cold, wondering how I'm going to explain that I'm living with a guy I haven't known for that long when there's a whoosh sound, and flames leap up from the pan Killian's handling. My heart jumps to my throat as the smoke detector activates at the flambé attempt gone wrong. The last thing I need is for the sprinklers to go off and soak the entire apartment.

"Killian, turn that off!" I shout, glaring at the still flaming pan in his hands.

He blows on it. But the fire in the pan is stubborn, dancing merrily as if to mock us. With a curse, Killian grabs the pan and, with no other options, shoves it under the running water in the sink. A cloud of steam erupts, accompanied by the hiss of the dying flame. The scent of char mingles with the now wet smoke filling the apartment while dinner is ruined.

We all scramble to open the windows, letting the cold evening air rush in to disperse the smoke. I climb onto a chair and also disarm the smoke detector just in case. Heart pounding in my chest, I'm grateful at least that the emergency sprinklers haven't gone off and turned our apartment into a soggy mess.

Once we're sure the crisis is averted, Killian turns to me, a sheepish yet apologetic grin spreading across his face. "Well, that didn't go as planned," he admits, rubbing the back of his neck. "How about I go grab us some takeout instead? Are tacos good?"

I can't help but laugh, the tension easing from my shoulders. "Tacos are great." I also can't help giving him a kiss before he goes out.

The moment he's gone, Ivy wheels on me as if the flambé accident never happened and asks, "Are you living together? *Already?*"

I stare back at the half of the closet filled with male clothes. At least the emergency break has given me time to come up with a plausible explanation. "Only temporarily," I say. "He tried to fix the dishwasher at his place and flooded the house. He's a typical man, convinced he's handy and can fix anything when he can't." I point at the taped-over bathroom door for confirmation.

"Uh, so how is it living with a man?"

I smile. "If you don't mind sitting on the toilet rim from time to time because they forgot to put the seat back down, it's not that bad at all."

We chuckle and lay the plates while we wait for Killian to come back. As per the lack of a table in the apartment and with us having only two bar stools, we set the kitchen bar. I then remove my laptop from the small desk and drop it on the bed. Ivy and I lift the desk and bring it closer to the bar, so we can all dine in the same area.

Killian arrives shortly after and distributes the tacos.

We all scarf down a few bites before Ivy asks, "So, how did you two meet?"

Panic swells in my chest again. Killian and I haven't discussed our origin story. I completely forgot to come up with a plausible scenario, and whatever we tell Ivy now, it's what is going to stick —forever. We can't tell the real story, but I still want our official meet-cute narrative to be epic. I will spare my non-existent single friends the saccharine, but the "coupled wise humans" that have taunted me for years with their perfect relationships bliss? No! I want to rub my happiness in their faces as much as possible. I want my meet-cute to beat all of their meet-cutes.

Only, of course, my mind goes completely blank now.

My mouth opens and closes, but nothing comes out.

From his place at the desk, Killian drops his fork and wipes his mouth on a paper napkin, his lips twisted in an amused grin as if he knew exactly what I was thinking.

"Mind if I take this one, Sugar?"

"No." I play nonchalant. "I know you love to tell the story."

Killian nods. "It all started with a book..." he begins, and then, with a wink at me, he launches into a tale that I'm as eager as Ivy to hear.

36

LOVE IN THE MARGINS

"I'm a huge reader," Killian starts.

And already, *swoon*. There's nothing sexier than a hot man with a book in his hands. I can already see the little hearts forming in Ivy's brown irises.

"You are?" Ivy asks, surprised. I can't blame her. Killian's appearance doesn't exactly fit in the bookworm category. He'd fit better in a mafia romance.

"Sure am, nothing better than a good book to curl up with at the end of the day." He turns to me and winks.

My heart responds with its usual flip. At this point, I'm not even sure if he's kidding about the book thing or if he's for real. He always seems to know a lot about romantic tropes, but I had pinned it down on him being *literally* from a romance novel. But he did say he's read all the Jane Austen novels. And he seems a bit too up-to-date on the tropes to be faking it. Also all the dog-eared scars I found in my novels are proof that he at least reads *some* romance.

"Anyway, I like to shop at used bookstores sometimes. So one day I pick up this book from the bargain cart that is a total mess

—annotated on almost every page. Still, it was only a dollar, so I bought it. When I started reading, I laughed at the same passages as the previous owner. More even, her little comments on the margins made me laugh harder still. And the romantic bits she had highlighted? They resonated with me deeply. I felt an instant connection."

Ivy squeezes my thigh, making me realize I'm gaping at Killian, enraptured in his narration—which I probably shouldn't be, considering this is supposed to be my story, too, and I should be well versed in it. I close my mouth and clear my throat, shifting on my stool as Killian continues.

"By the end of the book, I was gutted. The happily ever after did nothing to lift my mood because I knew there was no chance I'd ever meet the woman behind the annotations."

Ivy seems really worried at this point. "And what did you do?"

"I went back to the beginning of the book and searched every inch for a clue... and there it was on the title page, a little embossed circle in the lower right corner."

I smile because aww... the story Killian came up with is beyond perfect... also more proof he's perused my shelves.

Ivy turns to me now. "Oh my gosh, the custom stamp I gave you last Christmas?"

"Yep." I nod, unable to stop beaming.

"It didn't have her name on it, but it was easy to find the BookTok account she was running. I followed her and sent her a picture of the book. She replied. We started chatting almost every night."

"Wait." Ivy frowns. "Was this before or after you met Oliver? Because you were definitely single before."

I blush, feeling guilty about lying to her one last time. But I can't tell her the real way I met Killian. "Yeah, before I met Oliver. We were messaging, but it was mostly about books."

Killian sighs right on cue. "I knew she must be from around here since she dropped off the book at a local used store. But it took me way too long to finally muster the guts to ask her to meet me in the real world." His lips twitch at the inside joke just before he makes a distraught face. "And then she told me she was already seeing someone else."

"Oliver?" Ivy asks.

I shake my head. "Tinder Tim, actually." I wave it off. "You missed him entirely. Then I had the blind date with Oliver and you guys. But when Oliver and I decided to be just friends, I wrote back to him asking if he still wanted to go out…"

Killian lights up the room with a cute, warm, slightly-embarrassed-but-totally-smitten smile. "And as they say, the rest is history…"

"Aww." Ivy joins her hands over her chest. "This is so romantic…"

Yep, a perfect, *revoltingly* romantic meet-cute. If I'd heard this story as a single gal, I would've sworn off dating for good and adopted six cats. I glance at Killian and find him staring at me. Our eyes lock, and a million unspoken words pass between us.

How did I do, Sugar?

You did great and you know it.

He gives me a subtle nod.

"Wait, wait," Ivy interrupts our silent conversation. "What was the book?"

Killian's mouth curls at the corner, flashing us his knees-weakening lopsided grin. "Oh, I believe it was a billionaire cowboy romance."

Ivy blinks in rapid succession. "You read cowboy romances?"

Killian shrugs. "The smut is just too great."

We all burst out laughing at the comment. But for me, the giddiness is soon replaced by a deeper something sneaking up my chest and wrapping around my heart. A tether. It's like a warm, gentle new awareness slowly unfurling inside me, reaching into places I didn't even know were cold. My breath catches slightly, a fluttering in my lungs that mirrors the flutters in my stomach. It's a strange, exhilarating mix of nerves and excitement, like standing on the edge of a cliff overlooking a beautiful vista.

I subtly rub my clammy palms on my jeans, trying to calm the sudden surge of energy pulsing through me. My heartbeat quickens, drumming a rhythm in my ears that syncs with the surrounding laughter, yet seems to beat only for him. Ivy, the apartment, it all fades into a soft blur. All I can focus on is Killian —his smile, that scar over his right brow, his voice, the way his eyes light up when he's amused.

The realization hits me anew in a wave of profound clarity: I'm in love and there's nothing fictional about it.

37

BEYOND WORDS

The second Ivy is out of the apartment, I turn to Killian and pull him down into a kiss.

It's impulsive, an action born of that sudden clarity and two days of missed connections. Maybe it's reckless, but absolutely electrifying. His surprise lasts only an instant before he responds with equal fervor. His lips are warm and sure against mine, and his strong hands confident as they come to rest on my waist, drawing me closer until my chest is flush with his. Every point of contact sends electricity skittering across my skin. The kiss deepens, and with it the room seems to spin slightly, falling away until there is nothing left in the world but Killian and me, locked in this moment.

I pull back just enough to catch his gaze. Killian's eyes search my face, a hint of curiosity mixed with fond amusement dancing in his irises.

I love you. I say the words in my head but I want to shout them to the world.

"I—I—" I stop myself just in time.

I was about to tell him that I love him, and everyone knows a woman can't be the first one to say it. Relationship suicide 101. The fact that he already said it in Lakeville Hills doesn't count. He has to say it first in *this* world. To the real me.

"You love me." Killian nuzzles my neck. "It's okay, I know."

"W-what?" I make to push back, but he doesn't let me go. "I didn't say it. You can't just appropriate thoughts."

"I can, and I did."

"I'm pretty sure you can't read my mind, so, no, you can't."

"Your mind, maybe not." He drops a featherlight kiss on my temple. Then he trails a finger down my neck, over my collarbone, and brings it to rest just on the swell of my left breast. "But I'm pretty sure I can read your heart, Sugar."

I might need a good heart-reading right at this moment. I'm sure an ECG would show a severe case of arrhythmia because that poor organ is hammering against my ribs like it's trying to break free.

Killian's smirk is smug. "Don't worry, it's good that you love me."

"Why?"

"Because I'm a very traditional man in some senses, I don't give up the goods"—he needlessly waggles his eyebrows—"without those three little words."

"Which I haven't said."

"But that you're thinking."

I scowl. "And what are *you* thinking?"

I swear there's smoke swirling in his eyes as he talks next. "I've already told you how I feel."

"Yeah, but that was about a different me."

"Different world, same you." He cups my face in the most gentle gesture. "I love the pixie version of you who bakes, drives trucks, and saves innocent calves, putting her life in danger. And I love the bookworm version of you who is smart and driven and a little rough around the edges sometimes, but so soft to hold in bed. I would love you if you were a singer, a lawyer, a florist, a librarian—"

"Are you making a list of your sexual fantasies now?"

"No." He shakes his head, dead serious. "I'm trying to tell you that I would love any version of you in any world or dimension that existed. Because I'm in love with you, with your beautiful soul. I don't care about what profession you have or what car you drive. And what I'm hoping to hear is that you feel the same. That you loved the version of me that could whip out millions with a snap of my finger and the version of me that came to you with literally not even the clothes on my back. That for us, time, distance, and space mean nothing. That our love transcends everything, even our bodies."

I nod, too choked up to speak.

It takes me a few more breaths before I can finally speak. "I do. I love you as Killian St. Clair, billionaire cowboy, and I love you as Oswald Finch, penniless barman—possibly even a little bit more. I love how kind and caring you are, how you light up every room you enter with that easy smile of yours. I love the way you always seem to know exactly what I need, whether it's a joke to make me laugh or just a silent hug when words fail. I love your passion for life, and how you take every challenge head-on, yet always have time for the little things that matter. You make me feel seen, heard, and cherished."

Killian's expression softens, the smugness replaced by a warmth that makes my heart swell even more. He leans in, his breath a whisper against my lips. "That's all I ever wanted to hear."

Our lips meet again, and this time the kiss is gentle, at least at first, because soon, we break apart just for a moment before we crush our mouths together again. And then I find myself spun around and flattened against the wall.

Killian's hands drop on my shoulders, then move down my back, trailing lower until they're at waist height and they sneak to the front, pulling my sweater over my head.

Next, his deft fingers reach for the top button of the shirt I'm wearing underneath that he begins to undo. Each button takes forever, but I suspect it's by design.

"No r-ripping tonight, St. C-Clair?" I wanted to sound teasing and confident, but I think the stuttering gave me away.

He grazes his teeth on the sensitive skin behind my ear. "I already owe you too many buttons, Spoon."

His lips never leave my neck as he slowly exposes the skin of my chest to the chill of the room. But the cold is nothing compared to the heat that radiates from his touch. The air between us is charged with anticipation and each tiny clink of a button being released is like an electric shock passing through me.

He removes the shirt. His mouth gently nibbling at my shoulder now, his hands flattened on my belly but not yet where I want them to be.

I whimper in protest and feel his responding smile over the skin of my back.

"Patience," he whispers in a voice so gravelly it turns me even more impatient, especially as one of Killian's knuckles traces my spine, a featherlight touch that sends shivers cascading down my back and sparks a flood of adrenaline to course through my veins.

He gathers my hair up next, tousling it and kiss-biting the skin it previously covered.

When he murmurs, "I love your hair," I have to lean on the flat of my palms against the wall for support. "How wildly it falls on your back." He twists it now around his fist, gently forcing my head backward as he gets better access to my throat.

Killian's actions are deliberate, his movements calculated to draw out each second, each breath that surrenders from my lips. The wall is cold against my palms, but his body is an inferno, pressing behind me, erasing the chill with every inch of proximity. My head tilts further back, exposing more of my neckline to his fervent explorations. His lips trace a path of fire from my throat to my jaw, eliciting a cascade of goosebumps that ripple across my skin.

"Killian," I gasp, the word half plea, half sigh. This dance of restraint and urgency we're tangled in feels like more than I can bear.

His name is my surrender to the building storm. He responds with a low chuckle, the sound vibrating against the column of my throat. The heat of him envelops me entirely now, his hands finally journeying to the waist of my jeans. They pause there, as if in a silent question.

"Please." I'm burning. If he doesn't get the rest of my clothes off me now, I might die.

The sound of my plea seems to electrify him, to break free the last of his self-imposed restraints. His fingers pop the button, then draw the zipper down with a tantalizing slowness that borders on torture. The rasp of metal teeth unmeshing rings in my ears much louder than it must be in reality.

Killian's breath is hot on my neck, his hands now possessive as they guide the denim over my hips, encouraging it to fall like shed skin to the floor. And then I can't stand it anymore. I turn in his arms and sink my fingers into his hair, pulling his face to mine.

But it's not enough. I need skin.

I sneak my hands underneath his sweater and other layers,

dragging my nails over his back as he shudders in response, a low growl escaping his lips.

Soon, even that contact isn't enough. I tug at his clothes, wanting them off. Killian pulls back for just a second, reaching backward with his hand and pulling all his layers off in a single, swift motion.

Finally, my eyes can feast on every plane and curve etched into his skin. Then the privilege moves to my hands. Then my mouth.

We tumble to the bed, and Killian loses his pants on the way. Then the rest of our clothes are gone, and he's on top of me, looking down at me with a reverence that's almost disarming, as if he can't quite believe that I'm real. And there's a small part of me that still can't believe he's real. Really here. Really mine.

His eyes search mine, seeking permission. I give him a single nod in response before we become one. And nothing has ever felt more real than this, the union of two souls crashing together. The promise of a shared future. Whispers of forever etched into every movement, into every breath until everything explodes.

38

MY NUMBER ONE

The first light of dawn seeps into the room, casting a soft glow on Killian's face as he opens his eyes. I'm surprised by how awake I feel despite the early hour. My core melts when he reaches over and gently pulls one of my curls, the first thing out of his mouth a quiet, "I love you."

My heart stumbles over itself as I search those silvery eyes. There's no hint of doubt or teasing there, only sincerity.

"I love you too," I breathe. The words slip out unbidden. I've lost all control and left my heart unguarded. But I can't find it in me to regret this leap of faith. I'll cherish every moment I'm given with him, be it minutes or forever.

Our words hang in the air, the weight of them settling around us as we lock gazes. I grin and lean in to kiss him, soft and slow. We take our time, hands roaming, relearning each other's bodies in the new morning light as we make love again.

I must doze off afterward because I wake again with the sound of the front door clicking open and then shut.

I stretch my arms above my head and sit up, gathering the

sheet around me just as Killian walks in carrying two steaming paper cups of coffee and a white cardboard box.

"Morning, Sugar," he says with a grin.

He sets the coffees and the box on the nightstand and leans down to give me a quick kiss.

"My hero."

He picks up one of the buns from the box and hands it to me wrapped in a paper napkin. "How many of these do I have to bring over before you declare me a true and authentic cinnamon roll?"

"Still hung up on that?" I pat his cheek, chuckling. "I'm sorry, Bun, once a beautiful bastard, always a beautiful bastard."

"You still haven't told me how they do in bed?" He winks.

"Oh, what can I say? I'm more of a show, don't tell kind of gal," I steal his line.

I take a long sip of the hot coffee, letting the bitter liquid warm me from the inside out. Killian grabs his own cup and slides over the covers next to me. Then he leans over with a voice like velvet. "No need to say anything, Sugar, the way you dragged your nails down my back last night gave me a pretty good idea."

"I did not."

"Did, too. I might bear the scars for a while." He licks frosting off his fingers. "But don't worry, I'll wear them with pride."

"Jerk." I playfully push him aside. "Definitely still a beautiful bastard."

We eat the rest of our cinnamon buns in comfortable silence, shoulders touching.

After, I reluctantly crawl out of bed and get ready for a class that I wish I could skip to spend the morning in bed. Killian walks me to the door, pulling me in for a lingering kiss.

"See you later for body pump?" Killian has joined the fitness ranks and is now almost a fanatic of our workouts.

"Sure." I flash him a smile, stamp a quick kiss on his mouth, and head out the door.

* * *

We meet again on campus a few hours later, holding hands as we stroll the outdoor paths headed to the gym. It's a great day that mirrors my mood, the sun is shining, and it isn't too cold—even by Illinois standards.

As we pass the science building, I spot Dr. Hammond emerging from the front doors.

We're on an open pathway with nowhere to hide. I still hope my advisor won't see me, but when our eyes meet across the distance, I know there's no escaping saying hello.

"Dr. Hammond!" I call out, flashing him a strained smile.

"Ah, Leighton!" Dr. Hammond huffs, waving as he strides over, briefcase in hand, and sporting an amiable grin that doesn't quite reach his eyes. "I meant to email you... your article evaluating the efficacy of generative language models in natural language processing has been published in *Nature* in their 'Machine Intelligence' section."

He rummages into his briefcase and hands me a copy of the magazine. Excitement bubbles up in me as I take the publication from him, flipping through the pages until I find my article.

"Congratulations," Killian says, smiling at me.

My eyes widen with satisfaction as I stare at the glossy four-page spread. But as I reach the end of the article, my heart sinks. There, in black and white, is only Dr. Hammond's name. No mention of me whatsoever.

I look back up at my advisor, crestfallen. "Dr. Hammond," I begin, trying to control my disappointment, "I don't understand. My name isn't anywhere in this article."

Dr. Hammond shrugs. "Well, they likely wouldn't have published it without an established name attached."

Anger flares inside me. "You could have still put me as second author. This was my research!"

"Leighton, let's not make a fuss about it, shall we? You're lucky to have been involved at all," he dismisses me, ready to walk away.

Killian has kept quiet for the brief exchange, but now his eyes narrow as a low growl rumbles in his chest. His gaze is fixed on Dr. Hammond, his jaw set. And this one time, I don't even mind that he's growling. In fact, I might start snarling myself.

"I'm sure you can call the editor," Killian says, his voice steady and cold. "Leighton deserves recognition for her work."

"Excuse me?" Dr. Hammond raises an eyebrow at Killian, clearly not expecting external input.

Killian takes a single step forward, ready to go alpha male on me. But I stop him with a hand to the chest. I look at him in a way that says, "I can handle this."

He gives me a curt nod and takes a step back, leaving me free to direct all my fury on my advisor. "Dr. Hammond, I'm sure you didn't intentionally mean to appropriate work that isn't yours?"

"It is standard—"

"Great." I don't let him finish. "Otherwise, I'm afraid I would've felt compelled to file an official complaint with the faculty board."

I stand tall, unwavering, channeling my inner boss girl.

Dr. Hammond seems to consider my words for a moment. The staring contest goes on until he finally lowers his gaze. "Fine," he mutters. "I'll see what I can do."

"Thank you, Dr. Hammond," I say, trying to keep my tone even. The professor nods and walks away, leaving Killian and me standing on the narrow campus path.

I let out a sigh of relief as Dr. Hammond scurries back into the science building he just left—that might have more to do with him clearly being intimidated by Killian's quiet fury than my newfound resolve to be respected. But I don't care, I finally stood up for myself and I'll make sure my name is on that article if it's the last thing I do.

"That felt good." I beam, turning to Killian. "Thank you."

He gives me a small smile. "I didn't do anything."

"No, but I appreciate the moral support and you having my back. But also that you let me fight my own battles."

"Of course. You did the work, you deserve the credit."

We start walking again, heading toward the gym.

"Are you really going to denounce what he did?"

Looping my arm with his, I say, "Yes, if he doesn't make things right, I've had it with him."

Killian stops, looking at me seriously. "I still don't understand why you haven't changed advisor."

"There's a certain stigma in academic circles about... making a fuss, especially if you're a woman." I lower my gaze because I'm not exactly proud of being such a pushover when it comes to my advisor. "I picked wrong. I shouldn't have gone with Dr. Hammond. But, with less than a year left before I graduate, it's just easier to finish my research, get my master's, and move on. I'll no longer have to deal with him next year."

Killian passes a hand through his hair. "Do you already know what your plans are after grad school?"

The question sounds a little too casual. And there's the hand through the hair thing. "Why?"

"That thing Mitch wanted to talk to me about the other day at the bar. Well, turns out he's looking to retire soon. And he's asked me if I'd be interested in managing the bar for him."

I smile brightly. "Well, that's fantastic. You owned The Outlaw in Lakeville Hills, so maybe that's your calling in both worlds."

"Yeah, but here's the thing." He stops. Hand through the hair again. Uh-oh. "The bar would be here in Evanston, will you?"

"Will I what?"

"Stay in the Chicago area, after school. I don't want to make any promises to Mitch if you're moving somewhere else."

A rush of warmth floods through me, so potent that it almost leaves me dizzy. It's like a sudden summer storm of happiness, overwhelming and unexpected. And then the floodgates open. Unbidden tears fill my eyes. I hide them burying my face into Killian's soft sweater, snuggling into the little space where the zipper of his jacket is lowered.

"Hey, hey, what's happening right now?"

I just shake my head, probably smearing snot all over him, because I can't talk.

Killian gently strokes my hair with one hand while he squeezes me reassuringly with the other. "Talk to me..."

"Can we go home?" I blubber between muffled sobs. He has to go to work after lunch, and I really don't want to have this conversation in the middle of campus. Or wait until body pump is over.

Killian agrees, not even mentioning the gym class that he'll hate to miss. But at the moment I'm not equipped to deal with squats and burpees or whatever else the instructor would've tortured us with today.

We keep quiet as we walk back home, but Killian keeps a protective arm wrapped over my shoulder the entire time. Once at the apartment, he eyes me, slightly worried, as we shuffle out of our jackets. And he has every right to be skeptical seeing how I'm behaving like a lunatic and had a complete meltdown on his sweater.

I want to explain myself, but my lower lip is still wobbling dangerously and I honestly don't know that I can keep up an entire conversation.

Killian raises both his eyebrows. "I didn't know me potentially managing a bar could be so upsetting."

I shake my head. "I'm not upset."

"Are those happy tears then?"

I nod before going to him and hugging him. I press my cheek into his chest and his arms wrap around me. I take a few steadying moments before I start talking, still not looking at him because I can't bear the intensity of his steely gaze right now. "In all my past relationships, if you can even call them that, I couldn't get a guy to commit to weekend plans in advance, or holidays, let alone think months or a year ahead..."

"Give me names, I can—"

"Shhh, Killian." I squeeze him harder. "I'm trying to make a speech here."

"I'll mute myself."

A small breath of laughter escapes through the tightness in my chest. His heartbeat is steady against my ear, a grounding rhythm in the chaos of my emotions.

"Okay," I begin, and my voice sounds small even to my own ears. I try to gather my thoughts as he strokes my back in a regular pattern as if he could somehow smooth out the tangle of emotions within me. "What I was trying to say is that when you asked me about my plans for the future. How I'm—I'm a factor in your decision-making, even if we just got together like a day ago—"

"Hey, I wouldn't say that." He tilts my chin up gently to look into my eyes. "We've been on more than a few adventures, hey."

"Still, Killian, this means a lot to me. To know we're in a real relationship where we can plan ahead, one where you're as invested as I am. That you're willing to adjust your life to mine. I never had this kind of commitment with anyone and... I'm just so happy."

I blurt out, "I love you."

"I know."

I smile at his cheeky answer, then kiss him, then one thing leads to another and we take our morning workout between the sheets instead of at the gym.

We're still naked under the blankets when Killian sighs. "I have to go to work."

"No." I wrap myself around him, squishing him on the mattress so he can't get out of bed. "Call in sick."

"I can't, the bar's going to be crowded today. The Paris Masters is on."

"What sport even is that?"

"Tennis."

I pout. "Well, I officially hate all sports."

"Does that hatred extend to all sports bars, too?"

"Especially sport bars."

Cute frown. "So I should definitely tell Mitch no?"

I get serious now and cup his cheek. "You've already moved worlds for me. If you want to take over the Blackhawk, I won't ask you to also move cities."

He rubs his stubble on my palm. "Are you sure? What if you can't find a job around here once you graduate? Or if your dream job ends up being somewhere else? I can find a bar in any city."

"Yeah, but you probably won't find someone who likes you so much they'd ask you to become the manager right away."

Killian pouts, mock offended. "I am very likable."

I roll my eyes. "And very modest."

"But you make a fair point, not all bar owners will be looking to retire and have someone else manage the place in their stead."

"See, becoming manager at the Blackhawk is a unique opportunity."

"It is, but it wouldn't matter without you."

"Are you actively trying to make me cry again?" I ask, fanning my face to stop the floodgates from reopening.

"No, I'm not." He tickles me. "Don't cry. Please, don't cry."

"I'm not," I protest between chuckles, rolling off him. "Please stop."

Killian stops the tickling but keeps his hands on my sides, just above my hips. "Anyway, I don't have to give him an answer right away. Mitch says he still has a few months under his belt."

"Then that's perfect. I will graduate next semester, and I'll do my best to find a job in the Chicago area. And if that doesn't happen, we'll reevaluate from there, okay?"

"Yeah. I can tell Mitch I need to see where my girlfriend is headed next year before I give him a definitive answer."

"I love it when you call me your girlfriend." I can't help the silliest smile from spreading on my face. "I still can't believe we're making plans, that you don't have commitment issues, or aren't emotionally unavailable." I gently grab his chin but with determination. "Hey, if you become boss at this bar, you won't turn into a workaholic who's never home and puts his job above everything else, right?"

He shrugs free of my grip and nuzzles my neck. "No, Sugar Spoon, you're always going to be my number one."

39

RIDE ME

A few days later I come home early, eager to surprise my boyfriend and make love to him non-stop on his day off work. But when I get to my building, the apartment is quiet and still. A coil of unease winds its way around my heart.

"Killian?" I call out. No answer.

Did he go for a run? Disappear like he never existed at all?

I know now that fear of him melting out of existence is mostly irrational, but I'm still about to freak out big time, when the doorbell rings, making me jump. I rush over, heartbeat thudding, and push the buzzer. "Yeah?"

"Sugar Spoon!" Killian's voice calls out. "Come downstairs, please, I have a surprise for you."

"Killian?" Relief and a mild curiosity flood through me—but mostly relief he hasn't vanished. I don't know when I'll stop expecting him to poof out of existence. Probably never. "What surprise?"

"Come down and find out!"

"Alright, I'm coming!" I call, curiosity now taking the lead.

I rush down the stairs, nearly tripping over my own feet in my eagerness to see what Killian has in store for me. When I burst out of the apartment building, there he is, standing next to a shiny pink bike with a big red bow tied around the handlebars.

"Oh my gosh, is that for me?" My hands fly over my mouth.

Killian grins, his gray eyes twinkling. "Promised you I'd teach you how to ride one day."

"Killian! It's beautiful!" I gush, admiring the brown leather saddlebags hanging over the back wheel and the cute basket on the front. My eyes linger on a scratch on the paint of the frame, but it doesn't bother me. Killian must notice, though, because he suddenly looks sheepish. He passes a hand through his hair, nervously explaining, "I had to buy it used… you know, I still don't make a manager's wage."

"Killian, shut up." I go to him. "The bike is perfect. You're perfect." I grab him by his jacket and pull him down into a kiss. The bike is crushed between us, adding pointy and awkward angles to our embrace, but neither of us cares.

I smile against his lips, the warmth of his body pressing against mine, a pleasant reminder of how real he is.

As we break apart, Killian gives me a lopsided grin. "You ready to give it a try?" he asks, gesturing toward the bike.

"Yeah." I laugh, feeling a thrill of excitement. "But you'll have to be patient with me."

"Sugar Spoon." He circles the bike and nudges my hips with his. "I've been nothing but patient."

I laugh again and shove him playfully with my shoulder as we walk toward the park. "Alright, Mr. Patience, let's see if you can handle me on wheels."

Once we're in a paved section of the park, I approach the bike with an exaggerated caution that makes Killian chuckle. Gripping the handlebars, I throw a leg over and settle onto the saddle, unsure.

But Killian's hands are steady on my waist as I wobble slightly, helping me find my balance.

"Just remember to look ahead, not at the ground," Killian instructs. "I'll push you along until you get the hang of it."

Gulping nervously, I nod and grip the handlebars until my knuckles turn white.

"Easy now."

"I've got a feeling that's your talking-to-a-horse voice, cowboy."

He laughs a deep, easy sound that does wonders to soothe my jittery nerves. "Maybe it is, but it works, doesn't it?"

Killian starts to push me forward gently. His hands are warm and reassuring. I pedal tentatively while he walks beside me, his presence like a security blanket.

He gives me a couple of laps, before warning, "Okay, I'm letting go now!"

His hands leave my waist, and suddenly the world is spinning out of control. But instead of toppling over, I find myself moving forward—actually balancing. The wind catches in my hair, sending it flying behind me, and I can't help whooping triumphantly just before I spectacularly crash to the ground.

"You okay?" Killian is by my side at once.

"Yeah, I think the jeans saved me from scraping my knees. My pride might be dented."

"Want to give it another go?"

I beam at him. "Absolutely."

"Maybe next time, drop your feet to the ground if you lose balance."

"Noted."

We keep going until I can make a turn on my own without dropping my feet to the ground for stability. We're both exhausted, me more from the excitement than the actual amount of pedaling I did, Killian from having to run after me in circles.

We sink on a bench in the park, watching the sunset over Lake Michigan.

As we sit there side by side, the orange and purple hues of the dropping sun reflect on the lake's surface, turning it into a canvas of light and color, reminding me a lot of the first sunset we watched together.

I reach out and take hold of his hand, smiling at him even as tears prick at the corners of my eyes. "I love you, Killian. Not the cowboy billionaire, not the bartender, but you. Just you."

"And I love you, Leighton," he says. "Just you, with your stubbornness and your wild laugh and your terrible sense of balance."

"Such a beautiful bastard."

We kiss in the fading warmth of the sunset and in this moment, everything feels right. The past and the future merge into a beautiful present, where love exists beyond the pages of a book.

40

EPILOGUE

Maggie's wedding takes place on a bright late-summer day. I walk down the makeshift aisle—a white carpet rolled over luscious green grass—feeling the opposite of how I'd imagined I'd feel on this day.

Happy instead of grumpy. Optimistic rather than cynical. In love, not jaded. No scowls for me today, I have my dreamy rainbows and unicorns face on. *Gah.*

As I reach the middle of the aisle, Killian winks at me from his spot on one of the white chairs artfully arranged on the lawn of the eco-chic farm where Maggie and Corey are hosting their wedding.

And even though we've been dating and living together for almost a year now, my heart skips a beat. Perhaps it's seeing that familiar, fond grin on his face, the same he had the day he taught me how to ride a bike, or maybe it's just the way his eyes light up when he looks at me. Or it might simply be him wearing a black suit that has my knees wobble as I stumble forward.

The last time I saw him in formal attire was all those months ago in Lakeville Hills when he strolled into my bakery. So much has changed since then. Killian had to reinvent himself to fit into my world and has not made me feel guilty about it for a single second. Each day, he tells me how lucky he is to have me in his life and that he wouldn't trade me for all the billions in the world. My heart melts. Every. Single. Time.

The only thing Killian refused to accept about this new life was his alias. He ended up changing his legal name from Oswald Finch back to Killian St. Clair. I opposed the decision with everything I had, thinking it was a move too risky to put in place just for the sake of a name. But Killian refused to stay Oswald Finch for the rest of his life and brushed off my concerns with a simple, "What's life without a little risk, Spoon?" Which resulted in me spending the night before his courthouse appointment in a jittery state of nerves. But the application sailed through with no hiccups and, on the plus side, Killian presented the petition to request all new documents. So now, he has legit, government-issued papers that make us both sleep better at night.

As for me, I graduated this past June and found a job in the AI department of one of the biggest consulting groups in the country. Is it my dream job? Maybe not, but it's interesting enough and it pays the bills. And the best part? It's based in Chicago. It has allowed Killian and me to move out of my old shoebox apartment to a nice little house in a less expensive suburb halfway between his bar—he's not simply going to manage the Blackhawk, Mitch has offered to make him partner —and my office. We have lots of space and a large backyard. Having an outdoor outlet was something Killian confessed he missed the most about this new life, and I'm grateful we could find an affordable house with a garden. It's still not a ranch, but it's perfect for us. And when something inevitably breaks, Killian has learned to call for professional help.

We've also bought a used piano, and I'm teaching Killian how to play. After coaching me on how to ride a bike, he's also convinced me to take riding lessons. We go to a horse-riding camp every Saturday and I love it.

As for my graduate research, Dr. Hammond shut down the project the moment I got my degree. He probably thought he was slighting me. What he didn't consider is that if the university doesn't develop the research any further, the intellectual property reverts back to me in five years. Suits me just fine. And who knows, one day I might develop it into a business venture.

I take my place next to the gazebo functioning as an altar and wait with the rest of the guests for the bride to make her entrance.

The ceremony is beautiful, a perfect reflection of Maggie and Corey's love for each other as they exchange vows under an archway of flowers.

* * *

The sunset casts a golden glow over the gardens of the farm as we make our way from the ceremony to the reception. The scent of freshly cut grass and blooming flowers fills the air, creating an atmosphere of pure magic.

Rays of warm light glint off the champagne flutes as we weave our way through the tables, searching for our assigned seats as laughter and music ripple through the crowd, adding to the cheerful vibe.

I can't help but marvel at how much I'm enjoying this wedding. Who would've thought? Me, Leighton, the gal who used to hate weddings, finally embracing the joy.

I drop my clutch at our table and ask Killian to get us one of those glasses of bubbly as I go get some food for us.

The appetizer buffet is set up on long, beautifully decorated tables, with guests mingling and chatting as they load their plates. Once everyone has had their fill, we all sit down to enjoy the main courses served at the table.

"Gosh, I'm stuffed," I say as a server takes away the second course. "I'm never eating again."

Killian smirks. "Are you sure? You still haven't had the cake."

As if on cue, another server announces that the dessert buffet is now open.

A dessert buffet? Come on, that's unfair.

"Go get all those sweet treats," Killian teases. "You know you want them."

"Okay, cowboy, but don't complain if you have to carry me to our room because I'm too full to walk."

"I wouldn't dare complain." Smirk. "I might even enjoy tossing you over my shoulder later, Sugar."

Bet he would. I give him a mock reproaching look and go get in line. As I survey the mouthwatering array of treats before me, I catch the eye of another one of Maggie's bridesmaids in front of me in the line. Her cousin Felicity.

We're not close friends, but I've known her for as long as I've known Maggie. We've also been on a trip together once. I mean before the bachelorette getaway last April.

She gives me a side glance and smiles sarcastically. "You screwed me, you know?"

I blink, confused. "I what?"

The smirk is back on her face, but now I can see that it's playful, not angry. "You were supposed to be the other single gal in the wedding party, but you showed up with *that* instead."

She points behind her back at Killian, who, even seated at a table doing nothing, still looks like a secret agent ready to save the world and melt lots of underwear in the process.

I'll never stop obsessing over how hot he is in a dark suit. This one might not be designer, only a cheap number from the mall. But, gosh, the man can rock it. He looks like an Armani ad.

"Sorry," I say, not really meaning it but also meaning it a little bit. Before Killian splashed into my life, I was her. And I would've hated to be the only single bridesmaid at the wedding.

"I was counting on you not to be the only one wearing a scarlet S on her chest," Felicity continues, grabbing two empty plates and handing me one. "At least I could've told my parents. See, Leighton is also single. She's smart, cool, nothing wrong with her."

"Thanks, I guess." I drop a mini tiramisu glass on my plate. "If it's any consolation, when Maggie told me she was engaged, I was 100 per cent sure I'd be the ninth wheel at this wedding. But love —" I stop myself short.

Felicity raises an eyebrow at me. "Were you about to tell me love hits you when you least expect it?"

"Nope, no." I so was, but thankfully I stopped my wise coupled human brain just in time. There is really something about being in love that turns you into a pink-glassed, soppy romantic. But I'm trying my best to remain normal. Especially around people who don't deserve obnoxious optimism.

"Good, because I don't think I could take someone else telling me that."

On impulse, I drop my dessert plate and hug her. "You're a wonderful person," I say, squeezing on for emphasis. "Having a man in your life or not isn't a definition of your worth. Meeting someone you can fall in love with is just dumb luck and doesn't reflect on your character in any way whatsoever. You rock, girl, and don't believe anyone who tells you otherwise."

I squeeze her one last time and let go.

She stares at me in slight shock before saying, "That was

super weird." Then she reaches out and pats my arm. "But also appreciated. Thank you."

Her eyes get a little shinier.

I nod and we move along the line before the people behind us start a mob.

"You know," I continue, getting *all* the chocolates on my plate, "technically, you're not the only single person in the wedding party..."

"You mean the brother of the groom? He's a notorious asshole."

"A hot asshole, though."

"Are you trying to matchmake me now?"

"Not exactly," I say, even if I am a little, can't help it, the instinct has taken over. I'm out of my mind happy and I want everyone around me to be, too.

"What does that mean?"

"That I don't want to set you up for life." Lie, I've been waiting all night to tell her this, after running a background check on the man in question with Maggie, of course. "But if you want to take the edge off this horrendous celebration of love, the best man has been staring at you all day."

"Has he?" She scans the crowd until she finds him leaning against the bar, drink in hand, looking at her like she's more appetizing than any of the desserts on display.

Felicity turns away quickly. "He sure gives intense eye contact. You think I should pursue it?"

"Depends on what you want. He might be good only for a night of fun and nothing else."

"Then perhaps not."

"You could always ask him for a dance. Get all the wise coupled humans off your back."

"Who?"

"People in couples, we get less restless when we see a potential relationship in the making. Your parents might get off your case for the rest of the night as well."

She beams at me. "You're funnier than I remembered." She covers my hand with hers. "And rest easy, I'll be putting myself out there..."

We both laugh, then she nods at me and goes. I watch her walk back to her table. The best man promptly chucks down the remains of his drink and detaches himself from the bar in hot pursuit.

Nothing might come out of it, but the wise coupled human in me likes to think it can be the start of a great love story.

"You look awfully pleased with yourself," Killian comments as I sit back at our table.

I pop a chocolate in my mouth. "I might've just master-minded a best man and bridesmaid trope."

"You mean those two?"

I turn around and find Felicity being thoroughly kissed by the best man. "Wow, that was fast."

"Yeah, Cupid, clearly *your* doing. Anything for me on that plate?"

I stand back up and sit on his lap. "We can share."

I spoon-feed him bites of the various desserts, fully aware that I'm being offensively cheesy. But what can I say, weddings are just so romantic.

At my unshakable dreamy expression, Killian chuckles. "So, you into these kinds of things?"

"What things?"

He twirls a finger around. "Big days with white dresses, emotional toasts, and lots of dancing."

"Oh, you know." I try to play it cool as I shift slightly in

Killian's lap, the plate of mini desserts balanced precariously in my hand.

"Want to have another one soon?"

"No one's invited us so I don't—"

"I meant *us*, Sugar Spoon." His voice is teasing, his fingers tracing idle patterns on my arm.

"Ah, oh... well, I wouldn't be completely opposed to the idea."

"Then let's do it soon. But maybe a little less fancy."

"What do you mean?"

"We could ask the guests to come in casual clothes, no dresses allowed, only jeans and cowboy boots."

I see all my fairy tale wedding fantasies crumble and almost drop the plate. "That could work." I let out a nervous chuckle. "It'd be original for sure."

He flips a finger under my nose. "When, Sugar, will you learn to tell if I'm messing with you?"

"You're messing with me about the wedding? Because it isn't funny..."

"Not the wedding, Sugar, just the cowboy theme. You can have your princess wedding. Let's just do it outdoors on a summer night. You in a flowing white dress, fairy lights strung up between trees..."

I give him a scrutinizing look. "How long have you been thinking about it?"

Small shrug. "A little while."

"Only a *little* while, huh?" I tease, leaning into his chest. "You've got quite the details for something you've only thought about 'a *little* while.'"

Killian's arms wrap around me in a gentle but firm hold. "It was just a suggestion. My only wish is for you to have everything you've ever wanted."

I nestle into Killian's embrace. "Careful, St. Clair, that's almost cinnamon roll sweet. You're not going to propose with a ring hidden in a cupcake next, are you?"

Killian lets out a hearty laugh. "I was thinking more of a cinnamon bun, but if that's off the table, I'll have to think of something else."

"And the good part is that the only thing I really want, I already have, and it's you."

"Who's being corny now?"

I ignore his sarcasm and swipe a smudge of chocolate from the corner of his mouth. "I used to think love was just a beautiful lie, a fantasy spun in stories. But you, Killian St. Clair, you made it all real. Every dream, every silly hope I've ever had." He holds my hand now, his steely gaze becoming impossibly intense. "I still don't know how it's possible that you're here. But I like to think that you were right, that our love is so strong as to transcend time and space, that"— I pause, searching for the right words— "that our souls were destined to find each other, no matter the impossibility of it."

Killian smirks. "Oh, so now we're fated mates, uh?"

I swat him playfully. "Such a beautiful bastard."

"It doesn't matter what we are, Sugar. Our story, our rules."

ACKNOWLEDGEMENTS

Well, we did it—or more accurately, you did it. If you're reading this, you've made it through the chaos and charm of my latest creation, and for that, I'm eternally grateful. Whether you laughed, cried, or both, you breathed life into these pages. Your messages, reviews, and support make the long nights and endless revisions worth it. If this book made your day a bit brighter, then I've done my job.

Now let's talk about the village it took to raise this paper child of mine.

Hats off to the caffeine suppliers and local bakeries that fueled this endeavor. Your lattes and croissants are the unsung heroes of this manuscript.

To my family, thank you for understanding that 'I'm writing' was code for 'I love you, but please leave me alone with my imaginary friends.'

Mom and Dad, thanks for always believing I could do anything, except maybe putting my shoes away instead of leaving them scattered across the living room. That's my husband's problem now, and I know he has your deepest sympathy.

Endless gratitude to my editor, Rachel Faulkner-Willcocks, who helped me sort the world-building of a book boyfriend becoming real and asked for more spicy scenes. Thank you for not letting me get away with any plot line too far-fetched, and for always asking the tough questions.

Thank you to my copy editor and proofreader, Cecily Blench

and Susan Sugden, for taking care of the grammar and my liberal usage of comma splices.

To the production team at Boldwood Books for making this book so pretty, and to the sales and marketing department for helping me put this story in the hands of readers like you.

To the obscure and mysterious recommendation algorithms, they might also be the reason why you're reading this.

I owe a big thank you to the literary community, from the bookstagrammers and BookTokers to the bloggers, who champion my stories and stories like mine. Thanks for spreading the book love.

Here's to many more stories and shared smiles. We're just getting started, and I'm glad you're here for the ride.

ABOUT THE AUTHOR

Camilla Isley is an engineer who left science behind to write bestselling contemporary rom-coms set all around the world. She lives in Italy.

Sign up to Camilla Isley's mailing list for news, competitions and updates on future books.

Visit Camilla's website: www.camillaisley.com

Follow Camilla on social media:

instagram.com/camillaisley

tiktok.com/@camilla.isley

facebook.com/camillaisley

x.com/camillaisley

bookbub.com/authors/camilla-isley

youtube.com/RomanceAudiobooks

ALSO BY CAMILLA ISLEY

ALSO BY CAMILLA ISLEY

The Love Theorem

Love Oracle

The Love Proposal

Love to Hate You

Not in a Million Years

WHERE ALL YOUR ROMANCE
DREAMS COME TRUE!

THE HOME OF BESTSELLING
ROMANCE AND WOMEN'S
FICTION

 WARNING:
MAY CONTAIN SPICE

Boldwood

Boldwood Books is an award-winning fiction publishing company seeking out the best stories from around the world.

Find out more at www.boldwoodbooks.com

Join our reader community for brilliant books, competitions and offers!

Follow us

@BoldwoodBooks

@TheBoldBookClub

Sign up to our weekly deals newsletter

https://bit.ly/BoldwoodBNewsletter

Milton Keynes UK
Ingram Content Group UK Ltd.
UKHW040633090624
443911UK00008B/18